Hooker

BROOKE BLAINE

To Fryze -

So happy to
meet you, rooster!
are you too!
-A. Chata
Plains

Also by Brooke Blaine

L.A. Liaisons Series
Licked (Book One)
Hooker (Book Two)

Romantic Suspense
Flash Point

Co-authored with Ella Frank
Sex Addict

To one of my favorite hookers—my Jordan.
Thank you for letting me oh-so-casually insert myself into your family. Stuck with me, you are.

Chapter One
How I Lost My Pants
on the Red Line

"TAKE YOUR PANTS off!"

The war cry from the naked man streaking down the sidewalk didn't do much to ignite the crowd gathered at the corner of Hollywood and Highland, but then neither did the way he bounced around the pedestrians like a pinball.

Living in L.A., I was used to dodgy public displays for attention, which were usually in the form of someone golden-showering the sidewalk in broad daylight as I passed—I know. Sweet, right?—and it was best just to ignore them and not engage.

Poor tourists, on the other hand…

Gasps from a pair of female fifty-somethings to my right caught naked man's attention, and he dashed through the crowd in their direction, waving his spindly arms up in the air like one of those inflatable dancing-man balloons.

Oh Lord. Here it comes.

As my friends and I watched the train wreck happen with sympathetic stares, naked man reached the tourist duo—their fingers still white-knuckling their pearls—and then a maniacal grin crossed his face. Quicker than they could react, he dacked them.

Oh, sorry. Dacking is what Americans would call pantsing. As in pulling their loose trousers down to their knees to expose all the gloriousness that is hiding underneath. Err...or not, as it were, unless faded, flowery granny panties were in fashion. And I seriously doubted the hipsters were trolling vintage shops in search of those right now.

Groaning, I wondered how I'd let myself get talked into this. And by *this*, I mean the annual Pantsless Metro Ride, not the voyeurism I was currently engaged in. And yes, you read that right—I said pantsless, meaning those poor grandmas weren't the only ones walking around half-naked.

Nope, dozens of bodies around me sported various undergarments as they headed to the Metro station around the corner. Apparently, this annual event took place at over sixty cities around the world every January. I couldn't even tell you why the hell it was a "thing," since, at least in L.A., it seemed like just another way for the whacked-out to completely lose their minds.

I glared as I faced my three best friends, Quinn, Paige, and Ryleigh, who were still watching the chaos running rampant around us. When we'd made New Year's resolutions a couple of weeks ago to, and I quote, "do stupid tourist stuff and things we'd never usually say yes to," I had no idea that riding the subway half-naked in the middle of winter would fall into that category. This whole thing was a nightmare for me, mostly because I towered over my friends, which made blending in with the crowd almost impossible. And *that* meant more eyes on my undies.

I pulled my jacket tighter around me.

"You better hurry and take yours off before he does it for you," Quinn said, nudging me in the side. "I'm sure you don't want to hear what your horoscope said today about strangers in your life."

"No, I don't. And that's easy for you to say," I mumbled. She looked as badass as ever with her glossy black hair trailing down her back, dressed in her signature leather jacket and a pair of black combat boots. You barely noticed she was wearing a pair of faux-leather bikini bottoms for pants. It looked like she'd left the house that way on purpose.

"I'm not sure why I have to take off my—" My words were cut off as a gust of wind whipped up my coat and had me shrieking. "Fuck, it's bloody freezing."

Paige, ever the showgirl, stepped away from us and made a big show of unzipping her flared jeans. "It's not that bad," she said, bending over as she pushed her pants down to her ankles and then stepped out of them. Whistles of admiration from male passersby had her grinning as she straightened and tossed her blond locks over her shoulder. She was positively indecent in a pair of skimpy lace panties that were almost see-through. I was more shocked that it wasn't a G-string, to be honest.

Ryleigh laughed as she grabbed Paige's pants from her and shoved them into the oversized bag she'd brought to hold our clothes. Then she held her hand out to me. "All right, hooker. Off with 'em."

I glanced around me, at all the people passing by us all rugged up, and shivered, but this time not from the cold. "Did you know winter cold kills more people than summer heat does? I'm not really up for dying today, and even if I didn't die from frostbite, it's a known fact that cold weather increases your appetite, which makes you gain weight, and then your libido drops, and when that happens, it means you don't feel like having sex, and I just don't think—"

"For fuck's sake," Paige said as another blast of bitter wind whipped our hair wild and had us huddling together for warmth. "If you don't take your pants off right now, Shayne Callahan, I'm doing it for you."

Oh hell. She used my full name, which meant I had about five seconds before smoke blew from her ears. I decided to push my luck anyway.

"Tell you what. I'll hold the bag while you guys parade around naked, how's that?"

When a low growl sounded in response, I put my

hands up. "Okay, okay. But if this causes me to lose my sex drive, I'm suing you all for damages."

Squeezing my eyes closed, I unbuttoned my jeans and hesitated. *Just rip it off like a Band-Aid. It's not like anyone's watching...*

In one quick move, I slid my pants down, stumbled out of them, and then held them away from me for Ryleigh to grab. When whoops and exclamations rang out from my friends, I opened my eyes.

"Lookin' good, hooker," Ryleigh said with an approving eye before linking her arm through mine as we headed toward the Metro escalator. "I totally need those in my life."

"I can't believe you wore Star Wars boyshorts," Paige grumbled as she trailed behind us with Quinn. "Didn't I buy you bitches gift cards to Trashy Lingerie for Christmas?"

Quinn snorted. "I bet she gets more attention in those than you do in yours. What guy can resist gorgeous *and* nerdy?"

"This sounds like a bet," Paige said.

"No," I said, wagging my finger in her face. "No way am I going after numbers dressed like this, and I'm not doing the bend and snap in front of guys to see who can get the loudest whistles either."

Paige's bottom lip popped out. "You're no fun."

After we tapped our Metro cards and walked through the turnstile, we headed down another escalator to the packed platform. As I glanced over the wide variety of people gathered below, I couldn't believe there were so many willing to strip down to their underwear for no reason at all.

There were hipsters in their fedoras and glasses with underwear that was trying too hard (a.k.a. *not* granny panties); there were giggly college kids that hadn't yet gained what Ryleigh referred to as "their freshmen fifteen," wearing size-zero jackets and brightly colored, barely there bikinis; a small group of technogeeks sported their vintage Mario Kart boxers; there were the parading glamazons who could've rocked the Rodeo boutiques without even putting their pants back on; and then...there were the rest of us.

The "normal" lot, with our lumps and curves—or stick-straight body with no curves, in my own case—and dressed in our everyday wear, which for most were heavy jackets (it was a freezing-for-L.A. fifty degrees outside), boots, and our nicest cotton underwear—the ones that provided the most coverage. Mine just happened to have a picture of Boba Fett on the ass with the tag line "I have a Boba Fett-ish."

"See," Paige said, smiling broadly. "This isn't so bad."

A shudder went through Quinn, and she wrinkled her nose. "I dunno. I'm all for embracing your body, but some people really shouldn't be naked in public."

I followed her gaze to see a guy wearing *Where's Waldo?* boxers and knee-high socks shaking his...*Waldo* at a few frightened passengers as his friends high-fived behind him.

Ryleigh put her hands on her hips, looking ever so sassy in her vintage pinup top, peep-toe heels, and a pair of hipsters. She'd taken to wearing her long chestnut hair down more often than not when she wasn't working, and we all knew the reason behind the change—her dreamy boyfriend Hunter Morgan's preference for running his fingers through it every chance he got. The two of them were so damn cute together, I couldn't even pretend to hate on them for what would normally be a little gag-inducing for anyone else.

"I thought we were supposed to pretend like nothing unusual is happening," Ryleigh said. "Of course L.A. would fuck up the rules."

As we reached the bottom and maneuvered our way through the crowd to the head of the platform to wait for the train, we earned more than a few stares and comments. If I were a blusher, my face would no doubt be as red as my hair from all the attention our half-naked bodies were getting.

I think I would've preferred the frostbite. Fuck. Me.

A fully dressed man chewing on a toothpick stepped out in front of me then, causing me to lose my grip on Ryleigh's arm. When he gave me a long once-over and raised his thick unibrow in invitation, I skittered away, pulling the bottom of my shirt down as far as it would go— which, unfortunately, wasn't over my ass.

Strike that on the fuck me part. Definitely no fucking.

"The only rule in my book is to come in your

naughty best," Paige was saying as I caught up to the girls. "And if we get a bit of eye candy in the next two hours"— she nodded at a sharply dressed businessman…with bulging grey boxer briefs—"then I'd consider this day a success."

Oh God. No doubt there would be more "suit guys" like that one. You know, the hot men from your daily commute that you fantasized about and would finally get to see what was hiding underneath all that stuffy attire. Not that I was looking for that guy or anything. With my freckled toothpick legs bare, I'd prefer *not* to see that guy.

A light breeze wafted against my exposed skin then as the train heading for downtown slowed to a stop.

Quinn took the lead, and as we followed her inside the car already crammed with passengers, she said, "This would make more sense if we were raising money for a charity or to protest working conditions for kids in Indonesia or something."

Paige laughed. "Feel free to ask for donations. I'm sure you'd get quite a few dollars stuffed into your underwear."

The girls squeezed into the center aisle, grabbing on to the silver bars as the doors closed and the train started moving again. I tried to follow, but a woman with a stroller was blocking my path, so I sighed and gave the girls a shrug before reaching for the bar next to me.

I rode the train a lot to and from work, but I still couldn't get used to the bodies crammed on all sides of me.

At the end of a long day, the air was always hot and musky with sweat, and though it was still early afternoon, having less train cars on weekends meant it was especially crowded...and steaming. There was no way to avoid physical contact today, and as the train swayed to and fro, the bumps against my arms, hips, and ass had me missing my pants something fierce.

As the train slowed to the next stop, I tightened my grip on the bar to keep my body from knocking against anyone else, though no one else seemed to have the decency to do the same.

I'm naked, people. Fucking naked. Please don't touch my private bits.

More passengers crammed themselves onto the train, and I sighed, giving up the fight. Ryleigh caught my eye and shrugged as she was pushed farther down the aisle.

"Excuse me, everyone, may I have your attention?" a male voice coming from a few squished bodies away from me shouted loud enough that his voice had to have carried to the far end of the car. Against my better judgment, I glanced in his direction, and when I did...the most gorgeous pair of hazel eyes met mine.

Standing just behind the loudmouth was a man who had my lips parting and my breath catching in my chest. Like me, he was a head taller than the majority of those gathered, with thick brown hair that looked stylishly windblown. And as our gazes locked, I was...speechless.

Now, I'm a career matchmaker, so I don't preach the

whole love at first sight, "you just know from the moment
you lay eyes on someone" spiel that others do. I've always
said it takes more than a look to know if you're compatible
with someone, but at this moment I'd take back all my
words, stuff them into an old suitcase, and toss them out on
the side of the PCH. Because that guy…

I couldn't even finish the thought. My heart seemed
to be expanding in my chest at a rapid rate, all the blood in
my body rushing to accommodate the growth, leaving me
lightheaded and tightening my grip on the bar so I wouldn't
fall over. A hint of a grin lifted the corner of his mouth, and
as I stood there blinking, it slowly grew until a blinding,
brilliant smile lit up the car. It seemed to scream several
things to me all at once:

Hello.

You're beautiful.

And I feel that too.

Still I could only blink, not quite believing the flurry
of stars and hearts and flowers exploding inside. The
reaction didn't make sense. I'd never seen the guy before in
my life. What if he was a rapist or murderer, or worse…a
Republican?

My thoughts were interrupted as a glass-shattering a
cappella rendition of something that vaguely resembled a
Michael Jackson song assaulted my ears. Serenades
happened on a daily basis on my commutes, and let's just
say this was not New York City, where the casts of
Broadway shows made surprise appearances. We're not that

lucky. Because of those pop-up singers, I always made sure my headphones were attached to me, and I was sorely missing them now.

My forehead wrinkled as I cringed from the shrill sounds destroying my eardrums. Across from me, gorgeous guy's smile had morphed into a pained expression that matched mine. As he shook his head and rubbed at his ear, I couldn't help but laugh, which made him smile again.

Geez, how did anyone get through life sounding like a dying donkey? And worse—who'd want to share that with the world? I couldn't imagine anyone giving him tips for his vocal stylings, but maybe he made his money by people paying him to shut the hell up.

Tempted to do just that, I reached down to grab the five-dollar bill in my back pocket, but stopped short when my fingers grazed my thin panties.

Oh fuck shit ass and hole. Ryleigh had my pants. Which meant I'd been making googly eyes at Mr. Gorgeous without them, which *also* meant I'd have to exit the train with my underwear on full display.

Oh my God. Oh my *God.*

As my eyes widened, I quickly looked away from his gaze. Anywhere, anywhere but looking him in the eye. I felt suddenly exposed, because not only could he see the reaction he'd had on me, but…well…what if the pulsing between my thighs would show quite another…*ahem*…response?

Was it possible to stroke out from embarrassment at

twenty-eight? Because my face felt numb and I was positive anything I uttered would come out in a slur, like I'd had one too many of Ryleigh's Slippery Slutbag boozy shakes. I could've been drooling and I wouldn't have felt it. Or drooping. There could be major droopage on one side of my face…

There was no way to get the attention of the girls to check for me unless I shouted over the human fucking loudspeaker still "singing," so instead I stole a glance at Mr. Gorgeous. His eyes were still on me, and the way he was staring made me feel pretty sure half my face wasn't melting off, though I did brush the corner of my mouth to make sure I wasn't salivating.

Nope. I seemed to be okay, even if my panties weren't.

Gawd.

His head cocked to the side as his eyes trailed over my lips—and damn if I didn't feel *that* all over. And yeah, okay, maybe I sort of beamed under his appraisal. Not because I was an "ooh, that boy is staring at me" virgin, but because, hell, who wouldn't want *his* attention? I wished I could see the rest of him, but I was also grateful for the squished sardines currently separating us.

As the train rattled on, I made sure to look elsewhere often before ever so casually glancing in his direction—as though I was simply skimming over the crowd instead of forcing myself not to blatantly stare at him. I even attempted to watch the man singing "Dirty Diana," though I didn't dare make eye contact with him either. I mean, hello—no pants, no money to give.

The Seventh Street/Metro Center stop came into view before I was ready, and my eyes immediately shot to Mr. Gorgeous. He'd glanced out the window and then back at me, and I got the feeling this was his stop too.

My stomach flip-flopped at the possibility of more outside our eye-fucking commuter ride. Then he looked down at himself, his mouth twisting. Before I could analyze what *that* look meant, the doors opened and he was lost in the rushing tide of passengers exiting the car, while others shoved their way inside like assholes.

As I peeled myself out of the train, I searched the crowd for him, but he was nowhere to be found. Disappointment filled my gut, but what had I expected? That he'd wait for me to get off? And, honestly, did I really want him to see me without my pants, *especially* with the reaction I'd had?

Hell. No.

Still. That connection had been so intense, I couldn't imagine what the purpose had been if I'd never see him again. But he *had* gotten off on this stop, so maybe he was still around...

As the girls filed out of the train car, I pulled Ryleigh aside.

"Quick, I need my pants back," I said.

She arched a brow in a you're-fucking-crazy kind of way. "Uh, let me think. No."

"I need them. I'm serious."

"No can do, my sweet. Time to hit the bar." Ryleigh hefted the bag farther up her shoulder, and as she started to walk away, I took hold of her sleeve.

"Hand over the bag and no one gets hurt."

"Shayne, you can't put your pants on yet. We haven't gotten to the—"

I grabbed the side of the bag and it fell off her shoulder, but she caught it just in time and yanked it back.

"You don't understand," I said, my fingers tightening on the bag again and pulling it toward me. "There's a guy—"

"Dude. No—"

"Just give it to me—"

A back-and-forth war ensued as we each struggled for the tote.

"You're being ridiculous—"

"And you're being a cuntba— Oh *fuck*." As I jerked it toward me, something dark went flying out, littering the train tracks. And wouldn't you know it—my jeans were the victim.

"Oh no." I stared at my True Religions spread-eagled across the track. Without thinking, I took a step forward over the yellow line, and a stern voice to my left rang out.

"Don't even think about jumping down there."

I glanced over my shoulder to see a security guard coming toward me, his hand moving to the belt at his hips. "Consider those our property now. You try to make a play for them, and I'll be forced to take you in."

My mouth opened and shut several times as I searched for a response, but since I wasn't in the mood to be arrested—especially half-naked—I kept silent. Except in my head. There was a lot of *fuckingfuckityfuck* going on in there.

Holding my hands up, I backed away slowly and swallowed. Fine. I'd just steal one of the girls' pants and rock them as high waters. Or walk home in an epic trench coat walk of shame. No big deal. Really.

Ugh.

"Hope you enjoy," I muttered, and then one of the girls wrapped their arm around my waist and led me up the escalator as a sick feeling settled in the pit of my stomach. It wasn't like I could afford to throw away a pair of hundred-dollar jeans. Those had been a rare extravagant purchase for me, and not one I'd be able to afford anytime in the near future if my cheapskate boss Val had anything to do with it.

"Cheer up, babes, I'll get you another pair," Quinn said, rubbing my arm.

I sighed. Feeling like the constant charity case in the group was the last thing I wanted, even though I appreciated the gesture. "Thanks," I said as we stepped out of the Metro station, "but I think I'll stick to something from T.J. Maxx from now on."

"Don't be silly. It's not— Hey, watch out for the—"

With her warning too late, my boot landed in a pothole, and I tumbled down onto my knee, the scrape of the concrete stinging to high hell and no doubt leaving a bright red souvenir.

Cut. Wrap. It's official.

I'm never taking my pants off again.

Chapter Two
Rockin' the Cradle

"SO, SHAYNE. ANYTHING you want to tell us?"

I raised a brow at Quinn before I finished off what was left of my Pretty in Pink drink. The liquor went down smooth, which should've been a tip-off that I'd indulged a bit too much over the last two hours we'd been sitting at the corner bar at The Vortex for the official Pantsless after party. But who the hell cared at that point? It had not only numbed my super-sexy scraped knee, but also my inhibitions, which had been desperately needed so I could relax and enjoy myself in the midst of half-naked partygoers.

"Yeah," I said, holding up my drained glass and rattling the ice around. "I think I'll have another."

"Wrong." Quinn gave the other two girls a look, and

they must've picked up what she was throwing down because they all turned on their barstools to face me.

I froze at their expectant expressions. "Um. Why do I feel like I'm about to be interrogated? This isn't about my resident card again, is it?"

"You better spill it, Shayne," Ryleigh said, with a shake of her head. "We already know."

I searched each of their faces, trying to gain a hint as to what the hell they were talking about. "Spill what? You guys are freaking me out."

"I thought we were your best friends. I can't believe you'd hold out on us like that," Paige said.

"Oh please. I tell you all everything. Even the things you don't want to know."

Wait a minute. Wait just a freaking minute. Surely they couldn't know about—

"Your date," Quinn confirmed. "Cash Adams? Partridge Inn? A table by the water. Candlelight. Any of that ring a bell?"

"You were even wearing the royal-blue dress with the slit up your thigh that I helped you pick out," Paige said.

Quinn nodded. "And we heard the two of you were in quite a hurry to leave after the main course. Didn't even get one of their famous desserts—"

"Oh, I bet that dessert was to go." Ryleigh winked at me. "You're a dirty, rotten whore for not saying anything sooner, but we'll forgive you if you tell us every little detail."

"And every big one too," Paige said.

My jaw was on the floor of the bar as I blinked at my friends. My so-called date with Cash Adams was not something I ever wanted to relive, at least not without copious amounts of alcohol. "How...did you even find out about that?" I managed to squeak out.

"Zoe's latest sugar mama owns that place and she happened to be there that night," Ryleigh said, referring to the manager of her ice creamery and booziery, Licked.

Busted. So busted. "I was going to tell you guys, but I was waiting for, you know. Vodka."

Paige tapped her foot and motioned for me to start talking. "Well, now you've had plenty of that, so out with it."

"Okay, okay," I said, pushing my glass away from me. "It was just... It was a complete disaster." Such a disaster, in fact, that I didn't even know where to begin. Cash Adams was a B-list, mostly indie actor who'd gained industry attention by playing the autistic son of Meryl Streep last year in a movie up for an Academy Award. Though the date hadn't been my idea, he was intriguing enough that I didn't put up too much of a fuss.

Big. Mistake.

Pulling at my shirt as if it would somehow stretch down to my knees, I said, "So...well, do you remember that story that came out a couple of years ago? The one that claimed he did voices on dates? The baby-talk story, remember?"

Paige's brow furrowed. "Oh, I forgot about that. I

thought it ended up being fake?"

"More like he sued and won that defamation case because the girl was deranged and hoping for her fifteen minutes," Quinn said, before focusing back on me. "What does that have to do with anything?"

"Are you sure you want to know?" I asked. "It might crush a few fantasies for you." When the girls crossed their arms in a "we don't give a rat's ass" way and waited, I sighed. "Fine. He does it. The voices."

Paige let out a disbelieving snort. "He did baby talk to you?"

"No," I said. "Not baby talk. French."

"He spoke to you in French and you're trying to tell us it wasn't hot?" Paige shook her head. "Bitch, I will let a guy talk dirty to me in any language he wants—"

I held up my hand and prepared to blow her mind. "No, he didn't *speak* in French. He did this horrible accent thing where he zpoke like zis ze whole time."

Ryleigh's eyes were so wide I thought they'd pop out of her head. "He did not…"

"Yes," I said. "Ze whole time."

"Holy shit," Quinn said, a roaring laugh coming out of her petite frame. "Did he say it was for a movie role or something? One of those method actors?"

"I doubt it. The guy is a headcase."

Ryleigh leaned across the bar, pointing at me. "See, if I didn't know you to be one of the most honest people on the planet, I'd call your bluff, because that has to be the stupidest thing I've ever heard."

"No, stupid is when he tells the waiter, 'Ze lady will 'ave ze pan-zeared zalmon wiz ze lemon zauce.'"

Paige collapsed onto the bar top, trying to catch her breath from laughing so hard. "Jesus Christ, I knew that guy was weird."

"You did not," I said. "You were just obsessing over him last week when you saw the trailer for *A Man Called Gaylord*."

"Hey, I'm the first to admit the guy is pretty hot in an off-the-wall sort of way, and I heard he's hung like a—"

"Paige!"

Paige straightened and shrugged. "Well, he is. *Allegedly*. But he dated Mina Radetsky, who has to be one of the strangest people in Hollywood. Anyone associated with that girl has to have a few screws loose in the head, let's be real."

"I bet Mina started that voice shit," Quinn said. "Thank God you didn't sleep with him. Hung or not, if he started wailing, 'Geev eet to me, Zayne, ah yez, right zhere!' your clit would probably shrivel up and die."

"Please yell that next time, I don't think the people at the other end of the bar heard you," I said, ignoring the looks I could feel aimed our way. Not that it ever bothered me. We had foul mouths. We owned it.

"You should consider yourself lucky for dodging a bullet," Ryleigh said. "How did that date even happen, anyway?"

I sighed. "Val. Always Val."

Val Barberie. My boss and owner of HLS—Hook, Line & Sinker Matchmaking Company. She was hell on wheels and a nightmare to work for, but we'd been working together for more than five years, and I was expecting a big promotion and pay raise any time now. Val had a habit, though, of setting me up on client dinners that turned out to be dates. In her mind, a single matchmaker went against everything we stood for, and if I were somehow attached to a higher-profile man—say, in the entertainment world—it would give the company better visibility, and therefore more clients. Which meant more money in her pocket for the myriad vices she didn't bother hiding.

Ryleigh tsked her disapproval. "That woman has set you up on more bad dates than I could possibly count on my hands *and* yours. How the hell can she even be the head of a matchmaking company? She couldn't find a love match if both people slapped her in her too-big-for-her-body bobblehead."

"If she's gonna set you up on dates with celebrities, why not that guy?" Quinn nodded at the TV over the bar where the trailer for an upcoming action blockbuster was playing. "I bet *he* doesn't do shit accents, *and* he looks like he could throw you up against the wall for some super-hot wall-banging."

"That guy as in Ace Locke? Uh…yeah, okay," I said. "Maybe if I was a blonde who partied on yachts and I'd been on the cover of *Sports Illustrated* half a dozen times. He *is* cute, though. A bit muscly."

"Yeah, I'm not usually into the big 'n' bulky type, but I'd fuck him." Paige threw back the rest of her drink and slammed it on the bar.

"Please," I said, rolling my eyes. "Like you have a type."

Ryleigh's eyes were still glued to the screen, her forehead wrinkled as if she were in deep thought. "Does he wax his eyebrows?" she asked.

Okaaay, so not quite so deep.

"I doubt Val has connections to any A-list celebrities, hence my amazing dates so far. You're aiming too high."

"Ugh. It's unfortunate that Val is the face of the whole operation while our Shayne here is the brains," Paige said.

"No," I said. "She's got a great mind for business sometimes, not to mention the finances to back it up. I am but a lowly woman on the totem pole."

"Oh hell no, don't you dare sell yourself short." Ryleigh looked ready to stamp her foot in disapproval. "You have a gift, Shayne. It doesn't seem to extend to your own personal relationships, but it's still a gift. Hence why you're the finest hooker-upper in the city."

I shrugged. "It's just about reading people. And did you really just say 'hence'?"

Ryleigh waved me off and said, "Tell me, how many wedding invitations do you have collaged on your wall?"

I knew better than to answer that question, and let

her continue while she was on a roll.

"I believe at last count it was one hundred and fifty. *One hundred and fifty*, Shayne. That's three hundred people in this city alone that you've helped find their soul mates. That doesn't include those that are still dating. If that's not a gift, I don't know what is."

"Hell yes it is," Quinn said, as she passed us a fresh round of Nutty Irishman shots. "And if I ever decide I want to settle down, you're my first call."

"Thanks, but you're not my type," I said, giving her a wink.

"Maybe not, but *that* guy checking you out certainly is." She inclined her head in the direction of someone behind me, and I twisted on my stool to follow her gaze. And then I almost dropped my shot glass.

Mr. Gorgeous from the train was across the room in the middle of a group of guys, a beer in hand. A slow curve tipped his lips when our eyes met, as if he'd just found something he liked. I almost turned to see if there was someone else behind me, but I knew instinctively who that look was for.

Without the crowd of cramped subway passengers between us, I could clearly see the white collared shirt he wore, the sleeves rolled casually up his forearms, and his dark pa— Wait.

He wasn't wearing pants. Nope. He was wearing black boxer briefs. *Just* boxer briefs. *Oh hell on fire.*

"Hello, handsome," Paige said. "You better get on

that stat."

Ryleigh narrowed her eyes. "They both look a little young."

"Both?" I asked.

"Yeah, the twins. Is that not who we're talking about?"

"Twins?" Looking around, I tried to find whom she could be talking about. "I don't see any twins, Ry."

Paige let out a loud laugh. "Well, looky who's drunk and seeing double."

"Shit. Maybe I should call Hunter to come get me," Ryleigh said, fumbling in her bag for her cell phone.

"Oh hell no you don't." Quinn grabbed the bag away and tossed it to Paige. "No way are you getting out of Sunday Funday with us today. You can save that sexy-time crap for later."

"Yeah, you practically live together," I said. "Really, it's almost sickening."

"Almost," Quinn agreed.

Ryleigh shrugged and grabbed her half-empty drink off the bar. "Pretty much. Although..."

"What?"

A faint blush appeared on her cheeks. "We've talked about it. The whole moving-in thing—"

High-pitched shrieking cut off her words as we all jumped off our barstools and surrounded her, asking questions a mile a minute. Ryleigh laughed and put her hands up.

"Guys, I haven't said yes yet."

"But you haven't said no," Quinn said.

Paige hopped back on her barstool. "Just so you know, I refuse to wear salmon-colored anything, so keep that in mind when you're picking out your wedding colors."

Ryleigh's mouth fell open. "Wedding? Let's not get crazy over there. And when the hell would I ever gravitate to anything salmon-colored? Really, Paige, it's like you don't know me at all."

Laughing, I planted my ass back on the stool and looked up to see Mr. Gorgeous's eyes moving back to mine as if he could feel the moment I looked his way.

I'll be damned. Hot train guy was all about...*me.*

"Okay, can we please get back to the guy giving Shayne here mad fuck-me eyes?" Quinn kicked my shoe with her boot and bit down on her straw before saying, "He's seriously cute. Go talk to him."

I whipped around to face her. "What? I'm not going over there. He can come over here."

"You're a *matchmaker*, and you believe the guy still has to make the first approach?" Paige put her hand over her heart in mock disgust. "Such a disgrace."

"No, I don't believe that, I just...well, I..." I tried to come up with some sort of good excuse because the truth was that I did believe that. Call me old-fashioned, but I still wanted the whole "guy courting the female" thing to happen. "I've just had a lot to drink, and I'd probably end up ass over face. Not to mention I'm in my underpants

and—" Looking down, I saw that my leg had started
bleeding again, bright red rivulets running down my shin.

"Oh hell," Ryleigh said before grabbing a stack of
serviettes from the bar and thrusting them in my direction.
"Maybe you should go rinse it with cold water in the
bathroom?"

"Um…probably a good idea," I said, sliding off my
chair and bending over to pat down my leg with the
serviettes.

Quinn's hand shot out to steady my back as I
stumbled. "I'll go with you."

"Are you implying I'm clumsy? I'll be fine. I'm just
gonna clean off so I'm not such a bloody mess."

"But—"

"You could order another round of those nutty shot
thingies while I'm gone."

Quinn's head tilted to the side as she thought it over
for about two seconds and then nodded. "Yeah, okay.
Coming right up."

"You're just gonna break the seal while you're in
there. Loserrrrrrr," Paige called out.

Resisting the urge to flip her off, I carefully made my
way to the back hall where the bathrooms were, though the
crowd of people didn't make that feat easy without
stumbling more than a few times. I was never the most
graceful person, even sober, so add alcohol in the mix and it
was surprising I didn't have more cuts and bruises all over
my body. My mother called me Gracie for a reason.

A wave of dizziness had me teetering as I reached the back of the line, and my hand slapped against the wall to steady myself. *Damn alcohol.* I was used to shots mingled with boozy shakes, not just shot after shot after shot. I'd be feeling it tomorrow, but for now, I needed to focus on not falling on my ass. My pantsless ass.

I could feel a warm stream of blood flowing down from my knee again, and I reached down with a serviette to wipe it away. Only this time, I lost my balance completely, and as if in slow motion, I began to tumble to the floor. Just before I went splat, a strong arm caught me and lifted my upper half straight again.

"Good catch, thank you," I said as I turned to face my hero. "I think that last shot might've—" *Oh fuck me.*

It was him. Mr. Gorgeous, a.k.a. hot train guy. Up close and freaking personal.

"Uhh…" I lost my train of thought as his hazel eyes pierced mine, causing my head to spin and my brain to short-circuit.

The hand on my waist gave a comforting squeeze, and I hadn't, until that moment, realized it was still there. It had felt natural, like a part of me that had been there all along.

"Caught you just in time." He smiled, and the room lit up with him.

I wasn't prepared for the sheer perfection of what he looked like up close. Light stubble coated his jaw, and this close I could see not only the shallow grooves of his dimples—bloody hell, *dimples*—but also that one of his front teeth was just slightly ahead of the other. Somehow, though, it suited him perfectly.

"You sure as hell did," I said, still dazed and taking his meaning in an entirely different way than he'd meant it.

"Lucky me," he said, and then removed his hand from my waist to take my hand. "Nate Ryan."

I stared at it for a moment before my brain kicked in and I squeezed his hand back. "Shayne Callahan."

"Shayne...I like that." His warm hand stayed wrapped around mine as we stood there staring at each other for what felt like minutes.

The sound of a curse and something clattering to the floor knocked us back to reality as a woman behind us fell to her knees to scoop up what had fallen out of a purse she was holding by the broken strap.

The gorgeous man in front of me bent over to help her catch a few wayward pill bottles rolling away, and when he did, his black boxer briefs pulled tight against his muscular ass, and I got a close-up of the words *Wanna see my lightsaber?* scrawled across them in bright yellow letters.

Hot *and* a Star Wars fan...

And, evidently, he wanted to show me his ~ahem~ lightsaber.

Um, check please.

Crouching down, he picked up all the fallen items and handed them to the woman now eyeing him with a lustful expression. Then his gaze landed on my legs, and I felt the heat of his stare as his eyes paused on my bloody knee before traveling up higher to linger on my panties. I shifted uncomfortably, pulling the edge of my shirt down as if that would help me maintain some semblance of modesty. It wasn't that his attention was unwanted—it was wanted, and that was the problem.

As he stood, a sly grin spread across his face. And the dimples. *Oh help me*, the dimples were back.

"Those might be the hottest pants I've ever seen," he said, a sexy smirk on his face.

"Thanks, I really like your ass." My mouth clamped shut then, as I realized what I'd just said. "Fuck, uh...I don't mean I like your ass, I meant I like what's written on it. Not that I don't like your ass, you have a great ass, I just meant— I mean, not that I was looking or anything. I just saw what was on the back and...um...never mind."

He laughed then, the most glorious sound coming from that delicious mouth. He really shouldn't draw attention to said mouth. Some people—not me, of course— would try to molest it.

"It was a dare," he said. "My friends never thought I'd wear this in public, so I had to prove them wrong."

"I thought maybe you were just a huge Star Wars fan."

"That too. But who isn't?" His eyes dropped back down to my underwear. "A Boba Fett-ish, huh?"

"He's the best."

"Boba—" He shook his head. "No offense, but no one

thinks that. I don't believe you've watched the movies now."

"There's nothing more badass than a bounty hunter."

"I'm pretty sure a Jedi turned Sith Lord would trump that statement."

"Palpatine's little bitch, you mean?"

He raised his eyebrows in disbelief. "A hot nerd. I never would've guessed that."

"You're only saying that because I'm half-naked," I teased.

His eyes roamed down my body at a glacial pace, making sure to take in every inch of my skin, and while half of me was horrified he kept glancing at the freckled toothpicks I walked on, the other half was patting myself on the back for actually shaving and using a light self-tanner to cover the blemishes. You know, the ones from running into benches, the end of the bed post, etc.

"I won't deny that," he said. "But did you get in a fight with a sidewalk today?"

"Excuse me?"

"Pretty nasty cut you have there."

Oh. Oh, that's right. Somehow in the span of minutes, I'd completely forgotten about my graceful exit from the Metro station. I wasn't sure if my brain obliteration was from the multitude of shots or the effect he had on me.

"Well, I didn't want everyone else to feel bad from all this sheer perfection," I said, as I tried to play off my embarrassment.

"Cute, nerdy, and a klutz. An intriguing

combination."

Now, I knew I should've laughed off the comment, but that womanly insecurity flared, heightened by alcohol. I couldn't stop the irrational annoyance I felt at those words. Whatever happened to beautiful and intoxicating? *Those* were the words a woman wanted to hear.

Instead, I was a clumsy ass. Cute. And a super geek. In front of a hot guy. *Great.*

"You sure know how to flatter a girl," I said, moving with the line toward the bathrooms.

He fell in step next to me. "Those aren't bad things."

"Yes, what all women want to hear—how klutzy and adorable they are. Sounds like you're describing a six-year-old."

Shut up. Shut up now.

His forehead wrinkled as his head tilted to the side. "I'm sorry, did I offend you?"

"Of course not. I barely know you."

"So get to know me."

When I glanced at him, one of his eyebrows was raised in a challenge. Facing him, I crossed my arms over my chest. "All right, Nate Ryan. Tell me about yourself."

His eyes dropped to my defensive stance and he exhaled. "Okay, well…I grew up in Orange County, I've got two sisters, both of whom wouldn't know what a lightsaber was if it hit them in the face. I'm an adequate surfer, I can cook the shit out of an omelet, and my favorite color is blue because it's the only one I can see."

Ah, colorblind. "So you can't tell I'm a redhead?"

"Oh, I can tell…"

Huh. Whatever that meant.

"I'm getting my master's in fine arts in film and television production at USC, and I intern at—"

"Whoa whoa whoa," I said, waving my hand. "What did you say?"

"Oh no. Don't tell me you're a Bruins fan," he said.

"You're still in school?"

"Oh." His forehead smoothed out. "Yeah."

"So you're, what, like twenty-five?"

"Twenty-four."

My eyes popped wide. "Twenty-*four*? You're twenty-four years old. As in…not even able to rent a car yet."

Holy shit, when did I become older than everyone in this bar?

He frowned. "Is that a problem?"

"Let's just say you're closer to six than I am."

With a shrug, he said, "That doesn't matter. Besides, you look good for your age—"

"For my *age*?" My voice went up an octave.

"Don't take that the wrong way, all I meant was—"

"You're barely old enough to be in this bar!"

"I'm a few years past that—"

"I'll be thirty next year. Wait. No, the year after that."

He paused. "And?"

I let out a tight laugh. "Oh my God. Can this day get any better?"

"Look, can I help you with your knee? It's starting to run pretty bad—"

Wiping at my leg, I said, "Help me because I'm some old, decrepit woman who falls down and may break a hip?" A scoff escaped my lips as I shuffled forward again.

His fingers ran through his hair and settled on the back of his neck. "I think we got off to a bad start. Can we try this again?"

"No worries," I said as the door to the women's bathroom opened. I went inside and then turned to face him. "It was nice to meet you, Nate Ryan, but I think I've had enough fun for today. Good luck in school."

And with that, I shut the door.

AFTER SPENDING A good ten minutes on blood patrol—and also kicking myself for being an idiot—I headed back to the girls, thankfully evading Nate. Yeah, I'd overreacted, but guys in L.A. were all the same anyway, and it was better not to waste my time. I was saving myself for Prince Harry and that was that. We redheads have to stick together.

When I plopped my "clumsy" ass back on the stool, Quinn kicked my foot again.

"So? We saw you talking to Mr. Fuck-Me Eyes. How'd it go?" she asked.

I shook my empty glass of ice and sighed. "Not so

well."

"Uh oh. Spill."

"I think…we argued about Star Wars…and some other stuff."

Dead. Silence. And then Quinn cleared her throat. "Hold up. I must've heard you wrong, because it sounded like you said you argued about a movie."

"Um. I did say that."

Her head looked like it was about to jack-in-the-box off her body. "What?"

"How does that even happen?" Ryleigh asked.

I shrank back and fidgeted with the edge of my shirt. "People get…passionate about things they like. I mean, he tried to say Darth Vader was this deep character when really he was just Palpatine's minion with a mommy complex, and then he said Boba Fett was this—"

"Oh my God. Stop," Paige said, rubbing her temples. "I love you, but my brain will literally self-destruct if I have to listen to this."

"Well, on the bright side, at least you have something in common, even if you disagree on the specifics." Quinn gave a meaningful glance to the girls before settling her eyes on me. "Right?"

"Ugh. I'm pretty sure I just blew that one out of the water," I muttered.

As the girls gave me sympathetic looks, I cursed myself, trying not to think about the fact that I'd just gone off on the most attractive guy I'd seen, probably ever. Even if he *was* younger than me. Damn foot-in-mouth disease.

Oh, what the hell. He thought I was just "cute" anyway. And he thought a spineless character like Anakin was a badass. What a loser.

But a gorgeous loser.

A gorgeous loser with a killer smile. *Dammit.*

Nope, I wouldn't think about those things, nor would I turn around and apologize.

Another round of shots were pushed our way, and without hesitation I grabbed one and downed it.

I'd deal with my embarrassment, throbbing leg, and massive hangover tomorrow. At least in a city as big as Los Angeles, I'd never have to see that guy again.

Ch❤pter Three
Single in the City

SIX A.M. CAME way too early the next morning. It was amazing I heard my alarm over the jackhammering in my head.

No more Nutty Irishmen. Well, at least not in a glass.

I took the Metro to work, as I tend to do most days if I don't have meetings outside the office. Don't get me wrong, I don't mind driving, but if you've ever had to endure spending an hour and a half in traffic to go nine miles, you'd be a train convert too.

At least I kept my pants on for the ride this time.

After getting off at my station, I grabbed my requisite flat white from Starbucks and made my way down Figueroa to the historic building that housed HLS. I say historic, but really, fifty years is ancient here, so don't go thinking we're in Rome or something. As much as I loved our previous office on the west side—and missed my daily ice cream fixes from Ryleigh's ice creamery, Licked—there was something about the hustle and bustle of downtown that always energized me.

As I pulled open the heavy glass door to our building, a wild gust of wind whipped my long mane into a frenzy, plastering it to my face. Aaaand now I was a coffee-drenched mummy. *Just gonna go on with my bad self.*

"Good morning, Miss Callahan," Roberto, our always-smiling, fiercely protective security guard greeted as I stepped inside the warm lobby.

Pulling the curly strands away so I could see his face, I said, "The 'good' part of that statement is debatable."

"Rough morning?" he asked, as he reached inside one of the drawers behind the security setup and then handed me a wet wipe.

I took it with a grateful smile and set my cup on the counter. "You're the best," I said, as I cleaned off the remnants of the sweet 'n' sticky from my skin.

"There an event going on today that I need to make a note about?"

"An event? Not that I know of. Why?"

"Crew's all here. Been here for—" he glanced at the clock above his head— "'Bout a half-hour at least."

My hands stilled. "Even Val?"

"Mhmm, and from the looks of it, you might have

your hands full today."

"Fantastic." I tossed the wipe in the trash and grabbed my cup. "Nothing's on the books, but I'll let you know if that changes."

After giving his arm a quick squeeze, I headed toward the elevator that led up to our fifth-floor office.

Everyone is already here? That was unusual. I was usually the first one in, last one out. Something was definitely up, and I hoped my morning so far wasn't an indicator of how the day would go. I doubted my hangover could manage.

As I got off the elevator, I could hear a flurry of activity going on just behind the mahogany door. When I pushed it open, a state of frenzy greeted me, something exceptionally hard to do considering there were only four people there. Well, five including me.

I looked around, bewildered. Nicole, our front desk screening and scheduling coordinator, was running back and forth from her desk to the fax machine, papers scattered all over her desk, and a pencil escaping her loose bun. At the desk behind her, Jenna, head of PR and marketing, was pacing around her desk, talking animatedly to someone on the phone and clicking her retractable pen nonstop. I could hear shouts coming from Val's back office, as she and our image consultant and dating coach, Xander, seemed to be trying to outdo one another.

What...the...

I toed my way around the papers littering the floor.

"Did I miss something? What's going on?"

Nicole gave me a glare so frigid I was surprised icicles didn't pop out of her eyeballs. "Where the hell have you been? Your line has been ringing off the hook, and I don't have time to take your messages all day long. I have rather important things to do."

"Where have *I* been?"

"That's what I just said," she sneered. "Val's freaking out, and we've been calling you. Didn't you hear?"

"Calling me? But my phone hasn't—" Wait...where *was* my phone? I hadn't seen it all morning, come to think of it. Surely I didn't leave it yesterday in—

Shiiiiiiiiiiiiiiiiiiiiiiiiitballs.

My.

Fucking.

Pants.

My eyes closed as I took a deep breath and counted to five. *Will deal with that later.* When I opened my eyes, Nicole was sweeping the mess on her desk into a pile.

"You mind giving me a heads-up?" I asked, but I may as well have been Patrick Swayze talking to Demi Moore in *Ghost* with the way she ignored me. I mean, hello? Who ignores Patrick Swayze when he's trying to get your attention? *Sighhh.* Best movie ever. But I digress.

When I still didn't get Nicole's attention, I smacked down on the stack of papers she was lifting. "Speak clearly and in complete sentences. What. Is. Going. On?"

Nicole huffed, and the escaped tendrils of hair

covering her face flew up, as if they knew to get the hell out of her way. "Do you not read the news? Ace Locke is back on the market. Val's going nuts trying to snag him for our new campaign."

A laugh chock-full of "yeah right" came out of my throat then, but it was cut off quickly when I caught a glimpse of her no-bullshit expression. "Wait, you're serious? *Ace Locke?* As in…the actor that only dates supermodels?"

Nicole's eyes narrowed. "No. The Ace that is starring in the biggest action blockbuster series of the last decade who also happens to be drop-dead gorgeous and currently in *Celebrity Weekly's* top fifty bachelors in the world issue. *That* Ace Locke."

You've gotta be kidding me. This was a little too coincidental after yesterday's conversation with the girls.

"Uh…what makes Val think she could possibly land supermodel guy for our little agency?" I asked.

"Only the fact that she met him at a party last week and he expressed interest in our 'little' services. Seriously, how do you not know this already? What is it you *do* all day long?" She snatched the papers out from underneath my hand and click-clacked her heels back to the fax machine.

"Shayne! Is she here yet? Where the fuck is Shayne?" my boss's voice thundered down the hall, and it had Nicole and Jenna freezing and looking in my direction.

Yep. That was my cue. I flew past them, tossing my bag on my neatly organized desk as I went by. It was the only thing organized about this place this morning.

The door was wide open, with Val holding court in the center of her enormous corner office, a bubblegum-pink dress in her hands held out as far away from her body as she could manage, as if she wouldn't deign to touch it.

I cleared my throat as I stepped inside. "I'm here, madame. What is your will?"

Val's shrewd, heavily lined eyes focused on me. "Don't be cute with me, little Juliet. I need you to please tell Xander that I will not be wearing this pink monstrosity he picked out for me for the dinner tomorrow because it makes me look like a giant vagina." She whipped her head back to Xander. "Is that what you want? For me to look like a worn-out, flappy pussy? I should fire you." She tossed the dress into a heaping pile of clothes on the floor. "Next!"

I stayed close to the exit and watched as our poor man of the office rummaged through the rack of clothes for a more flattering option. "Does this dinner have anything to do with trying to land playboy of the year?"

"Ah, look whose brain decided to come to the *cock*tail party," Val said, waving her hand at the next ensemble option. "Yes, Ace will be *coming* to dinner, where I'll be doing some heavy-duty...*convincing*."

I wasn't about to ask what her version of heavy-duty convincing entailed. She was licking her lips in a way that said exactly what was running through her head.

Ew.

Val snatched the red sequined gown Xander proffered and held it up. "What do you think, Shayne?

Cherry-poppin' red for his first night?"

"Gorgeous. But do you really think this is a good idea? I hardly think a guy who drapes himself in *Sports Illustrated* models is looking for a serious—"

"Stop." Val's heels pounded on the hardwood as she sauntered over to me, her hips throwing off a bunch of Jessica Rabbit, screaming confidence, both sexual and otherwise.

With the point of her blood-red nail, she lifted my chin up and assessed my face as though she were checking for wrinkles. From the way her skin remained blemish free, even as she tipped the fifty scale, I got the feeling she assumed this position with her Botox injector often. "You don't actually doubt my abilities, do you?"

"No—"

"And don't you think he would be a fabulous little fuck to plaster all over the billboards of Los Angeles?"

"He would, but—"

Her lips curved into a wicked smile. "And doesn't director of client relations have such a sexy ring to it? Shayne Callahan, director of client relations. Hmm. A step up from matchmaking coordinator, don't you think?"

Director? Me? Yessssssssssss! Long-awaited promotion, here I come.

"Of course, if I don't land this account, that won't be possible. Such a shame. You really are quite talented. Now," she said, dropping my chin, "I need to choose an ensemble that'll make him come in his pants." Then she called over her shoulder to Xander, "And not the pink taco."

AFTER HELPING VAL pick out a dress that properly
showcased her assets, I headed to my work area. The chaos
up front had died down a bit, but Nicole's laugh rang out
every now and again, and it was enough to make your ears
bleed. I'm not kidding. Have you ever heard pigs squealing
toward an orgasm? Me either, but I imagine that's what it
would sound like. The other tenants on the floor had sent
the building manager so many noise complaints regarding
her laugh that it was shocking she didn't get slapped with a
restraining order for assaulting everyone's eardrums.

    And that was only one reason I wanted to muzzle
her.

    Even with just a clear privacy divider and no door,
the square office that comprised my work area still felt like a
safe haven of sorts. The rug was black flokati, the chairs an
ebony and white damask that had been my favorite design
for years. To my right was a small window view of
downtown, and behind me, a black wall with a collage of
wedding announcements and invitations from couples I'd
worked with. And my favorite thing in the office—the new
amethyst-colored desk Ryleigh had gotten Hunter to make
for me as a birthday gift a couple of months ago. It was
adorned weekly with fresh calla lilies, courtesy of my visits

to the flower market a few streets over.

The office itself was an homage to the city—I'd found everything in the fashion district on super sale, and I could never resist buying local, especially when it was a bargain. If you're going to spend the majority of your time at work, you may as well make the space you inhabit pretty, no?

After powering up my computer and kicking off my joggers—yes, commuting required those if I actually wanted to be able to walk—I traded them in for a pair of work flats. I rarely ever wore heels, and not just because I was tall. After all my super-embarrassing run-ins, I'm sure you can guess why.

Scrolling through my email, I starred the ones with the subject line "Ask the Matchmaker" so I could come back to those when I started my weekly column. I responded to the rest in a matter of minutes, mostly requests from local media for Val, as well as advertising proposals, which I redirected to Jenna to deal with.

My phone buzzed.

"Yes, Nicole?"

"Your nine o'clock is here."

I glanced at my watch. "It's eight fifteen."

"So?"

I sighed. "I'll be out in a minute."

Clicking open the eager client's file, I made a note: *Forty-five minutes early. Prompt in L.A. traffic or overenthusiastic due to desperation?*

As I headed toward the front desk, I noticed the

frazzled energy had further dropped to a simmer and the mess was cleaned up. The man sitting in one of the fine white Italian leather pavilion chairs that Val had picked up on vacation last year had a head of slicked-back inky hair, a finely pressed suit, and a superior smile on his face.

Oh God. I knew the type right off. *Please don't let this guy hit on me. Not this early in the morning. My hangover can't take it.*

I forced a pleasant smile on my face and held out my hand to introduce myself. His eyes roamed up and down my body, and his hand lingered a little too long on mine. His body language screamed "too confident," but his limp, clammy handshake said quite another thing.

"Miss Shayne Callahan, I was expecting an interview, not a date."

His smile broadened, and I was instantly blinded by the bleach job he must've paid his dentist thousands of dollars for. It was harder than it should've been to keep from squinting.

"This is definitely just an interview. Please follow me, Mr. Harburger."

As I turned, I shot a death glare at Nicole, who sat there with an innocent look on her face. No doubt the little twatbag had scheduled this one on purpose. *Screening coordinator, my ass.* If you couldn't tell, we had a hate-hate relationship going on. She routinely sabotaged me with clients that weren't a good fit for HLS, and there was not one thing I could do about it. Not to mention there was the God-awful hyena laugh. It was enough to drive you batty.

I could feel my backside burning from the holes the eyes of the greasy Hamburger—as I now thought of him—were boring into it. He was exactly the kind of guy that kept me from wanting to date or ever put anything on besides sweatpants. But, shocking as it was, there would probably be a perfect match out there for him—and I would have to find her. God help us all.

"Have a seat. You're early, so we'll go over your application together, if that's all right with you." I motioned to the chair in front of my desk and took my seat behind it before maximizing his online profile once again.

"I'd love to tackle this thing together."

I suppressed a groan and kept my eyes on my screen, frowning when I reached the section describing his background.

"It says here you're twice divorced, no children. We have a strict policy regarding divorced clients—no more than one previous marriage. I also see that you're a friend of Val, which explains why she overrode that policy." And explained a lot about the kind of people Val associated with, didn't it?

"Yes, well, I made a generous donation to her last business venture, so you could say I'm calling in a favor from a friend."

"Of course. So, Mr. Ham—Harburger, could you tell me what it is you're looking for in a potential partner?"

He studied my face for a moment before answering.

"Well, I don't mind a feisty redhead with grey eyes," he said, his eyes scanning down. "Thin. Mid to late twenties, preferably."

And wearing black trousers with a white collared shirt like mine too, no doubt.

"That's a bit specific."

"I'm sure you can find someone who fits the bill. I hear you're the best."

Ignoring his advance, I continued with my questions. "According to your application, you're seeking a female with a steady job…no kids…common interests would include traveling, wine tastings, sailing, and…sex."

"Saved the most important for last." He winked at me.

I glanced again at his age. Fifty-four. He should probably add shopping and sugar daddies to that list. I decided to play a hunch.

"Mr. Harburger, when was your last relationship?"

"Well, I've never been a big relationship kinda guy—
"

"Then can I ask why you're wasting my time?"

The smile left his face. "Pardon me?"

I leaned forward and clasped my hands together. "From what I've gathered about you in just the short amount of time we've had together, it seems as though you're looking for something a bit more casual than what our company offers. I understand you have a personal tie to our CEO, but I'm afraid I can't help you."

I got the feeling it took a lot to shock the man, and I'd
succeeded—he looked flabbergasted. I was normally a bit
more patient, but my head was throbbing, my schedule was
full, and I wasn't in the mood today for time wasters.

Peeling off a large sticky note, I scribbled the names
of a couple of escort services that catered to his crowd and
handed it to him as I stood.

"These will be more helpful to you in your search.
Make sure to let them know I sent you."

He briefly looked at it and shook his head, anger
boiling beneath the surface if the under-the-collar flush was
anything to go by. "Unfuckingbelievable. Is Val here? She's
going to have your ass when she hears about this."

"Val is out of the office for the day, but I'll be sure to
give her that message."

"The hell you will. I'll be giving her a call now, so
you might want to start packing your desk, Red."

"That won't be necessary. You see, our company
caters to those looking for long-term relationships, not
casual sex. I was going to invite you to come back once
you'd decided you were ready for more than a fling, but I've
just changed my mind. Now, you can exit the way you
came, or I can have our security guard escort you out." I
gave a nonchalant shrug. "Your choice."

He crumpled the paper in his hands and then
thought better of it, sticking it in his pocket instead. I stood
there, unblinking as he turned on his heel, muttering
obscenities. Once I heard the front door slam, I made my

way to Nicole's desk.

She was chatting with what sounded like a friend on the main line—a stark difference to her demeanor than when I'd come in earlier—so I reached around her and hit the button to end the call.

"Hey!" She whirled around in her chair.

I bent down and placed my hands on her armrests, my voice low. I hadn't worked for a no-nonsense boss like Val for years and not learned anything, even if my ballsy side rarely came out.

"You are not irreplaceable. You pull a stunt like that again, and I'll make sure the only job you can get is scrubbing the loos at Taco Bell. You got that?"

She nodded, eyes wide.

"Filter. The. Applications. Say 'Yes, Shayne' if you understand."

"Yes, Shayne."

"Are there any other whack jobs coming in today that I should know about?"

She shook her head.

"And if by some chance there was, you'd go ahead and cancel them or risk Val's wrath?"

She lifted her chin. "Of course."

"Glad we understand each other." I straightened up and headed back to my desk, not even bothering to stop when I heard her mutter "bitch."

THE REST OF the day passed uneventfully compared to the first interview.

My second prospect was a sweet woman in her mid-thirties looking for a decent guy who could not only keep a job but keep his pants zipped. Easy enough.

My one thirty went a little something like this:

"Mr. Fisher, you wrote that you enjoy photography, collecting rare coins, and taphophilia." I furrowed my brow. "I'm not familiar with what that is. Could you tell me a bit about it?"

"It's a term for those of us who enjoy and are passionate about cemeteries and graveyards. We call ourselves 'tombstone tourists.' I've got a website devoted to the gravesites of all the famous celebrities buried in Los Angeles for the last sixty years if you wanna check it out. Gets about ten thousand hits a day."

I blinked.

"And you would like to find someone who shares those interests…?"

And my three o'clock:

"What I'm really looking for is someone outside of the entertainment industry. And preferably not a lawyer, either. I've had bad experiences with those." The woman flipped her platinum locks and pulled the strap of her brand-name purse back onto her shoulder. "Someone with a respectable job. But not anyone in the medical field, since they work too many hours. Not a cop, either, that's too dangerous; I don't want to worry every day like that. Oh, and no army guys. I don't want to relocate anywhere, and I've heard they have a girlfriend on every continent from what my friends have said…"

By the time six thirty came around, I was beat. I'd made complete profiles for all the candidates (bar the Hamburger), put together a few potential matches for each, and even scheduled a first meeting for taphophilia guy with a woman I'd met that worked at her family's funeral home.

So there you go—a successful day in the life of a full-time matchmaker. Glamorous, I know. Are you starting to see why being a single girl in the city is the smart idea?

Chapter Four
Meals for One

THURSDAY NIGHT AND there I was again. It wasn't like I planned these things. They just…happened. Just happened four weeks in a row now, so this was starting to border on pathetic. Actually, pathetic would be having to escape my cramped apartment to avoid the rich-bitch reality show marathon my twin roommate pains in the ass had blaring in the living room.

After my longtime roomie had moved in with her boyfriend a couple of years ago, I'd been desperate to find someone to make up the other half of the rent, and damn if I didn't get a two-for-one deal straight from Miami. Just out of high school, super mouthy, and with a wardrobe that consisted solely of glitter bikinis—you can probably guess I couldn't wait to get the hell away from the Doublemint twins.

Unfortunately, my tight financial situation had me stuck, although if Val landed an Ace in the hole and I got promoted…surely that would mean a giant bump of a raise too…

And then—freedom.

But for now, my situation consisted sadly of three little words that were grating on my nerves. I glared at the little red sign hanging in the aisle. The ultimate bane of my existence.

Meals for One

That stupid sign was designed to make single people feel bad about themselves. Specifically those shopping in a deserted Target on a Thursday night.

Ugh. Target was an asshole.

As I browsed the choices behind the meals-for-one refrigerated doors, a blaring, unfamiliar ringtone went off, and it seemed to be coming from my purse. After the realization earlier in the week that I'd left my phone in my pants, and therefore sure to be crushed on the train tracks, I'd had to get a new one.

"Hey hey, almost birthday girl," I said, when I answered Paige's call.

"So there's been a change of plans."

Uh oh. Knowing Paige, it meant her low-key birthday shindig planned for tomorrow was about to turn into something massive. "You mean you've decided against spending all day at the beach followed by a night of strip club hopping? What could possibly top that?"

And then she said the word I'd been dreading.

"Vegas."

My eyes closed as my head lolled forward. *Fuck me.* There was no way I could afford Vegas right no—

"And before you stroke out about it—because I know you will—the room is covered, the drinks are free all night, and we're taking my car. Which means be at my place by nine and make sure to get your beauty sleep tonight. Oh, and bring your damn heels this time, and also that dress you wasted on ze faux-French loser."

"Paige—"

"Don't start with me, Shayne. It's my fucking birthday, and I'll do what I want, spank you. I'm not going without you, and I *am* going, so that means too damn bad if you'd rather spend a night at home with Netflix and *The Shining* twins."

I suppressed a groan. They were why I was trolling the grocery aisle in the first place. There was no way I could fight her on this, since she was always such a stubborn pain in the ass, and honestly, a weekend away with the girls sounded like exactly what I needed.

"Like I could say no to you," I said finally, and I could almost see the self-satisfied smirk on her face.

"Right answer. See you mañana, hooker."

The call disconnected, and a small smile crossed my lips. Quick and to the point and refused to take no for an answer—that was my Paige.

Okay, so I needed to grab and go so I could get home and pack a bag. *Let's see...lasagna for one...southwestern egg rolls...spinach and mushroom pizza...bingo. Yep, that sounds healthy.*

After yanking the door open, I grabbed two of those bad boys. On second thought, I needed enough for another workweek. I'd hate to miss my weekly Target date, but them's the breaks. I reached back in and loaded up three more.

"I see you decided to wear pants this time."

I froze at the male voice behind me. *Wait. I know that voice... Oh please let me not actually know that voice.* Slowly, I turned on my heel, my arms full of pizzas.

My heart dropped into the pit of my stomach then, because, what were the odds, it was fully pantsed Mr. Gorgeous. Nate Ryan. In a white button-up shirt and black pants with matching suspenders, he looked almost as good as he had without pants on. Or maybe he looked better. Just wow...suspenders.

The effect was beyond hot. Hot and boyishly charming and completely unwanted at this particular moment, especially with him staring at me all amused and holier than thou.

And yes, it was a holier-than-thou face—I mean, I would know.

The arched brow, his lips listing up on one side, which only showcased one of his sexy-as-hell dimples. *Oh bloody hell. Is this really my life?*

"Hi," I managed to say.

He nodded toward my legs. "Your pants are making me hungry."

Aaaand that was the point where I stopped breathing. Except to say, "What?"

His eyes trailed down my body and rested on my thighs. Self-conscious, I looked down, almost sighing with relief when I realized my lower half was indeed covered this time, but that feeling went away pretty fucking fast when I saw the ice cream cones on my pajama pants practically flinging themselves at him.

Yes, I'd gone out in public in pajamas, so sue me. I hadn't counted on running into…well, anybody.

"Oh. Oh yeah, um…I like ice cream," I mumbled. "Especially from Licked, my friend Ryleigh's store, although I have to say, her boozy shakes are unreal, especially the Make Me Quake Shake, which has these amazing pieces of those Ferrero Rocher balls in them, and they just give it the perfect amount of crunch so that you—" I stopped and took a breath when I noticed his grin getting wider. I swallowed and then said, "Not that I go there all the time or anything. Because I don't. I mean, I've only been once or twice. You know…to taste test. Actually, I never eat sweets."

He laughed then, and those penetrating eyes, tinged with more green than brown today, made their way up my body once more, pausing with what looked like amusement at my full hands. Then his gaze was on me and those dimples were out in full force.

"That's too bad," he said. "I've got a helluva sweet tooth."

Wait...was he *flirting* with me? Was that a come-on? Or just stating a fact?

"Yeah, well, in that case your dentist probably hates you," I said, readjusting the cold-ass meals in my arms. I'd be damned if I let those suckers go now. I'd tied my jacket around my waist, and my thin tank top would reveal a tit-bit more than I needed him to see.

He chuckled at that. *Hmm.* He had a nice chuckle. And a husky laugh. Both of which made my eyes zoom in on his throat. I wondered if it was as warm as it looked. He must've caught me staring, because he coughed, bringing my attention back to his face. His eyes were twinkling something wicked.

"You might be right about that," he said. "Maybe I don't like people telling me what to do. Or dictating what I can and can't put in my mouth."

My mouth dropped open, but I quickly snapped it shut. This guy was obviously a charmer, and after dealing with guys like him all day, the last thing I would do was fall prey to another arrogant playboy. Nope. Not me. Not gonna happen.

"So do you come here often?" I asked, throwing out the first thing that came to mind that wasn't sexual in nature.

He pinched his eyebrows together at me a bit and

looked around. Guess my badass conversation style caught him off guard. Oh, who the hell was I kidding? I was so off my game with this guy I shouldn't be allowed on the court.

"Sorry, I was just checking to make sure I didn't stumble into a bar. Yeah, I find the store pretty essential for keeping my fridge stocked. And occasionally I do laundry too, so detergent comes in handy. You?"

"Yeah, I do laundry."

"Any more sexy pajama pants where those came from?" he asked with a wink. At least I thought it was a wink. He could have an eye twitch. But I was so annoyed at myself for looking like a slob that—once again—I snapped at him.

"That's a personal question. I don't think I invited you to snoop into my underwear drawer."

"I wasn't asking about your underwear. I barely know your name, Shayne Callahan."

"I'm sure that wouldn't be the first time you didn't know the name of someone whose underwear you inquired about."

Immediately I wanted to slap myself, but seeing as my hands were full, I had to settle for an inner kick in the pants. *What the hell is wrong with me? Shut up, Shayne.* But something about the guy made me want to fight with him, and as any of my friends could tell you, I'm a lover, not a fighter.

I couldn't pinpoint what it was...his self-assured smile? The way he'd caught me at my worst on both occasions I'd met him? The fact that he looked so damn good in those suspenders that my mind could only visualize him using those to tie me up? *Wait…what?*

Dammit, why did I have to come to Target in my freaking pajamas?

His head cocked to the side. "Are you always this combative?"

"Are you always this arrogant?"

"I just came over to say hi."

"And inquire about my panties."

"Which I've already seen, remember?"

Oh. Oh yeah. I didn't have anything to say to that, did I?

His head fell back, and I was pretty sure I heard a growl of frustration escape.

Yeah. If this wasn't proof I suffered from foot-in-mouth disease, I didn't know what was. I just can't control it. The word vomit just comes spewing out without a care. Or a bucket. *Cleanup on aisle four.*

Nate straightened and shook his head at me before moving in my direction. I backed up at his approach, until my back hit the frosted door. His hand pressed against the glass by my cheek, and as he leaned in, his breath tickled my ear. I shivered and squeezed the boxes in my arms tighter, though I was sure my trembling was from the cold, not from the proximity of his body.

I was almost sure.

"Listen, Shayne," he said, in a voice low and throaty,

belying his age. "If I wanted to know about what else is hiding under your clothes, trust me, I'd find out." He pulled away slightly, bringing his face in front of mine. "And maybe next time, you'll want me to."

Next time? I thought as he backed away, the red shopping basket in his hand swinging back and forth like a pendulum clock counting down to our inevitable third meeting. My knees felt a bit wobbly as I watched him retreat, and I didn't trust myself to push off the glass just yet.

No, I'd stay here, mute and staring, while he got the last word. And do you want to know the saddest thing? All I could think when he left and I was tossing the frozen food boxes into the cart was, *Thank you baby Jesus that I chose the healthy spinach ones.*

Chapter Five
Viva Las Vegas

LAS VEGAS.

EVEN after visiting more times than I could count, the city always called to me. I wouldn't consider myself a materialistic person, nor am I usually comfortable around grandiose displays of wealth—hah, because I don't have any!—but I love seeing those enormous structures all lit up and sparkling. The blast of perfumed air hitting my face upon walking into each one gave me goosebumps—a sign of exciting, unpredictable times ahead.

Bright and early the next morning, I was throwing my bags into the boot of Paige's Tahoe when my phone rang.

"Good morning, Val," I said.

She didn't waste any time with pleasantries. "What's this I hear about Vegas?"

Shouldering my phone, I pushed the bags farther into the boot to make room for Paige's stuff, not that there was much space left after Quinn and Ryleigh's piles. To say we never traveled light would be an understatement.

"Happy Friday to you, too. Want me to pick up a souvenir flask for you?"

"Cut the small talk. You goin' cock-calling, Callahan?"

Such a way with words. "If you're asking do I plan to visit the animals at Circus Circus, I hate to disappoint you, but the answer's no."

"Well, in case you were planning on a few rounds, don't. You've got a meeting with Ace at The Chandelier at eight tonight."

Her words pinned me to my spot. "No, I don't."

"Yes, you do."

"Val..."

Her voice, like melted butter, tried to smooth me over. "Such a happy coincidence that he'll be there at the same time, don't you think?"

No, no. No way did I want to meet yet another up himself celebrity, and definitely *not* during Paige's birthday weekend. Why would she give him up to me anyway? Miss Cherry-Poppin' red dress and all.

"But...I thought this was something you wanted to handle," I said, even though it was pointless to waste my breath. I'd be going whether I wanted to or not, but I wasn't going to be a pushover.

"And I was under the assumption you wanted a promotion."

"What am I supposed to be meeting with him about exactly?"

"Oh, I'm sure you'll find plenty to talk about."

With a sigh, I said, "So you're telling me you want me to meet with Ace, as in Ace Locke…at a bar…alone."

"A bar isn't exactly private, Shayne."

Realization hit me in the face with the force of a Mack truck. *Oh bugger.* "Is this a date? This is a date, isn't it? Please tell me you're not setting me up with him at a bar in Vegas while I should be celebrating my best friend's birthday."

"I don't know why you have to put a label on everything—"

"And not just a date," I said. "A date with a celebrity, which I told you after the Pepé Le Pew disaster I'd never do again."

"Okay, now you're just being picky. I'm positive Ace doesn't do voices. For Christ's sake, he's not method."

With a frustrated growl, I slammed the boot shut. As I came around the car, Ryleigh and Quinn were giving me curious looks, but I shook my head and pointed to my phone.

"I'm off this weekend, Val. I put in my request months ago."

"Most people would jump at the chance to be in your shoes."

I rubbed my forehead to alleviate the throbbing that had suddenly come up. Part of my job description was knowing how to pick my battles with my boss, and this was one I knew better than to cross her on.

"Fine," I mumbled.

"I didn't hear that."

"I'll be there."

"A 'thank you so much for this incredible opportunity' would've sufficed as well, but that would be too much for you, I suppose. Make sure to wear something skimpy to show off those toothpicks, would you."

"Right on top of that, Val."

"Don't drop the ball. Or balls," she said before the line went dead.

"Oh come *on*," I muttered, shoving my phone in my back pocket and stamping my foot for good measure.

"Please tell me that wench isn't making you stay here this weekend. I'll kill her," Ryleigh said.

"No...but—" Out of the corner of my eye, I saw Paige attempting to roll her bag down the long outside staircase, and I jogged over to help her.

"Oh, for the love of fuck," Paige said as she struggled to keep her oversized suitcase from falling down the stairs and dragging her behind it. I grabbed the handle from her and heaved it down the remaining steps.

"Thank you," she managed, leaning against the rail

and catching her breath.

"I'd ask you why you need this much stuff for a two-night trip, but I don't dare antagonize the birthday girl," I said, rolling her bag toward the trunk.

"I appreciate that, Shayne. Lemme go grab the other one."

I whirled around. "The other—"

Before I could get out the rest of my sentence, she was back inside the house. The boot was already full to bursting, so it would take a bit of maneuvering to pack it all in. When we were younger, my mum had somehow squeezed in a family of five's clothing *and* Christmas presents in one little tiny space. She'd said it was like fitting puzzle pieces together, trial and error. That sounded simple enough.

Too bad I hated puzzles.

Paige's door opened again and she placed a slightly smaller bag on the landing. "All right, I think that's everything. Damn. Liquor bottles are heavy."

"That bag is full of alcohol?"

"We've gotta pre-party."

"Of course we do. What was I thinking?"

I helped her heave the suitcase to the car, and when she noticed the contents inside, she stopped in her tracks and let out a loud laugh.

"There is no way in hell Ryleigh's stuff will fit," she said. "She brings two bags of just shoes."

"Actually, most of that *is* my stuff," Ryleigh said,

smirking as she joined us. "I came over early to get a head start."

Paige raised an eyebrow. "Smart fucker."

"And I brought the coffee," Quinn said, carrying a tray of coffee cups from her car.

"Ohhhh, you're the best," I said, running over to take one off her hands. Caffeine was a must if I was going to deal with what the night had in store for me. Scratch that—I needed something stronger.

"Hey Paige, you got any Baileys in that bag?"

She gave me a wary glance. "It's nine a.m."

"And I'm on vacation."

"Good point. Quinn, you're driving," she said, tossing her the keys and unzipping the bag we'd just hauled down to reveal a bottle of Kahlua. "Will this work?"

I nodded my agreement and we peeled off our coffee lids to spike the drinks.

And then we were off.

"Hey," Quinn said after we'd pulled out of Paige's luxurious Hollywood Hills neighborhood. "You know what this means, right?"

Paige stopped mid-sip and shook her head. "Oh no. No, no, no, no."

"Liquor up, buttercup. You're gonna need it." Quinn smiled in the rearview mirror in Paige's direction.

"Absolutely not. I changed my mind. Stop the car."

"Too late. It's my honor to chauffeur our beloved birthday girl, and to celebrate, I'll be playing all my favorites. A little seventies rock. Some hair-band eighties. Maybe a little nineties grunge."

Paige gave a loud groan. "Oh God, please no. Not the slit-your-wrists Nirvana shit."

Quinn gave an evil laugh. "You just keep pouring that liquor, and leave me in charge of the radio. Now cheers," she said, holding her arm out to clink her non-spiked with ours.

We were past Barstow before I had the courage to bring up Val's call.

"She what!" Ryleigh exclaimed, wheeling around from the passenger seat to face me.

"I know, I know. I'm so sorry, you guys, but I don't know how to get out of it," I said, leaning my head back against the seat. A light buzz was taking the edge off my nerves, but I was more concerned with letting the girls down.

"Don't you dare!" Paige cried out. "Quinn, turn that down. Did you hear what she said? First Pepé Le Pew, and now Ace Locke? Jesus, Shayne. Do you have a golden pussy we don't know about?"

Quinn flicked the radio off. "Holy hell. This is some vision-board shit coming true right here. Can you wish Henry Cavill into mine?"

"You have to go. Have to," Paige said.

I glared at her. "It's your freakin' birthday. I'm not supposed to be on duty, and I'm so tired of going on these stupid meeting date things for her. Besides, we've got plans."

Paige slapped the back of the seat. "Hell yes we do! We'll all go, then. He won't know we're there, and it's the perfect place to grab drinks before our night out. We'll just get ready a bit earlier."

Their excited faces told me I'd have the support I needed to get in and then GTFO. I breathed a sigh of relief. "That would be perfect. Thank you, thank you."

"See, now we can spy on you and save you when you give us the signal." Paige gave herself a pat on the back. "You're welcome."

Chapter Six
Ace in the Hole

HOURS LATER, AFTER we'd checked into the
Cosmopolitan, I'd gotten a full makeover from Paige,
including a smoky eye to go with the blue dress she'd forced
me to wear that was about ten inches shorter than I
preferred. *It's like the Pantsless Metro ride all over again,* I
thought, pulling at the hem.

Paige tousled my loose curls around my shoulders.
"Stop fidgeting."

"I can't help it. I'm showing my bum."

"You're not showing your bum," she mimicked in
my accent, and then she stepped back to inspect her
handiwork. "Okay, lip gloss, and then you're set."

"And here are your shoes, properly scored so you

don't fall on said *bum*." Ryleigh set down the not-quite-three-inch heels—as high as I would allow—and then flopped on the bed. By contrast, *her* heels had to be double the size of mine. How she walked in those, I had no clue, but she could probably run a marathon in them and be fine. It wasn't normal.

"Okay, so let's go over the signal again," Quinn said as she emerged from the bathroom looking like an assassin goddess. That was the only way to describe the diminutive strapless leather dress that looked like she'd have to get peeled out of later. Maybe that was the point.

"If he starts any baby talk, if he puts his hands in places you don't want them, or if you're at the point where you want to throw your drink in his face and smash the martini glass over his head, make sure to do this first and we'll come regulate." Quinn balled her fist, held it up to her cheek, and then rubbed the line of her jaw with her thumb.

My eyebrows shot up. "Yep. Got it. Not conspicuous at all."

"Won't be if it's done right," Quinn said, handing me my purse.

"Did you put mace in here too?"

"Watch it, smartass."

Now, it just so happened we were staying at the same hotel that the meeting with Ace would be taking place, so after the girls went down to assume their positions, I waited for five and then punched the elevator button for the level I needed.

Ugh, why did Val do this to me? My stomach always flipped with nerves every time I had to go on one of these "meet-dates," as I called them. And knowing I was about to meet someone I'd watched in movies? Not intimidating at all. *Really.*

By the time I arrived at the Chandelier, my stomach was in a chokehold so tight it was on the verge of tapping out. For Pete's sake, it wasn't like I'd never met a celebrity before. I once saw Tom Hanks at the farmers' market down the street, and when he smiled at me and said "Hi" as he walked by, I still didn't pass out.

So I could definitely handle Mr. Big and Brawny.

Ace wasn't at the top bar, so I headed down to the second floor, studiously ignoring my friends as I walked by where they were positioned at the main bar. When a wolf whistle sounded behind me, my heel skidded across the slick floor, my arms going windmill in an effort to stop the crash. Residual wobbling as I tried to stay on my feet and then…safe.

Bloody hell, that was close.

On an exhale, I tossed my hair over my shoulder, and that was when I saw my potential client. Had to be. A heavily muscled figure sat in a roped-off area hidden in amethyst shadows and blocked by a couple of bodyguard types. As I approached, they moved to the side, and I heard, "Miss Callahan," as one opened the rope.

Ace stood as I entered, and he wasn't nearly as tall as I thought he'd be. In my heels we matched each other pretty damn close, though I had no doubt he could bench-press me in a hot minute if his tires for biceps were any indication of strength.

"Thanks for meeting me, Miss Callahan," he said, as he shook my hand, his grip firm. "I'm Ace."

"Nice to meet you. And call me Shayne, please."

He motioned to the plush chair across from him and waited until I sat down before he took a seat. "I wasn't sure what your poison was or I would've ordered ahead." Then, as if on cue, a waitress was let inside the rope.

"Oh, that's okay," I said, taking the drink menu that was offered and quickly scanning over it for something sweet. "I'll have a Violet Femme, please."

"Excellent choice," the waitress said, before turning to Ace. Her ample cleavage was on display as she angled herself so that he'd have the best view. "Another bourbon for you, sir?"

"Keep 'em coming." Even though the woman was giving him permission to enjoy the view, he didn't so much as glance at her chest—or her bare legs in a skirt inches shorter than mine. When she didn't get the response she was hoping for, she frowned and exited the way she came. Then he unbuttoned his suit jacket and shifted back in his seat, as if ready for me to give him a spiel of some kind.

I hadn't been given a lot of intel on this meeting—okay, strike that, I'd been given *none*—so I wasn't quite sure what he was looking for exactly. I was about to, to use Paige's repulsive expression, "pull it out of my ass."

"Val said you had a meeting earlier this week," I said, crossing my legs. But as soon as I did, I could feel a breeze against my bum, so I readjusted so that they were crossed at the ankles instead.

No blowing bum breeze now. *Perrrrfect.*

"That we did. You came highly recommended by a friend of mine."

"Well, Val's done a great job of—"

He wagged a finger. "No, not Val. *You.*"

"Me?"

"I heard you're the brains behind this whole operation, so I wanted to meet with you personally to see if you're—and I don't mean any offense by this—as good as I've heard you are."

Oh…oh wow. Swallowing hard, I tried to formulate a response to what he'd said, but the words refused to come out.

People in his circle knew about me? That was more than a little mind-blowing. I briefly wondered if I'd unwittingly helped any supermodels find love lately, but *please.* Like a model needed help finding a boyfriend. Which raised the question…what the hell did Ace Locke need me for?

"I thought we could help each other out," he said, as if he'd been privy to my thoughts.

My brain finally snapped back in gear, and I nodded. "Right. Of course. And I know how much our company could benefit from working with you, but I have to admit

I'm curious what we can do for you?"

He grinned. "So you're aware of my prior dating history."

As tempted as I was to play dumb and clarify what he meant, I wouldn't be half as good at my job if I didn't keep up with couplings, especially those in the spotlight. "I'm not sure how accurate the reports are, but I think I have a handle on what you may be looking for." That was about as polite as I could make it, because somehow I didn't think "skinny blondes who take off their clothes for a living and consume nothing but cigarettes, champagne, and Ex-Lax" would be as PR—even if it *was* the truth.

He took a long swallow from his drink, and when he set it on the arm of the chair, his finger circled the lip of the glass.

"The thing is, Shayne, I'm looking for someone a bit...different than my usual."

"Different how?"

"Well, now that's the question." Again with rimming the glass. Heh. Rimming. Paige would have a joke about that. "I thought maybe we could get to know each other first before we get into the business stuff."

Oh... "Um, I'm sorry, I didn't bring my credentials, but they're posted on our website if you'd like to—"

"No, no, I meant tell me more about you. Your accent is...British?"

"Australian, actually. Although it's nowhere near as strong as my family's. They tend to call me a traitor to the country I was born in. Nice, right?"

"So you've been here a while, then?"

"About ten years, yeah. My family moved here when I was eighteen, and then after I'd finished uni they decided to go back. So it's just me here now."

"Must get lonely."

"Nah, we Skype a lot and I've got a great group of friends. And I love my job, of course."

"I understand that."

My head cocked to the side as I studied the solemn expression that kept peeking out when he wasn't forcing a smile. "I'm sure it gets lonely traveling so much. Always on location for movies or tours."

"It does, it does. I'd like to find…someone. You know? Not that I expect anyone to want to pack up and go with me all the time, but…" He shrugged. "It'd be nice."

The waitress came back with our drinks, and once again I couldn't help but notice he didn't pay her any attention. She was tall, thin, blond, and busty—exactly his type. Maybe he wanted to make a good impression by proving he wasn't just after a hot piece of ass.

We continued the conversation, and he told me about how he'd gotten into the movie business, about his strict Catholic upbringing, and how whom he dated seemed to have a big impact on his career. His specialty was action movies, and he explained that his handlers told him having a pretty young thing on his arm helped to boost his attractiveness to the female audience and had guys wanting to be in his shoes.

But even as we laughed about that, something passed in his eyes. Something tired, something pained…

Now, normally I wouldn't drink more than a glass of something if I was out with a client, but this wasn't an ordinary meeting, and hello—Vegas.

"A pair of lemon drops," a deep voice said, and I looked up to see a seriously attractive waiter holding a shot glass lined with sugar and a lemon out to me. I guessed blondie'd had enough rejection.

"I can't believe you're not making me do something I'll need a chaser for."

Ace winked. "Hey, these look like tequila but taste a helluva lot better." As he took his shot from the waiter, he pulled out a bill from his pocket, his fingers lingering when he handed it over. Then Ace flashed the guy a broad smile. "Thanks a lot."

Okay, hold up a second…

Even though I was beginning to feel the effects of the two drinks I'd already had, I knew I wasn't imagining what I'd just seen. And Ace wasn't hiding the way he watched the guy leave, though I doubted he would've been so obvious if anyone else had been with us. I was hyper-attuned to everything he was saying and doing as I tried to figure out just what he was looking for, so you better believe I just caught the message he was sending me.

My gaze followed his, and I had to admit, the way the waiter's tight black pants fit his ass was worth drooling over.

"I think we might need another round of shots soon," I found myself saying.

Ace's eyes met mine, a mixture of relief and something else I couldn't quite name swirling in them. He sounded cautious when he spoke. "Is that okay?"

I nodded and held out my shot for a cheers. "Most definitely okay."

After we'd downed the sweet and sour, we fell back into a casual conversation, but my mind was spinning. Several questions went through my head, but it seemed Ace wasn't quite ready to open up yet. Still, it had me wondering what my role in all of this would be.

Did he want our company to help him come out?

Did he want our company to help him find someone to keep on the down-low?

Wait, no, that couldn't be it. It was to be a mutually beneficial relationship, which meant he'd need to be seen with...

Ohhh. A woman on his arm and a man in his bed, maybe?

Yes, that could definitely be it. And while it wasn't something I had experience in, surely there were women out there willing to cover for someone like Ace.

"So would you like to meet when we get back to—" I stopped dead as Ace reached for his drink. Just past his shoulder I could see that the girls had moved down the bar and were now directly in my line of view, but they weren't who had caught my attention. Standing next to Quinn was someone completely unexpected, and I swear if it was possible for eyes to bulge out of your head from shock, mine would've been rolling across the floor already. Because just behind her was Nate.

Nate Boxer Briefs. Nate Target Aisle. And now Nate…Vegas.

No way. It couldn't be.

I squeezed my eyes shut to clear the obvious hallucination from my brain and then opened them again.

Nope. Still there.

And not only was he there, but from the way Ryleigh was excitedly gesturing toward his back once she saw I was watching, he was with our group.

"Sweet fuck," I said under my breath.

"Is everything okay?"

In those frozen seconds, I'd completely forgotten about Ace sitting there, and his voice made me jump halfway out of my seat.

I sat up and flashed a bright smile, putting my PR Shayne mask back on. "You bet. So would you like to meet at my office, or—"

"Do you know them?" he interrupted, inclining his head in the direction of my friends. The moment our gazes hit them they all spun around and pretended to be focused on the scenery.

Way to be stealth, guys.

Focusing back to Ace, I said, "Never seen 'em before

in my life."

He chuckled a bit and took a sip of his bourbon. "Never, huh? That guy seems to disagree."

I looked back up to see Nate watching us with interest. When he had my attention—and let's be real here, when did the guy not have my focus if he was around—he lifted up his drink to us, much like he'd done at The Vortex.

Though I tried to keep my face unemotional, my heart felt like it was going to explode. What were the chances he'd be here and that my friends had run into him? A snowball in hell would've stood better odds.

And it made me squirm in my seat to think he probably had the wrong impression of what was going on between Ace and me. Probably thought I was on a date, and my friends were just Peeping Toms. The latter was right. And really, I shouldn't care, because both times I saw him, it didn't end so well.

Maybe I should insert my foot in my mouth and leave it there when I saw him coming.

God. Why did the guy cause my stomach to flip-flop and my body to break into a cold sweat every time he was nearby? I mean, those physical symptoms are usually associated with someone you *don't* wanna see. With dread.

Not with…lust. Because that's what it was. It had to be. Dirty, *dirty* lust. But looking at the guy, could anyone blame me? No. No, they could not.

"Shayne?" Ace's voice cut through my inner monologue. When I looked at him, he smiled and said, "I've got to get going soon, but maybe another shot for the road?"

"A shot? Oh. Yes, great idea."

Well, I'll be damned. Ace was shaping up to be a non-douchebag. I was surprised to find I actually liked the guy. Not in a sexual sort of way—too much waxing going on for my tastes—but he was down to earth and seemed genuine.

Then again, he *was* an actor.

Hottie waiter came back to hand us repeats of the lemon drops, and then one of Ace's bodyguards approached and gave him a nod.

"And that's my cue," he said. "It was a pleasure to meet you, Shayne. I'll be in touch soon if it's a go on your end?"

"Definitely a go. We'd love to work with you."

"Well, uh." He rubbed the back of his neck. "If it's all the same, I'd rather work with just you. Val is a little…"

"Eccentric?"

"'Fucking crazy' are the words I'd use."

"Then I'll make sure to work with you directly," I said with a wink.

A wink? I totally winked at Ace Locke. How come this guy didn't make me ramble and stutter all over the place, but twenty-four-year-old over there had me falling over and lashing out at every turn? It made no sense.

After we said our goodbyes, I waited until he was out of eyesight to go meet up with my friends, who no doubt wanted every last detail of what went on. Imagine my

surprise when they didn't immediately bombard me with
questions, but instead ushered me over to where Nate was
standing with a group of guys.

With his face cleanly shaven, he looked younger than
he had with the scruff covering his chin and jaw. But still
ridiculously attractive. It made me want to kick him in the
shins.

"There you are," Ryleigh said, linking her arm
through mine. "Would you look who we ran into as we were
walking inside? Isn't this such an awesome coincidence?"

Leave it to the happily attached woman to set her
friends up so they'd be "happy" too. Wasn't that supposed
to be my job?

As much as I wished I could avoid meeting Nate's
eyes when I came to a stop in front of him, his gaze was
insistent. I gave him a tight smile. "And he's fully clothed
today. Miracles happen, I suppose."

"I don't have to be," he replied, and then he handed
off his beer to one of his friends and began to take off his suit
jacket. And wouldn't you know, he had on a pair of damn
suspenders underneath.

Fuck me, I'd never resist him if those were unleashed.

"Keep your clothes on, Romeo, this is a respectable
establishment," I said. "And let me guess. You put a tracking
device on me last night?"

"I was trying not to be so obvious about it, but…" He
gave me a cocky smirk before grabbing his beer and taking a
swig. "So…"

"So…"

The question was on the tip of his tongue. I could see it. The one about whether Ace and I would be seeing each other later…like maybe in bed.

"Come here often?" His grin cracked wider, an obvious attempt at teasing me about my lack of social skills last night.

Har har, ass.

"You're such a dag. Really," I said.

"A dag? Does that mean insanely good-looking and charming?"

"Sure it does."

"Sounds sexy in your accent, so it can't be too bad."

I narrowed my eyes. "Aren't you going to put your clothes back on?"

He glanced at the jacket draped over the back of a chair and shrugged. "Nah, I think I'll leave it off. It seems to bother you."

"I couldn't care less, I assure you."

"Sure. So…was that a date?"

"I *knew* you couldn't resist asking."

He put his hands up. "Just an innocent question. Big guy doesn't look like the type that would appreciate your Boba Fett-ish, so I was just looking out. Friend to friend."

"Are you trying to say only a guy who wears suspenders like yourself would be my type? Or perhaps a pocket protector and nerd glasses? Maybe I like big muscles and…really tight shirts. Or guys who have absolutely nothing in common with me. Because sometimes the whole opposites-attract thing is actually right on. Although in my experience it's been completely off, like the one time I went out with this fisherman guy because my mom was all, 'Shayne, give him a chance, or you'll wind up a bloody old spinster,' and it turned out to be the worst experience of my life. I've blocked most of it out, mind you, but I can remember the deep-sea trip with this glass floor, and then there was fish guts and their heads were chopped off, and I think I lost about five pounds puking up the lollies I'd eaten that day. Worst date up to now, I suppose, but there's always room for more mistakes."

A beat, and then, "So I'm guessing that's a no?"

"Oh. Right, yeah. Not a date."

His face relaxed, and then he said, "Well then, what can I get you?"

After I gave him my order, he went over to the bar, and I turned back to my friends. Who were all staring at me with identical expressions of horror.

I wiped at my face. "What? Is my lipstick everywhere?"

"What the fucking *hell* was that?" Paige hissed.

"What was what?"

"Oh baby girl," Quinn said, shaking her head and looking at me with *oh you poor thing* eyes. "You like him, huh?"

"Who, Nate? Of course not. I barely know the guy, and from what I've gathered, he's a typical L.A. wanker.

A.k.a. *not* my type." I tucked my hair behind my ear. "Why would you think that?"

"You only ramble like that around us or when you like someone," she replied.

"I do not."

"You do so," Ryleigh cut in. "It's totally obvious now."

"Shut up, you're giving me a complex. I don't ramble. And even if I did, it's not like it means I like the guy. I suppose his boxer briefs the other day were pretty hot and all, and the dimples are a total turn-on for most people, but I definitely don't like him. Like the wise Bridget Jones once said, 'He's just a knobhead with no knob.'"

"I'm glad we set that straight," Nate said from behind me.

I froze as heat flooded my body and then my mouth clamped shut. When the girls immediately ran off for drink refills, I knew I'd cocked up good and proper this time.

Shiiiiiiiiiiiiiiiitballonastick. Why does this always happen to me?

Chapter Seven
Rock Out with
Your Cock Out

I PIVOTED SLOWLY, and when I was facing him again, he held out my drink.

"Cheers to knobheads with no...*knobs*, was it?"

"Right...uh...I didn't mean that, I just—"

"No, it's okay. You don't know me, and from our brief run-ins, I've given you the impression I'm somehow...knobby." He frowned into the contents of his drink. "I'm not exactly sure what that means, but I'll have to convince you otherwise. Won't I?"

When he looked up, his eyes were full of a challenge, like he was daring me to let him prove me wrong. And as much as I knew my words had been full of the asshole variety, part of me wanted to get to know the real Nate

Ryan.

Okay, not just *part* of me wanted that. More like 93.9 percent. Which meant I was not. Giving. In.

With a shrug, I said, "Seems like a waste of time."

"Because you've got me figured out?"

"Look, it's my job to know how to read people." As he opened his mouth to protest, I shook my head. "Let me guess. You haven't had a steady girlfriend since you broke little Miss Mary Sue's heart back in high school."

He narrowed his eyes. "Beth. And that doesn't mean anything."

"Hah." I pulled the swizzle stick out of my glass and slid the cherry off with my teeth. Nate's eyes were glued to my mouth. "It means you're not looking for love. You're looking for hit-it-and-quit-its."

"And what about you? Is that internal marriage-and-five-kids clock or whatever it is women get ticking yet?"

"Hardly. I'm not looking. Period." But even as I said those words, I could feel the lie behind them. When you set up happy couple after happy couple and saw the bliss that could be... Well, it makes you wonder if you'll ever have that.

I had time, though. I mean, it's not like I had one foot in the grave, pushing around a walker and chomping my gums. I just wanted to be firmly established in my career first, and maybe Ace would be the client that sealed that part of the deal.

"Talking is overrated," Paige cut in, pushing herself

between us and handing us each a pair of shots. One sniff told me these weren't the easygoing lemon drops, but the one-tequila-floor real deals.

"I'm not gonna be able to walk soon," I said, eyeing the potent liquor.

Paige threw her arm around Nate's neck. "You're taking care of my girl tonight, right?"

As he crossed his heart, his eyes never leaving mine, he said, "I'll guard her with my life."

"Good. Now cheers, bitches, it's my birthdaaay."

We all held up our shots before throwing them back, and damn if that nasty stuff didn't go down like it was blazing a path to hell. Chasing it with my Violet Femme only flamed the fire, though. Where was water when you needed it?

"Hey, easy now," Nate said, as he pulled the glass away from my mouth. "I know I said I'd take care of you, but I have a feeling you'll fight me when I try to carry you out of here, and I'd like to enjoy you first."

"You are persistent, aren't you?"

"If I wasn't, you'd tell me to fuck off."

"I'm pretty sure I already have."

Nate grinned. "I know you don't mean it."

"Why would I say things I don't mean—" I started, but when I saw the trio of males rounding the bar in Paige's direction, a bubble of laughter rose in my throat.

"What's so funny?" Nate asked.

I shook my head. "Paige is gonna lose her shit when

she sees—"

"Oh, what the fuck are you doing here?" Paige's voice rose above the crowd as she shot daggers at the tall male in black smirking in front of her. Dressed in a suit, with his long, dirty blond hair pulled back at the nape of his neck, he looked like a rock star, guyliner and all. Super hot if you liked that sort of thing, which, according to his reputation, many, *many* women did.

"Just wanted to wish my best girl a happy birthday, of course."

"You can't come crashing in here like a goddamn wrecking ball, *Dick*," Paige said, hands on her hips.

Richard Dawson—a.k.a. the *Dick* she was referring to—looked around and spread his hands. "Looks like an open bar to me. And you look delicious as usual, Pita." Bringing her hand up to his mouth, he winked at her before planting a kiss on the back of it, and she growled in response.

"I'm guessing they know each other," Nate said as he leaned in, his breath tickling my ear and sending shivers down my body. "Ex-lovers?"

He was close, too close, but I didn't move away. Instead, I said, "Apparently their parents are best friends, and they grew up together. She swears they've never hooked up, but who knows with them. You can never tell if they want to kill each other or fuck each other. Maybe both."

"So all this fighting is…foreplay?"

His words felt like a double meaning. Was he talking

about Paige and Dawson, or did he mean us? I didn't have time to wonder about that, though, because Ryleigh and Quinn moved in front of us.

"I hate to interrupt, but you know where this is going, right?" Quinn said. She inclined her head toward the birthday girl, who was still trading barbs with her childhood buddy turned whatever he was.

Ryleigh nodded. "Dance-off. Totally."

"Did you say dance-off?" Nate laughed, but then it faded out when we all just stared at him. "You're joking. Oh, come on, you're not serious."

"It's not what you're thinking. It's more like...find the hottest partner on the dance floor and sex them up to make the other person jealous. Or something." Yeah, it sounded crazy coming out of my mouth too. "I know it seems a little suss, but trust me."

Quinn threw back the rest of her martini. "Let's grab her and go, then." Then to Nate, she said, "You and your friends brought your fake IDs, right?"

My mouth fell open. "Quinn!"

She laughed as Ryleigh pulled her toward Paige. "You know I'm kidding. But seriously, you guys should join us. Shayne would love it if you did."

"Quinn, shut up."

"What, so you don't want me to go?" he asked. "Not like I'd give you much choice on the matter. I did promise to guard you with my life tonight."

I turned to face him, and he didn't back up an inch.

The air between us grew static, crackling with electricity. It was a bad idea, letting him join us.

Tell him no. Tell him you like your life as it is, with your ice cream pajamas and trashy television show binges and your vibrator, Big Ben. Because this could get complicated and messy real fast, and a guy like him would break a heart without a second thought.

Of course I didn't say that. *No,* tequila answered for me. And tequila said, "Bring it the hell on."

Chapter Eight
Jam Out with Your Clam Out

LIKE A GOOD bodyguard, Nate hadn't left my side all night when we'd entered the club. Not when I went to the bar. Not when I'd headed to the bathroom to touch up my lipstick—though he was waiting just outside the door.

The butterflies that had started when I'd first noticed him earlier that evening hadn't dissipated either—they'd gotten worse. That hadn't happened with someone in so long that the sensation was unfamiliar, though not necessarily unwelcome.

With a final look in the mirror, I fluffed my hair out around my shoulders, grabbed my drink, and walked out of the bathroom. Nate was leaning against the opposite wall, arms crossed and his sleeves pushed up his forearms. His gaze traveled down the length of my body.

"Did I mention how much I'm enjoying the fact that you forgot your pants again tonight? If I hadn't seen those sexy pajamas, I'd be a little concerned you didn't own any."

"As if you would mind that."

"I think you like me looking at you."

I mimicked his pose as I leaned against the wall. "Well, I can't stop you."

"No, you can't." He cocked his head to the side. "Do you know what I love more than anything?"

"Stalking potential dates in the grocery aisle?"

"Gorgeous women who pretend they're not interested."

I rolled my eyes and pushed off the wall. "I'm not pretend—"

"You like the challenge," he said, stepping in front of me, his eyes flicking to my mouth. "And believe me, so do I."

"Wrong."

"Stubborn and in denial. I can work with that." He took the glass from my hand and tipped the liquid into his mouth.

"Let me guess. Girly drinks are your favorite too."

"Nah, just wanted to get a taste of what's going into that delicious mouth of yours."

"Jesus." I shook my head. "You don't stop, do you?"

His dimple deepened. "You like that too."

I tried to keep my lips from twitching into a smile,

really I did. He was so damn frustrating. But persistent. And persuasive. And so fucking sexy it was hard to remember why I was trying not to show my interest.

My mind blanked. *Why is that again…*

His stupid smile was winning me over, though. I had to try harder. And maybe not look at him.

Turning away, I scanned the crowd on the dance floor looking for the girls. Near the DJ booth, Ryleigh and Quinn were dancing solo and watching the dance-off in progress. Also known as Paige grinding all over one of the guys Nate had come in with while Dirty Dick had his hands all over a busty blonde nearby. It was so obvious that they were showing off for each other, and it was all about the one-upmanship with those two. They needed to just get it on and get it over with already.

Nate moved in behind me.

"Should I entice you to join me out there, or do you prefer voyeurism?"

"I enjoy a good show, but now I'm curious how you'd do that. Entice me?"

"I could tell you…or I could show you. Preference?"

"Tell me and maybe I'll let you show me," I said over my shoulder.

He put his hands on my hips, keeping me facing the dance floor, and I felt him lower his head, the warmth of his breath breezing across my neck. Shivers rippled down my body, giving away the effect he made on me with barely a touch.

His lips skimmed my neck so lightly I thought I'd imagined it before I heard, "I'd make sure you were looking at me as I let my eyes roam over you. This dress"—he fingered the hem of the material that reached the top of my thigh—"if I didn't know better, I'd think you wore it for me. Short enough that I can feel how smooth your thighs are without having to slip my fingers underneath. Not that that would stop me...because once I had you out there...had my arms around you...had you tight against me so I could feel every part of you...then I could let my hands wander."

I felt those same fingers move higher underneath my skirt, crumbling my already weakened defenses, and it took everything in me to push his hands back down.

"Tell...and then show. Those are the rules," I said, trying to not let myself get carried away by his words. But damn it was hard. Especially when he gave a light chuckle and moved his hands back to my hips to fit me flush against his body. My struggle to remain aloof wasn't the only thing that was hard between us.

Oh sweet Christ...

"Fuck the rules," he said, grabbing my hand and pulling me out to the dance floor.

As I squeezed through the bodies around me sensually grinding to the pulsing beat, I felt my heart accelerate in anticipation of feeling the man in front of me once again pressed against my body.

Maybe whatever happened in Vegas really *could* stay in Vegas. It wasn't like we had to get married or anything. I mean, he was just this really hot guy to have fun with for one night only, and if we could just get the explosive sexual chemistry thing out of our systems, we could go back to L.A. and be normal. Like it never happened.

At least, that was what I wanted to believe.

Once Nate reached the center of the room, he turned around and gripped my waist, pulling me forward until there wasn't a breath of space between us. Sweaty bodies crowded in on us, so close it was hard to tell where one couple began and the other ended. The lights were hot and flashing, and this close, I could smell his delicious scent—the salt of his sweat mixed with the faintness of his cologne and my drink that still lingered on his sweet breath. I wanted to run my tongue up his neck to taste him. But I didn't want to stop there.

As my gaze lingered on his neck before moving up to his mouth, his lips tipped up. "Feel like sharing what that look's about?"

I was dimly aware I was throwing caution to the wind, but after as many drinks as we'd had… *Oh, what the hell.*

My stare turned confident. "I was just wondering what you'd taste like."

His hold on my hips turned almost painful, and I could feel him growing hard against me. Hard and long…

I squeezed his arms tighter, and he responded by moving a knee between my legs and rocking with me so that I was straddling his thigh. My already swollen clit rubbed against his pants, the thick muscles underneath creating a delicious friction as his hands on my hips guided me, rolling me with him. Slow at first and then harder, my breath coming in irregular pants. My flimsy panties were no match for how wet I was, and I tried to push away.

"No," he growled, and pulled me tighter. I looked around to see if anyone was watching, but we were so immersed in the crowd that even with the hundreds of bodies surrounding us, it almost felt…private.

The pulsing between my legs needed to be sated, and I didn't try to escape this time. Nate kept one hand on my hip, still moving me against him, my thigh rubbing his hard length at the same time. His other hand moved to the edge of my hem, just as he'd promised earlier, and then disappeared beneath the fabric. The rough pads of his fingers slid up the back of my thigh slowly, moving up to grab a handful of my ass, kneading and drawing me even closer against him.

We moved to the pounding beat, and it was just the right amount of pressure to stoke the fire building inside.

Oh God…I could come right here. In the back of my mind, I knew I was with Nate, in the middle of the dance floor, surrounded by people, but all that registered was the way my sensitive flesh rubbed against him in exactly the way I needed.

Nate pressed a kiss beneath my ear. "You feel so good, Shayne."

With those words, I grabbed a fistful of his dark hair

and buried my face in his neck as my orgasm violently burst and shuddered through me. His fingers tightened on my skin when he realized what was happening, but he didn't stop moving or pull away.

Where the hell did that come from? Did I really just… On his… Oh my God.

As I came down from the high and loosened my grip on his arms, he slowed our pace down and moved the hand under my skirt up my back to hold me still while I struggled to get my breathing back to a normal tempo.

"Holy shit." He leaned back, his eyes wide on mine. "Hottest fucking thing…" he started, but then his hand went to the back of my neck, and he brought my lips to his.

He tasted even better than I'd imagined. Not that I'd imagined it…much.

Okay, maybe somewhere deep in my subconscious I had, and *hell*…he did not disappoint. As he swayed us to the music, his mouth stayed hungry on mine, his tongue a caress I wanted over my entire body.

I didn't care that I was kissing him on the dance floor like other couples I'd made fun of before. I didn't care—and I should've—that I'd just had an earth-shattering orgasm in the middle of a crowded room where anyone could see. And I certainly didn't care to pull away from him when I heard familiar voices around us.

I heard Quinn's wolf whistle and then, "Well, I'll be damned. Don't stop on our account."

"I think she's trying to give Paige a run for her

money," Ryleigh said.

"Who's giving me a run for my— Holy shit, Shayne. I'm so proud. Someone give her the room key."

As Paige's voice rang out behind me, I pulled away, but even as I turned, Nate's hands on my hips positioned me directly in front of him.

Oh...okay, that's hot.

The girls broke into slow claps when I faced them, which normally would've embarrassed the hell out of me, so what I did next was way out of character.

I curtsied. Fucking curtsied.

"Thank you, thank you," I said.

"Next showing in an hour," Nate said from behind me.

Paige fanned herself. "Hot damn, I'd like to see that, but our girl here is a shy one. So how about you two take the key and get the hell outta here?"

"What? I'm not leaving you on your birthday," I said, stepping forward and lowering my voice so Nate couldn't hear me. But Paige wasn't having it.

"Oh yes you are. Your birthday gift to me is to take sexy Mr. Suspenders upstairs before he combusts. In fact, I demand it." She winked and then handed me the key card Ryleigh pulled out of her clutch. "Just make sure it happens on your bed, not mine."

Chapter Nine
Well, Aren't You
a Right Bastard

ONCE WE'D LEFT the heated confines of the club and headed back to my room, it wasn't reality that set in. Nope, it was the buzz that had my skin tingling and my mind solely focused on Nate and starting round two of what had begun on the dance floor.

Amazing that alcohol could do a one-eighty on your brain.

When we reached my room, I ran my hands up and down his suspenders. It was a shame those would have to come off. "So...do you want to come in?"

Not like he was going to say no, but I figured I'd ask anyway because I wanted to hear him say yes. The girls were heading to another club and we had at least a couple of hours to be alone, so I wasn't about to waste time getting a repeat of what had happened only a short while ago.

While I wasn't big on the one-night stand circuit, especially not lately, I wasn't one to shy away from enjoying myself. And right now, I couldn't remember the last time I'd wanted to be with someone so much. Who would've thought hours ago that this was the way things would turn out...

Nate's lips brushed my throat in a kiss before he gently pushed my shoulders away and looked me in the eye. Through the haze of my alcohol-induced state, it took me a minute to work out what the expression on his face was. There was longing, there was lust, and there was...regret.

Wait—regret? That can't be right.

I squinted at him again and tried to figure out what else that look could mean. Nope...still there. An icy chill spread through my veins at what that look said was coming.

"Are you fucking kidding me?" The words were out of my mouth before I could stop them.

"Shayne—"

"No," I said, pushing away from him. I looked him up and down, trying to find some clue of what I'd missed, what signal I'd misread. His hands stayed by his sides and he didn't attempt to move toward me to tell me I was wrong. The blood pounded in my head, the alcohol adding fuel to the anger and hurt and embarrassment all fighting for dominance. *How the hell did I get this so wrong?*

"It's not you—"

I scoffed. "Don't. Do *not* give me the rest of that sentence. Was this some kind of game for you?" Then the realization hit me all at once, and I could barely make out my next words. "A dare... Was this a dare?"

"Christ, Shayne, of course not." He gripped the back of his neck as his eyes pleaded with mine for understanding. "I like you."

Seconds passed by as I waited for the rest of the ball to drop.

"And...?"

"And I'm not an idiot. We've both been drinking. I know you'd probably wake up tomorrow hating my guts again or picking a fight, and I'm not about to take advantage of the fact that you like me right now just to have one night with you."

"Nope, 'like' is not a word I'd use to describe how I feel about you."

He dropped his hand. "I'd like to see you again."

"And I'd like a Mack truck to run your ass over, but we can't all get what we want."

Nate took a step toward me, and I took two steps back.

"Don't do this. We had a good night tonight."

"'Had,' past tense, and now it's over. Good night, Nate." I turned and reached into my bra to pull out the key card, but pulled out a Post-it note reminding me of what time to meet Ace instead. Where the hell was the key card...

I felt around in my bra, but it wasn't in there. Did it

fall out? Still stuck in my dress? *Damn B-cups...* Ah, screw it. Tugging at the hem of my dress, I wiggle-danced until the dumb card dropped onto the floor.

Nate laughed. "Wait, can you do that again? I forgot to take a video." He pulled his cell out of his pocket and a light flashed on my face. "Okay, now again, but in slow motion."

"How about I slow-motion-slap you instead?"

"On the ass? Kinky."

"Oh shut up," I grumbled, and pushed the door open. My heels had me teetering—well, that and tequila— and I grabbed on to the frame before I fell over. After kicking my shoes into the room, I turned to slam the door in his stupid, arrogant face, but then his hand shot out against the handle and stopped me.

He got a glare for that. A big *screw you and your big penis* one.

"Let go," I said.

"Not until you agree to go out with me when we get back to L.A."

A rumble of hysterical laughter forced its way up my throat. So much so that I had to bend over to catch my breath.

Everyone check out the balls on this wanker.

"That's the most ridiculous thing I've ever heard. 'Hey, I know I led you on all night and when it came down to business couldn't follow through, but would you like to go to the Cheesecake Factory sometime so I can do it again?'" My eyes narrowed to slits. "Do I have 'gullible dumbass' written all over my forehead? Because that's the only way I'd ever say yes to you again."

I attempted to shut the door again, and he blocked it.

"You know," he said, running his hand through his hair, "I think you like to test my patience. And it's something of a game to you, so that's fine, but let's make things clear. First, you've never been a dare. I pursue you because I want to even when you make me crazy by spouting off mouthy shit I know you don't mean. Call me crazy, but it turns me on. And I really enjoy the way your forehead wrinkles up like that when you look at me like I've grown two heads." He looked down at the front of his pants and then grinned. "Well, I'm not far off on that one."

"Such a comedian. And my forehead doesn't have wrinkles," I said, reaching up to check.

"Shayne."

"Yes, asshole?"

"Can I finish?"

I raised an eyebrow but kept my mouth shut.

"Second, I like you enough that I don't want to be a one-night stand you can't remember."

I opened my mouth to retort, but he put his finger on my lips.

"You know I'm right about that. And I'll be honest, I know how much I've had to drink, and I'd like to remember the way you look under that dress the first time I get to see." His eyes trailed down my body, a look of appreciation in his eyes that I had to admit was mildly satisfying. But I kept my expression firmly in the annoyed zone. I think. It was feeling a bit numb, so hopefully it was cooperating.

"And second," he said, lifting his eyes to mine.

"You already said second."

He growled. "Fine. Third."

I nodded for him to continue, and he shook his head.

"Okay, third—trust me when I say you won't get away from me next time."

"Awfully presumptuous of you to assume there would be a next time," I said. "Don't the dorms close early?"

His fingers found their way into my hair, and he pulled my face close so I could feel his warm breath whisper across my lips.

"Please," I thought I heard him say softly. Unlike my stubborn mind, my body was quick to respond to his touch, and as my eyes closed, my lips parted. He brushed his mouth across mine once, twice, light brush strokes that set me on fire. *Damn him.*

"Say yes."

I kept quiet instead before moving forward for full contact. His grip on my hair tightened, and my eyes fluttered open.

"Shayne." His voice turned stern, demanding.

"So bossy for a twenty-four-year-old," I murmured.

"Almost twenty-five."

I sighed in resignation, and a wide grin took over his face.

"Good...that's good." He leaned and crushed his mouth against mine, and the irritation I'd felt at his rebuff seeped out of my pores until I could think of nothing but how perfectly his lips moved with mine.

Too soon it was over, and he was letting me go before we could build back up to *tear all the clothes off* mode.

His thumb brushed gently over my forehead. "Well, would you look at that."

"What?"

"It actually *does* say 'gullible dumbass.'" He pressed a quick kiss between my brows and chuckled before moving out of the way of my slap. "I'll see you soon, beautiful."

I stuck my head out the door and scowled at him. "Will that be before or after your trip to hell?"

He was still laughing as he faced me and walked backward down the hall. When he blew me a kiss, I extended my middle finger, kissed it, and returned his sweet gesture. Then I shut the door before he could see me crack a smile.

Chapter Ten
Hot Diggity Dog

"GET IN HERE, ya little cocktease," was the yell that greeted me from down the hall just as I'd sat down at my desk Monday morning. Everyone's heads swiveled my way, and I had to hold back an eye roll at the realization they must've all heard I had a meeting with Ace during my time off.

Nothing was sacred in this place.

As I closed in on Val's office, the sound of something being thrown to the ground made me jump. Then several somethings.

Peering through her cracked door, I saw Val flinging large coffee table books off the shelves that lined the left wall of her office. There was a pile in the center of the room that was already littered with books and magazines, and it looked like if she continued on the warpath, the rack of designer shoes that had been sent over was gonna get it next.

"Leave the books alone and no one gets hurt," I said, walking into the room cautiously with both hands raised, palms out.

"So did you seal the deal?" Val asked, not bothering to look my way. Instead, she flipped open the cover of a hardback, eyed it with disgust, and then tossed it onto the floor pile. "Eight inches? Nine?"

I ignored her assumption that I'd slept with a potential client and focused on the bigger problem. Books. On the floor. "Can I ask why the sudden aversion to reading?"

"Spring cleaning," she muttered, and then her eyes zeroed in on mine. "What, only seven inches? Six and a half? Really, why aren't you bursting to share?"

Only my boss would think my sex life was any of her business. *Well,* I thought when Nate sprang to mind, *lack thereof, anyway.*

"I didn't sleep with Ace Locke."

"Bah, of course not. I forgot your pussy is closed for business."

"It's not—" I sputtered. "I just don't sleep with clients or people I work with. That should be a good thing."

"You're a pitiful excuse for a matchmaker, you know that? How can you possibly put people together when you wouldn't know a cock if it slapped you in the face?"

Ew. "That's not...really...my thing."

Val's hands stilled on a copy of *Humans of New York*, and her eyes narrowed to slits. "Do you mean to tell me I hired a carpet muncher?"

"What? No." I rubbed my already throbbing forehead. "Look, Val, I'm not a lesbian, and even if I were, you would've still hired me because I *am* a great matchmaker. Besides, you can't go around saying that term. It's offensive."

"Well, I suppose with the invention of laser hair removal, the *carpet* part of that statement is a bit outdated." Val's lips pursed as she perused the hardback before slamming it shut and dropping it on the floor.

Cringing at the abuse going on, I knelt down and gathered the books into a neat pile. I didn't know what had set her off this morning, but it was clear I needed to rescue the victims of her wrath.

"What the hell do you think you're doing?"

"Since you don't want them, I'll find a good home—"

"Don't bother. It's trash. Trash, trash, trash, trash, trash," she said, rounding her desk and then flopping on the white-cushioned monstrosity behind it. After taking out a prescription bottle from the top drawer, she shook a few pills into her hand and tossed them back with a diet soda chaser.

At least I thought it was diet soda. No telling with her.

"Are you going to stand there and stare at me, or do

you plan on telling me some time this century how the date went with Ace?"

"The *meeting* went well… He's a nice guy, and I think he really does want to meet someone to settle do—"

Snoring from behind the desk cut me off. Then Val shook herself awake.

"All I heard was blah blah nice guy blah. Ace is not a *nice guy.* He's a multimillionaire box-office action star who fucks anything blond and on two legs, and he'll do wonders for getting our name out there. So tell me you've got a list of women who fit the bill."

"I don't think that's what he's after exactly…"

Val's heavily mascara'd eyes blinked at me. "And just what the hell does that mean, Shayne?"

"It means I don't think one of his usual model types is what he wants."

"Fuck me, this sounds like gibberish." Val swallowed another couple of pills, without a chaser this time. "Why do I have a feeling you're gonna tell me he wants a nice, sensible girl like yourself? Hmm? Do you have a golden pussy I don't know about after all?"

"Why does everyone keep saying that?" I said, throwing my hands up. "There's nothing golden down there, only cobwebs, like you said."

"That's an easily remedied problem. Remind me to get you an appointment with Raphael."

The woman's attention span was all over the place.

"I don't need your masseuse, Val."

"He's a helluva lot more than that. He always gives a happy—"

"Oh my God." With my hands on my hips, I craned my neck back and forced myself to remember why I'd come in here in the first place. Oh right. Ace. "The thing is…Ace is definitely interested in working with us, but it's a bit more complicated than he made it out to be."

"Complicated how?"

"Obviously this stays here, but I think he's looking for something of the…male variety. In private."

"Did you say male?"

"I did."

The only show of surprise on her Botoxed face was the slight arch of a perfectly drawn eyebrow. Then her chair rocked back and her red nails drummed across her desk. She stared me down for so long that I felt a bead of sweat fall down my back. I was used to mouthy Val yelling obscenities, so this mute version had me squirming.

When she finally stopped rocking in her chair, she spoke. "You're telling me Ace Locke prefers hot dogs to tuna."

My nose wrinkled, but I didn't bother correcting her or we'd be off on another tangent. "Yes, that's what I'm saying."

"And he wants it in private, you say. As in no publicity? That's not part of the arrangement."

"There's a bit more to it than that. We weren't able to get into specifics, but my guess is he's looking for…um…a cover of sorts."

"A beard, Shayne, you can say it."

On an exhale, I nodded. "Yes, a beard."

After another swig of her drink, she leaned back in her chair again, crossing and uncrossing her legs. Her gaze moved behind me to the mess she'd created. When I cleared my throat after what felt like several long minutes, she held up a finger.

Not *that* finger.

"Here's what we do," she said slowly. "You'll start going through the database and pulling potentials. I'm thinking at least high C-list. It worked for Katie Holmes, so let's get someone on one of those Netflix shows. What's hot right now?" She didn't pause for an answer before picking up her phone. "I'll call and set up a meeting with him this week—"

"Val—"

"Let Xander know I'll need another dress, stat—"

"Val, I—"

"—and to make sure it's not another angry vagina dress or he's fired—"

"Val," I said louder, causing her to stop and glower. "There's one more thing. I'll be working with Ace."

She lowered the phone back to its cradle. "Excuse me?"

Don't fidget, don't fidget.

"He, uh...said he'd like to work with me directly. I mean, if that's okay."

"Told you that, did he?" A fake smile stretched across her skin, and then she muttered, "Cobwebs, my ass."

Uh oh.

"I'm sure it's because he knows how busy you are running the company—"

"Don't bother making up an excuse. I can see right through you, and I don't mean your off-the-Goodwill-rack top."

Nordstrom Rack, actually, I corrected in my head.

She stood and sauntered to the front of her desk and leaned against it. "But since you think you're up to the task of handling this whooooole huge thing all by yourself, have at it."

"Wait, no. I don't mean to do it all by myself—"

"Oh nooo, I wouldn't think to tread on *your* territory. You'll find not just one perfect someone, but *two* perfect someones for our little gay bazillionaire." Then she pushed off the desk and stepped toward me. "But just a warning, hooker. Your ass is on the line. If you fuck up by even the smallest fraction of an inch, I'll have your freckled ass back on a Qantas flight to Australia to whatever podunk little town you escaped from so fast you won't have time to remove my stiletto from your rectum." Then she smiled, a friendly, evil smile. "We clear?"

"Crystal."

"Good girl," she said, and then went back to her chair.

As I headed toward the door, I noticed I was shaking

with adrenaline from the whole exchange, but I couldn't leave without making sure Ace's secret stayed, well, a secret.

"Val?" I said, pivoting back to face her.

"Hmm."

"You won't tell anyone, right? It's just if it got out, it would probably ruin his career, which is why he came to us in the first place. Because he trusts us."

She made the motion of sealing her lips. "I'd hate for that to happen. I always liked him as Ranger Joe Fox." Then she grabbed her drink and kicked the chair around to face her back wall of windows, the conversation effectively over.

With a sigh, I opened the door to leave and ran smack into front-desk Nicole.

"Hey, watch it," she said, as a stack of papers went flying out of her hands and she scrambled to get them.

But she'd been too close to the door. Like, so close she could've been eavesdropping.

"Hear anything interesting?" I asked after shutting Val's door behind me.

"I'm not sure what you mean."

"Really."

She made a show of looking around the empty hallway. "Shayne. Are you hearing voices? Do people speak to you in your head?" Her face was one of mock sympathy. "You really should get that checked out."

"Is there any reason you're standing outside Val's office?"

"Of course," she said, holding up the stack of papers.

"Val asked for these copies this morning, but then I saw the door was shut. Is she free now?"

I knew she was lying. Knew it like I knew that Gucci handbag she kept propped up on her desk like a trophy was a big, fat fake, though she claimed otherwise to anyone who'd listen. I'd seen her buying it in Santee Alley in the fashion district a few blocks away, a place notorious for fifteen-dollar knockoffs.

I gave her a long look. "You do remember you signed a confidentiality agreement when you started working here?"

"What does that have to do with anything? Seriously, Shayne, what is your problem lately?" She put her hand on the knob and then over her shoulder said, "Maybe it's time you hooked yourself up and stopped worrying about what everyone else is doing. You're so paranoid."

With that, she stepped inside Val's office and slammed the door shut in my face.

Now, I'm not a violent person, but this girl had a swift uppercut and gut punch coming. And probably sooner rather than later.

Chapter Eleven
Do You Accept This Rose?

I'D BEEN A zombie all day, my mind solely focused on the people I needed to call between each break in clients and what favors I could possibly owe them for any connections they could give me. If this was what it was like to grovel, I was not a fan.

I massaged my temples in slow circles as my to-do list loomed in my head.

Deal with hormonal, psychopathic, drug-addicted boss and deranged co-worker? Check.

Interview potential clients all day and ward off a total of two advances? Check.

Find a celebrity beard and *undercover boyfriend for A+- list movie star client ASAP or lose my job and end up singing off-*

key Michael Jackson songs on the train for money? Pshh, no big deal.

Really. It wasn't like I would end up in a shared apartment in Watts or anything. Or would I?

Ohhhhh God, what have I done? I thought, banging my head on my desk. I'd never been one to beg, but it looked like I would have to get my knees dirty.

Not in *that* way. I wouldn't be stooping to sexual favors. *Yet.*

When the clock neared six p.m., I gathered my things and closed up the office. Everyone was out the door before five, and that one hour of peace was heavenly before having to deal with train passengers and my roommates.

As I stepped off the elevators, I noticed my favorite security guard still at his post.

"Roberto?" I glanced up at the lobby clock. "It's a little late for you, isn't it?"

Roberto looked over his shoulder, his perma-grin stretched wide, and his eyes twinkling something mischievous. "It is, Miss Callahan, but I got caught up talking to this nice young fellow."

Then he moved to the side and there he was. Like a knight in a dark pinstriped suit, Nate Ryan stepped out from behind Roberto with a single pink rose in his hand.

I stopped moving, and my lips parted on an inhale.

Nate didn't look like a college guy in that tailored getup...*oh no he didn't*. Face freshly shaven and with just a hint of those dimples, he would've melted the panties off any woman he wished.

And to add to all that, I had a feeling there would be suspenders under that jacket. It was so twisted that it turned me on. *Right?* I mean, most girls get drooly over things like rock-hard abs, but nope. Suspenders. What the hell.

He took a step toward me and said, "I realized too late that I didn't get your phone number, but you'd mentioned what building you worked in…"

I did? God, I didn't remember that. No telling what else I divulged while under tequila's thumb.

When I didn't move or respond, Nate's smile faltered the smallest fraction.

"Um." He looked at Roberto and then back at me. "Is this okay? I hope you take it more like a nice surprise gesture than a crazy stalker gesture."

My mouth twitched at that.

Roberto's eyes were concerned as he moved up next to Nate. "If you want him gone, just say the word."

That shook me out of my stupor. "No, no, that's okay—"

"I mean it. I'll make sure he spends the night in the dumpster."

"Not necessary, I promise. Besides," I said, looking Nate up and down before smirking, "I could take him."

Roberto laughed. "No doubt about that, ma'am."

Relief swept over Nate's handsome features before he quickly replaced it with a cocky grin.

"Is that for me or Roberto?" I asked, motioning to the

flower in his hand.

"That depends."

"On?"

"Whether you'll go out with me."

"When? You mean now?"

He nodded. "Now."

After the hell day I'd had, all I wanted to do was take a long, hot bubble bath, especially considering how he'd left me in Vegas just a couple of nights ago.

"That's a nice offer, but I've got to work from home tonight—"

"Absolutely not."

"Absolutely yes, I do. I had a rough day, and besides, you can't just drop by unannounced and expect me to break my plans."

"With yourself."

"The best plans are always with myself."

"Until now," he said, twirling the long stem in his hand. "You can give me a couple of hours. We'll grab food, you'll feel better, and then you can work as late as you want to. Otherwise Roberto here gets the final rose for best date chat tonight."

Roberto cleared his throat. "And on that note, you two have a good evening. I'll see you in the morning, Miss Callahan."

"One day you're gonna call me Shayne," I called out after him before facing Nate again. "Look...I think it's sweet you came all this way—"

"Sweet?" he repeated, and shook his head. "Not sweet. Selfish, more like. Besides, you promised me a date, or did you forget Friday night already?"

I tapped my lips. "Hmm. Was there a promise? I'm trying to remember. If there was, I'm sure it was meant for a weekend. With lots of advance notice. A girl's got to plan for these things."

"What can I say, I'm impatient." He held the rose out to me, and as I reached to take it, he pulled it back.

"And..." he drawled, "persuasive." He held it out again, and I narrowed my eyes before reaching for it, only to have him repeat the fake-out.

"You're also a pain in the ass, has anyone ever told you that?"

"Probably not in the sense that you mean."

"You're disgusting."

"And charming?"

"And ridiculous."

"Does that mean you'll go?"

Snatching the rose out of his hand, I smiled sweetly. "I'm setting my timer, Romeo."

"Success," he said, giving me a broad smile. "And I don't even have a curfew tonight."

"I hope you're kidding."

"Obviously." He pushed open the door for me and we headed out into the windy evening. "Are you hungry? I know this great Italian place a couple of blocks over."

Running through the list of nearby restaurants in my

mind, I frowned. "I don't think there's anywhere like that nearby. Are you sure?"

"Positive," he said, so confident his chest practically puffed out. Then he grabbed my hand and took the side closest to the road. *Yes, I noticed.* It was the little things that caught my attention, and that was a point on the gentleman side of the scoreboard for sure.

"Well, then Italian sounds great."

We walked down the busy sidewalks, passing the happy-hour business crowd and the man on the corner playing his keyboard, with speakers blaring for all to hear. He was actually pretty good. I let go of Nate's hand to fish for a dollar out of my bag before realizing what I'd done.

I'd liked when his hand had grabbed mine. His grip was firm and strong, and mine had felt...protected. A ridiculous thought, since I'd never been one to need a man to make me feel safe. Not when I carried a pint of mace in my purse.

But still. I liked that he'd grabbed for me without a thought, like it was the most natural thing in the world to do. It'd made my stomach flutter and my toes tingle.

Again. *Ridiculous.*

I tossed the dollar inside the music man's tip jar and tried not to look at Nate's hand or think about the fact that I wanted him to reach out for me again. Instead, I looked at his face, all smooth skin and strong jaw, and noticed he was watching me with a curious expression.

"What?" I asked. *Do I have lunch leftovers on my face?*

He gave me a soft smile and held out his hand again.
I tried not to seem too eager as I took it and walked
alongside him.

"It's just around this corner," Nate said. "I used to
come here my first two years in college and work on
assignments for hours. They have the best meatballs in the—
" He stopped abruptly as we came to an empty storefront.
He looked up as if to check if the sign was still there, but
there was nothing.

"Huh," he said under his breath, and then peered in
the window. "I was just here a few months ago, and they
didn't say anything…"

I pointed to the paper taped to the outside of the
door. "It looks like they left a note."

Nate walked up and read the sign and then shook his
head. "Closed after thirty-five years," he mumbled, and
turned toward me. "Well, uh. Looks like Plan A is out. How
do you feel about Thai food?"

"YOU GOTTA BE kidding me." Nate pulled at the door
handle of Tiki Thai's Kitchen again, but it didn't budge.

I could only laugh and nod at the hours of operation
sign hidden in the corner of the window. "Looks like it's a
lunch-only place."

He ran his fingers through his tousled brown strands

as he groaned in frustration. Dropping his hands, he gave me an apologetic look. "I am so, so sorry—"

"Don't be, you tried. It's kinda cute."

He quirked an eyebrow. "Kinda cute, huh?"

"Yeah, you're basically the worst date planner ever, but it's fun to see you flustered. I'm sure that doesn't happen often."

He groaned again and then pulled out his phone. "Okay, let me see what's around here that *is* open."

"We could always go there," I said, pointing at the restaurant behind him.

He glanced over his shoulder and then looked back at me in horror. "Funny. You're a funny girl."

"Hey, why not? It's food. Plus I'm sure they'll have the heat on. I doubt we'll find much else close by, since most everything around here is for the day crowd."

"I'm not taking you there on a date." His voice was adamant.

"It's really not that big a deal. Look, I'm walking. I'm walking over there. Watch me go." I headed toward the crosswalk, and once the sign turned white to go, I began to cross the street and peeked to see him still standing on the corner. "Stubborn as a bull. Okay, you keep standing there. I'll be inside where it's warm, eating something super greasy and bad for me."

I faced forward just in time to trip over a pothole, but this time I caught myself before I could splatter all over the pavement. Good thing, since my knee was still scuffed up from falling pantsless. "Damn potholes," I muttered. "Way to go, Gracie." As I righted myself, Nate reached my side.

"You just wanted to get me to cross the road. I get it. No need for dramatics," he said with a laugh.

I glared at him but still took his offered hand to help me onto the sidewalk.

He shook his head at the sign above the door. "Just remember you asked for this."

Chapter Twelve
It's Not a Date without a Concussion

I SQUEEZED MORE syrup on my chocolate chip waffle and then took a bite, closing my eyes to enjoy the sweet mix of chocolate, maple, and buttermilk. "Mmm, so good. Waffles are dessert in Australia, so really it's like I'm skipping dinner altogether."

Nate watched me from across the booth with an amused look on his face. "You're going to tell all your friends I took you to IHOP on our first date. They're gonna call me IHOP guy and think I can't afford to take you somewhere nicer."

"How about shut it and eat your pancakes."

He chuckled and took another bite. He'd gotten chocolate chip too. "Bossy yet low-key. An unusual combination for an L.A. girl."

"Well, that's why. I'm not an L.A. girl."

"No. No, you are definitely not that."

"And what about you? You mentioned you grew up in Orange County, I think?"

"Yeah, I did, but I didn't move there until I was eight. My family's originally from Michigan's thumb."

"Michigan's what?"

"It's thumb. The state is shaped like a mitten." He held up his hand, fingers together, and pointed to a spot on his thumb. "I grew up right about there."

"Huh. You learn something new every day. That would explain why your jacket is off and your sleeves are rolled up even though it's freezing outside." I'd kept my peacoat on even in the restaurant, since the cold air kept filtering in every time the door opened. I'd have given almost anything for some thick sweatpants.

"It can't be less than fifty-five."

"Exactly. Anything under seventy and I stop functioning."

"*Now* you sound like an L.A. girl."

"Maybe it's rubbed off a bit. I've heard you mimic those you're around."

"That's true. So, I'm curious…" He sat back in the booth and wiped his mouth with his serviette. "You said you weren't on a date with Ace Locke the other night—"

"I wasn't."

"And it was just business?"

"It was."

"Well, I thought about that, and I came up with a few different ideas about what that business could be if I could run them by you."

"Knock yourself out."

He leaned forward and steepled his hands, resting his chin on top of them. "Director?"

"Of movies? Hah, no."

"Talent agent?"

"Negative."

"Stunt coordinator?"

"I can barely walk on two feet."

"Good point. Business manager?"

"Nope."

"Hmm. Professional escort?"

I choked on my orange juice and quickly covered my mouth as the liquid sputtered out. When I'd recovered, I said, "You're not serious."

"Hey, I saw you Friday night, and so did everyone else in that club. You're stunning, Shayne, and any guy alive would pay to get close to you if that's what it took."

I pursed my lips and wondered how to take that. On one hand, he could've been insinuating I used my looks for money. On the other, he'd just called me stunning...

"Stop analyzing that comment, please. I can see the wheels turning in your head. Take it as a compliment."

I pursed my lips and slowly shook my head. "Not an escort. Guess again."

"That's all I got. You've stumped me."

"And you didn't Google me. I'm shocked."

"Why? Are you Googleable? Should I do that now?" He pulled his cell out of his pants pocket, and I reached across the table to cover the screen.

"No need. I'm boring. Honest."

"All right," he said, tucking the phone away. "Spill your guts."

I took a deep breath, suddenly nervous. *What if he thinks what I do is silly or stupid or too superficial?* Luckily, the smart side of my brain took over, and it slapped the stupid thought back into the nether regions of my head.

"I work for a company called Hook, Line & Sinker." When he didn't say anything, I continued. "Basically, we, um. We're a matchmaking company. But not for casual hookups or anything; it's for people who are serious about finding a life partner. God, that sounds old, doesn't it, life partner. I suppose life and death partner is a bit morbid, but if you were looking for a life partner, I mean, wouldn't it make sense you'd want a life *and* death partner?" When I took in a breath, the way he was watching me so intently made me squirm. "Uh…anyway, I meet with potential clients and then I…pair them up. That's the short version, really."

He stared at me for a long time, and I fidgeted with my thumb ring under his gaze. *Why is he looking at me like that? Is he utterly repulsed? Or worse, does he want to be a client?*

"You're a matchmaker…"

I nodded.

"How the hell did you get into that?"

I told him the story about how I'd run into Val at a wedding reception of a mutual friend, and after setting her up with her fourth husband, she'd swept me off my feet, in a sense, with promises of a big, important title, lots of glamorous parties, and lucrative pay. Not that the job had ever amounted to any of that. Then I explained about the columns I wrote, the couples I'd personally paired. And he sat there, taking it all in, seeming to absorb every word.

When I was done, he grinned. "I never would've guessed that, not in a million years. It's interesting, though..."

"What is?"

"So far you haven't struck me as a starry-eyed, hearts and flowers kind of girl." He leaned forward. "You're a little combative when you meet someone, if you haven't noticed."

"I'm not combative with everyone."

"Just me, then?"

I thought back on recent first meetings outside of work and then shrugged. "Huh. I guess so."

"I'll take that as a compliment."

"That you incur my wrath? You're twisted."

"Mhmm." He took another bite of his pancakes and then asked, "So do you set up all your friends? The ones you were with last weekend looked pretty single to me."

"Actually, I'm not allowed to help them. I had to pinky-swear I wouldn't do it unless they asked or they'd revoke my green card."

He started to laugh with his mouth full and ended up coughing. "Fair enough. So is this what you always wanted to do?"

"I didn't grow up thinking this would be a career or anything, no. At first I thought I'd be a mermaid, but then I realized I would have to hold my breath for longer than thirty seconds underwater, so that was out. Then I saw *Jurassic Park* and wanted to be a paleontologist, but digging up bones didn't seem like so much fun. Not that being dropped off on an island with velociraptors trying to kill you was up my alley either, but desert life is not for me. Um, what else? Oh, I was obsessed with watching figure skating and made my mum take me to an ice rink so I could practice triple axles, but then I ended up spraining my ankle about twenty minutes in." I paused to take a sip of my orange juice. "And then one day in high school my best friend Jennifer had her heart stomped all over by this jerk-off Dave, so I convinced my neighbor Frankie to take her out and cheer her up. I think they have five kids and two cats now or something crazy. But anyway, after that, people would always ask for my help and it turned out to be something I was good at—" I stopped when I caught Nate staring at me with wide eyes. *Oh, shit, my friends are right. Zip it, Shayne, you rambling hot mess.*

He smirked and leaned back. "So you kind of fell into it."

Yep, that had been a bit more information than I

needed to throw out, I guess. "Sorry. Yeah, that's the short story."

"Don't be sorry. I like to hear you talk."

And didn't that admission have me squirming in my seat.

"I think I've talked enough," I said, laughing. "What about you?"

He spread his hands wide. "I'm an open book."

"Tell me some things on your bucket list."

"Hmm. I'd like to direct a full-length feature film with a decent budget. Cage dive with great white sharks. Learn a foreign language. And—" He stopped and shook his head. "What about you?"

"What were you about to say?"

"Nothing. I can't give you my whole bucket list."

"Was it skydiving? Bungee jumping?"

"Nah, already checked those off."

"So adventurous. Tell me what you were gonna say."

One of his eyebrows shot up. "Would it be terribly cheesy to say I'd like to fall in love?"

"The cheesiest."

"Well, it can't be too surprising considering your line of work."

"Is that really what you were going to say?"

He shrugged and gave me a dimpled smile. "Something like that."

"Tell me. I promise my lips are sealed."

"You know that bridge in Paris that people put locks

on?"

"Yeah, what about it?"

"I'd like to do that. Put a lock on the bridge, I mean."

My brow furrowed as I studied his face to see if he was pulling my chain. This had to be some kind of line he used on women, because what guy had putting love locks on a bridge on his bucket list? I wanted to ask if he was for real, but instead what came out was, "I'm pretty sure they cut them all off."

"What? No, they don't." Poor guy looked heartbroken.

"Not to crush your bucket list dreams or anything, but…yeah, I'm pretty sure you can't do that anymore. Maybe you could write a message in the sky as a declaration of love instead?"

"Or maybe I'll just find another bridge."

"Or you could do that."

A romantic. Who would've thought? And didn't that have my interest jumping up another level or five.

NATE INSISTED ON driving me home, saying the train after dark was no place for a "hot female." His words, not mine. Normally I'd never let a guy within a two-mile radius of where I lived until at least the third date, but hell, he'd already seen me without my pants, so it worked out.

He pulled up to the curb in front of my apartment complex—and no, the expensive BMW he drove didn't escape my notice—and shut off the engine. The night was surprisingly quiet as we sat there in the dark, and I knew there was no way he couldn't hear my heart pounding as I wondered at our next moves.

"I'm not too far from you," he said, breaking the silence and then spouting off the address.

Huh. He was only maybe a mile away. "That's convenient."

"For?" I could hear the smile in his voice.

Play it cool, Shayne. He may decide you and your ice cream pajamas are too lame for him and his Star Wars underpants.

"Oh, you know, in case I ever need a chauffeur." I unbuckled my seatbelt and bent down to grab my purse from the floor, but he reached at the same time. Our heads crashed together in a painful headbutt and I jerked back.

"Ah hell," he said, holding his forehead. "Sorry, I was gonna grab it for you. Are you okay?"

I rubbed my temple and nodded. "No worries. Happens all the time."

"I'm beginning to realize that."

When I reached for the door handle, he laid a hand on my arm.

"Don't move," he said. Then he jumped out and came around to my side to open the door for me.

A guy opening doors all night—another increasingly rare move that got another mark in the gentleman column.

"Thank you." Taking his offered hand, I stepped up onto the curb, and then we headed up the stairs to the main entrance.

Would he kiss me again? Sober this time? Did I want him to? *Oh, bugger off, Shayne, of course you want him to.* Actually, I wanted to invite him in, but there was no way that was happening after his first denial. Not to mention we had paper-thin walls and the twins were home...

"I'm glad you said yes to tonight."

"I only said yes for the waffle. But I guess the company was okay too."

"Only okay? This wasn't the best date ever? Not many women have the pleasure of going to a last-choice restaurant with me *and* getting a concussion."

His fingers brushed the tender spot on my head, and I shivered, and couldn't even blame the reaction on the cold. It was him. All him.

He took a small step forward, bringing his body within inches of mine. He was so close I could almost taste him in the air, our breaths forming puffy clouds that intermingled between us. Then his lips touched mine, soft at first and then crushing as my mouth parted for his.

His hands gripped my waist underneath my unbuttoned jacket before traveling up my back. Then he moved one hand out to grasp the back of my head, pulling me closer as I wound my arms around his neck.

I lost myself in that kiss, the slow, sensual pull of it, the taste of him mixed with chocolate and the sweet mint he'd sucked after—a heavenly combination. Our tongues moved in sync, like his mouth had been made just to fit mine. His body was warm, so warm that I barely noticed the frigid wind that had kicked up to scatter my hair around us.

He kissed me for hours or minutes, I couldn't tell, as it was so completely fulfilling and yet over too soon. Strong fingers threaded through the hair at the nape of my neck and drew us slowly apart, and his other hand came up to brush the hair out of my face. His lips touched mine once more, then twice, before asking, "Thursday. Can I see you then?"

I opened my eyes and tried to remember what day it was. Tried to remember my name. Anything.

His mouth tipped up on one side. "I know Thursday nights are usually reserved for sexy pajamas and Target visits, but maybe you could make an exception?"

"Or maybe you could take me there," I said, my voice returning, though a bit huskier than I was used to. "IHOP and Target dates. You're a total ladies' man."

"What am I going to do with you?"

I opened my mouth to say something inappropriate and then thought better of it and made the motion of zipping my lips shut. Instead of a response, he angled his head as if to kiss me again, but at the last minute he turned to kiss the sweet spot under my ear. Softly. Reverently.

"Thursday," he whispered, and I could only nod as he pulled away, a sexy, satisfied grin on his face.

There was only one thought on my mind as I

watched him walk to his car and drive away.

I was in trouble. Big, dirty, delicious trouble.

Chapter Thirteen
The Motherfuckin' Leak

I WAS WAITING for my coffee at Starbucks when it happened.

Bleary-eyed and half-awake at seven a.m. the next morning—to get a head start on project don't-lose-my-job, natch—I'd almost missed what the women next to me were gossiping about.

But can you blame me for still dreaming about the night before? I didn't think so.

The way Nate looked at me right before he kissed me on the front steps. How tightly pressed against me he'd been, so much that I could feel every part of him, even his—

"...and did you hear the news about Ace Locke? I had no idea."

I had to force myself not to whip around when I heard Ace's name.

News? What news? Good? Bad?

"Oh, please. They're lying," her friend responded. "There's no way. He dates supermodels, for Christ's sake."

"I just heard it on the radio on the way up here, and if Ryan Seacrest tells you, you know it's true. And apparently, not only is he gay, but he went to a matchmaking place somewhere around here that was gonna set him up with someone. Can you believe that?"

"MOTHERFUCKER!"

The room went silent, and every head swiveled around to look in my direction. Even the damn baristas.

I swallowed and unclenched the fists I hadn't realized I'd balled up.

"Uh…" I sputtered. "I just…lost my contact." Dropping to my knees, I swept the floor with one of my hands and held the other over my eye, as those around me backed up to give me room.

My whole body had to be turning a hundred shades of red, both from the ridiculousness of crawling around on the floor to cover my outburst, and also anger from the reason *behind* said outburst.

This had to be a mistake. A nightmare. Yeah, that was it.

"Got it," I said, grabbing at the imaginary contact and jumping up. Everyone was staring at me with wide eyes, inching farther back so they didn't catch my brand of crazy.

"Flat white for Shayne," the barista called out, and I practically ran to the counter to grab my drink before darting out the door. The cold wind was a slap in the face as I speed-walked to work.

Oh God. This was bad. So very, very bad. *How did that news get out?* Val? Eavesdropper Nicole? Shit.

Shitshitshitbigpileofmotherfuckingshit.

I picked up the pace, and when I reached my office building, I flung the door wide open and raced inside. Roberto wasn't there yet, but I yelled a quick "Mornin'" to the early morning guard and went straight for the elevator. I'd gotten up early to get a head start on going through my client file, but now that was the least of my worries.

Once I got to my office, which would hopefully still be empty for at least another hour and a half, I dumped my bag on the floor and logged in to my computer. I typed in the first entertainment site that came to mind, and there it was—"Breaking News: Ace Locke is Gay!" the headline screamed, and I cursed under my breath as I clicked it open to see the damage.

My eyes devoured the article, which attributed the leaked information to an unnamed reliable source, and went on to say that Ace had been seen meeting with the head of HLS at The Ivory Tower last week to discuss his participation in their upcoming "coming out" campaign, as well as spending a night out with matchmaking coordinator Shayne Callahan, in Las Vegas to scope out potential matches. There were even pictures of both Val and me, though the one of Ace and I at the Chandelier was a bit grainy. It then went on to give a few instances of "proof" of Ace's interest in men. One named source had been the waiter at the restaurant he dined at with Val, who claimed Ace was "flirtatious and made advances toward him" before tipping him more than triple the bill.

"That's not proof!" I screeched at my computer before dropping my head in my hands.

Did Val leak this information? Did Nicole? Fuck me, what a mess. I was gonna get fired. I should just pack up my stuff now. Then Ace's face popped into my head, and I fell into my chair.

Oh God. Did he know yet? He was probably still sleeping. At least, I hoped so.

Twinges of guilt twisted in my gut as I thought about what his reaction would be when he saw the headlines. No doubt he would think that I'd stuffed up. That I was the one who gave up his secret to the whole world, the one he'd wanted to keep under wraps.

Furious was an understatement. If it hadn't been for me, neither Val or Nicole would've known and none of this would be happening. *If*, of course, they did it. And I had a strong feeling my guess was right on.

On the other hand, Ace knew I'd be checking in with my boss regarding what we'd talked about, so…

Groaning, I collapsed on top of my arms.

How had everything gone tits up overnight? And the

bigger question: how the hell was I going to fix it?

I'D TROLLED EVERY entertainment news website and chewed through a whole pack of gum and half a dozen pen caps when Val decided to make her grand appearance three hours later.

She didn't glance my way or make any smartassed comments about my vanilla outfit, per usual, as she walked by. Finding that strange, I jumped up and followed, hot on her heels. I needed answers, and I needed them hours ago.

"Please tell me it wasn't you," I said, following her into her office and shutting the door behind me.

Her heels click-clacked on the floor as she breezed across the room and dropped her Louis Vuitton bag on the desk. "Tell you what wasn't me? And why are you following me around this morning? Don't you have a column to write? Some fornicating couples to match?"

Stopping in front of her desk, I tried to keep my voice calm and steady. "You know what I'm talking about. The Ace leak. The one that's all over the news right now. Please tell me it wasn't you."

"Course not." She flipped open a compact mirror and applied a coat of her signature red lipstick. *Traitor red,* more like.

"I'm serious. Did the whole world just find out

something private because you talked to the media? Please tell me the truth."

"Hey. Little do-gooder." Val glanced briefly at me before returning her eyes to the mirror. "In case you forgot the pecking order around here, I am your boss, and you are my employee. I don't have to tell you when I take a shit or how I decide to wipe my ass."

"But…you just said—"

"I know what I said, and that should be good enough for you." Val blotted her lips with a tissue and tossed it in the trash. "Now, having said that, you need to learn this business. Sometimes if you want to succeed and make a name for yourself, you have to do whatever it takes." She ran her eyes over me before narrowing them. "But, you know. I think I was wrong about you."

"Wrong how?"

Val wrinkled her nose in distaste. "I don't think you've got the stomach for dealing dirty to get to the top. Too sweet, too much sugar."

What does she mean dealing dirty?

Before I could ask, her phone rang and she gave an agitated sigh. "As you can see, it's going to be a busy day, so if you could…" She made a shooing motion with her hand and swiveled her chair around as she answered the call.

What just… Did she just… What the hell happened here?

As I walked out of her office, I felt numb. I'd never had her unleash on me before in that way, and it sent my mind whirling.

Was this how business was played? *Dirty?* She'd just called me out for having a conscience, but how was that a bad thing? Was I supposed to just throw people to the wolves to make a name for myself? Was that what success entailed?

Mulling over those thoughts, I headed to the sanctuary of my office—however temporary that would now be—and as I rounded the corner, someone grabbed my shoulders from behind. I whipped around to see sweet 'n' petite Jenna standing there with a concerned look on her face.

"You okay? Nicole was trying to get your attention…" She glanced over her shoulder to where Nicole sat with a supremely annoyed expression on her puss as she held up her phone.

"Hel-lo," she said, and I gathered from her condescending greeting that whatever was about to come wasn't something I wanted to hear.

Looking at her reminded me that I needed to install a punching bag in my office if I somehow kept my job. Or maybe one of those dartboards. It'd be too obvious if I stuck Nicole's face on it, but maybe every time I heard her obnoxious laugh from across the office, I'd throw a dart. *Good plan.*

"You've had about ten phone calls already from someone named Mr. Herschman who says it's urgent, so can you please call him back so he stops tying up the line? Some very important media calls are coming through that *I* have to take care of." Nicole flipped her long, dark hair over her shoulder as she spun around to slam down the phone, which promptly began to ring again.

Hold your tongue while you still have a job…

I had to physically bite down on my cheek to resist losing my shit on that sniveling little brat, and luckily Jenna noticed. She pushed me toward my chair and then went to retrieve the messages with the number of Mr. Herschman, whoever that was.

The last thing I felt like doing was dealing with a new client with the mess I had stockpiling in front of me. No, what I needed to do was get in touch with Ace and make him see it wasn't me and that we'd fix it, some-freaking-how. Any time God wanted to strike me with a brilliant idea on how to do that, it would be great.

Really, anytime now. Won't hold my breath or anything.

"Jesus, Shayne, it's him again," Nicole's voice rang out, and the sound of her voice made me want to scratch my skin off. Instead of a punching bag or dartboard, maybe I'd just go straight to a voodoo doll. One of my clients made them for scorned lovers, and I could— *Oh God, I can't even believe I'm considering that.*

With a sigh, I counted to five and then answered the line. "Shayne Callahan."

"Hi, this is Roger Herschman. I'm Ace Locke's personal manager."

Okay, now *that* had me sitting up straight.

"Oh…hi, Mr. Herschman. What can I do for you?"

"You can explain to me how the hell Ace is front fucking page news today."

Shit. I swallowed hard. "I've been asking that same question this morning, I assure you."

"You didn't go running your mouth to any of those tabloids, did you? Because I will find out, and God help me if it was you—"

"No, sir, I swear I was not the source. I'm just as outraged as you are."

"I highly doubt that. I've got paparazzi already lined up at the goddamn gate, and a client who's refusing to come out of his bathroom. Lots of bad shit happens in bathrooms, you get my drift? And if any bad shit happens on my watch, I'm taking you and that fucking company down so hard you'll be shitting last week's lunch out of your mouth."

Bloody hell.

"I understand," I said, sinking into my chair. Sinking. That was an excellent word for how I felt at the moment. "I'm not sure how I can help—"

"You can start by getting over here to explain the situation."

"Oh...right, of course. I was hoping to speak with Ace anyway, so just let me know where to go," I said, fumbling through my drawer for a pen. He gave me the address and hung up, and then I grabbed my bag, too nauseated to even think about bringing my still-untouched coffee.

"Where do you think you're going?" Nicole's

wretched nasal twang rang out, and I answered by slamming the office door shut behind me.

I was a girl on a mission—even if I didn't have the slightest clue what that mission was.

Chapter Fourteen
Does This Beard Make Me Look Fat?

AN HOUR AND forty minutes later, after having taken the train home to get my car, I was pulling up to the gate of Ace's swanky Beverly Hills neighborhood, and thank God for the security check-in station.

A crowd of paparazzi was gathered on the sidewalks, unable to get in, and they looked my way but lowered their cameras when they caught sight of my car. But as I showed my ID to the guard and passed through, a Jaguar pulled up behind me and the camera flashes went insane. No doubt they were snapping photos of everyone who came and went just in case it was someone they could use for a tabloid story…unless you drove a barely running, decades-old Saturn.

Nerves flooded my stomach as I followed the
directions I'd been given. I was trying not to think about the
fact that I was mere minutes away from entering a big
Hollywood star's house, but as I passed the ostentatious
mansions with their bright green manicured grass and high,
moss-covered walls, my heartbeat became erratic, and I was
sweating even though I hadn't turned the heat on and it was
freezing outside.

How am I even here? I was an impostor, someone
who'd been in the wrong place at the wrong time. I mean, I
was just a small-time freaking matchmaker, not someone
who knew anything about celebrity cover-ups and scandals
and whatnot. This was something Paige could handle, not
me. *Oh hell,* I should've called her. She'd know what to do,
though I doubted any of her advice would be anything less
than X-rated.

My hands were slipping off the steering wheel as I
pulled up to the gates of Ace's estate. If the properties I'd
passed along the way were any indication, his house was
palatial. My guess was confirmed when I saw the Spanish-
tiled roof looming over the gates and extending
down...down...down...

Jesus, how far does it go? That's not intimidating at all.

I stopped at the intercom and wiped my hands off on
my slacks before rolling the window down and hitting the
button for the speaker. There was a camera set up on top of
it, with two more on top of either side of the massive gate.

Maybe I could turn around and —

"Yes?" came a curt voice over the speaker.

"H-hi. Shayne Callahan for—"

A loud buzz and the gates parted. I drove Old Ouiser forward, which was sputtering in protest at the hill it'd just climbed, and I prayed no one would come out and send sniveling glances its way.

Wait. Would a butler or someone come out and valet the car? Did they have those at these types of places? God, that would be exceptionally awful, since I avoided valets like the plague. There was a trick to turning off Old Ouiser that no one else seemed to be able to do, and it was better just to self-park and avoid the embarrassment, if possible. I patted the dash with a soothing hand at the thought.

All right. All I have to do is come up with a solution to save my ass and the company, and offer a helpful solution to Ace's predicament. No big deal.

An entire car ride over hadn't given me any bright ideas, but I was pretty good at winging it.

Usually.

Sometimes.

Oh, fuck it all. I was completely out of my league.

Luckily, no one came out to help me with my car, so I gathered what was left of my wits and headed up to the gargantuan front door. Before I could ring the doorbell, it opened.

"You must be Miss Callahan," a portly man in a pristine grey suit said, moving to the side for me to enter.

"Shayne is fine."

"They're waiting for you in the kitchen." He led me through the largest foyer I'd ever seen, then past an enormous staircase with a long corridor just behind it. At the end was an expansive, open area with a wall of windows. The left side featured a sitting area with oversized plush couches facing a theatre-sized television, and on the right, Ace on a barstool, slumped over at the island counter in the middle of the kitchen.

Hovering nearby were who I assumed to be his handlers, one almost an exact Olivia Pope replica, even down to the white trench coat, and the other an older man who looked a little red in the face. Had to be Mr. Herschman, the same guy who'd given me a good reaming over the phone. They both cut off abruptly when I entered, and as they went silent, Ace lifted his head. The obvious anger and hurt were there in his eyes, but underneath that was something even worse—despair.

I stayed back, not wanting to get too close and invade his personal space any more than I already had. My mouth opened to say the first thing I'd thought, which was, "I'm glad they talked you out of the bathroom," but I caught myself before spouting off the insensitive remark and instead said, "I don't even know what to say other than I'm so sorry about what's happened."

"Sorry?" Red Face boomed, and yep, that was definitely Mr. Herschman. "Damn right you're sorry."

Trench coat woman put a hand on his arm, and then said, "Thank you for coming, Shayne. I'm Martina

Lankshire, Ace's publicist, and you've already spoken with Roger here."

Roger who was spitting licks of fire out of his eyeballs. *Yeah, I know him.* Nice guy.

"Any idea who's pulling this stunt? That boss of yours, maybe? She seems to have quite the mouth on her."

"It wouldn't make sense for Val to leak information when it only damages her company," I said, the words ringing false in my ears.

After confronting Val in her office earlier and what she'd said, I didn't fully believe she was above tarnishing Ace's name to get ahead. Didn't even half believe that. Yeah, it was hovering more in the twenty percent range, and that just made me feel like an asshole. But I didn't have proof, and I was holding out hope that if the leak had indeed come from HLS, that Nicole was the rat behind it all.

Martina raised an eyebrow. "Bad publicity is still good publicity."

Val said the same thing. Maybe I'm not *cut out for all of this...*

"Anything that was said between my boss and I is held in the strictest of confidence out of respect for client confidentiality. I'm hoping, just like you, that we can get to the bottom of all this."

A grunt came out of Mr. Herschman, but he didn't comment.

"Let's worry about damage control first, and then we'll figure out who's behind this and sue the pants off them." Martina flipped open a laptop, and began going over the statement they'd prepared to release to the media, and asked me questions about who I could bring in as Ace's "girlfriend."

To that, I had...no answer. I didn't have celebrity contacts, and I'd need more time to go through client files to find someone trustworthy. But time wasn't something we had in abundance. All the while, Ace sat on the barstool staring at his hands and not moving, not talking. I didn't even think he was listening to what was going on around him.

It struck me as strange that all through our interactions, it'd been like Ace wasn't even in the room. Were his manager and publicist the people who handled the big decisions *for* him? And why? *What's he thinking?* One way to find out.

I cleared my throat. "I was wondering...if maybe I could talk to Ace alone. Please?"

"There's nothing you could say to him that can't be said in front of all of—" Roger started, but Martina grabbed his arm.

"Let's just give them a minute. Smoke break?"

"Ah hell. I need one."

As they made their way out, I took a seat on a stool adjacent to Ace. There was nothing but silence at first, but before I could speak, Ace said, "I know it wasn't you."

Then his eyes met mine, those sad, dark eyes. I didn't want to ask how he knew or why he trusted me. It was just a comfort that he did.

"Thank you," I whispered.

Then his gaze drifted back down to the table.

Without his minders nearby, the house was deathly quiet. No phone ringing incessantly, no television blaring with the news, no swarms of people inside raising chaos anymore. He'd done exactly what I would've in his shoes— turned the outside noise off and unplugged everything.

"What," he said in a low voice, "do I do now?"

It was then that I realized he wanted someone to tell him what to do. How to fix the mess. This huge hulk of a man was like a little boy lost, and my instinct to protect this person I barely knew rose up inside me.

"Well," I said slowly, considering the obvious choices. "It seems like you've got two options. You can deny everything, or...you could come clean."

"I can't...do...that," he said through clenched teeth, his voice rising. He rubbed his face with his hands. "My terms. This was supposed to be on *my* terms."

I wanted to soothe him in some way, but I wasn't sure what to do here. Not being involved in the entertainment industry in any capacity, I was way out of my depth.

"What have Roger and Martina suggested?"

Ace scoffed. "They care about money. They couldn't give two fucks about me."

I bit my lip and looked out the screened glass door to where they were both smoking a few yards away from the house.

"Okay. Um... I guess first, what do you want?"

"I want this to go away."

"Time travel isn't in my special skills set, so I'm going to need you to work with me a bit here."

He sighed and lifted his head.

"What do you want, Ace?" I asked again softly.

"I can't come out, not officially. It would ruin me."

It was outrageous to think that his sexual preference would have anything to do with his career, but of course it would. Women wanted the fantasy when they watched his movies, and there was a strong possibility many men would think less of him. Discrimination in any other line of work wouldn't be stood for, but somehow the court of public opinion weighed heavily in his.

"Then you deny."

"Right, but that's not going to carry a whole lot of weight on its own."

"Is that why you need the...beard?"

He blew out a breath, his palms over his eyes, as if to keep them squeezed shut to block out the world. "Yeah, that could help. But at this point if some random new girl appeared on my arm, it would look mighty suspicious."

"Do you have any ex-girlfriends you could reach out to?"

He snorted. "I wouldn't put it past any of them to have leaked it, accidental or otherwise. Models aren't known for their discretion, so I've learned."

A thought crossed my mind. "What if it was a date?" I said out loud before realizing what I meant.

"If *what* was a date?" he asked, his brow furrowed.

"Uh." *Ah hell.* I decided to keep running with that train of thought. "What if your ties to HLS and Val and me were actually just ties to…me? As in, what if our meeting had actually been a date and not the alleged meeting to unveil your coming out? And um…well, maybe the meeting you had at that restaurant with Val was actually just a dinner because she's like a mother figure to me and I wanted you guys to…ahh…meet? Or something like that. And I'm sure the paparazzi saw me as I came into your neighborhood, but if I was your girlfriend, it would make sense that I'd be here for you this morning. Right? I think that's… I mean, that's plausible, yeah?" When I stopped and took a breath, Ace was frowning at me.

"You're offering to cover for me?"

Oh hell. Was that what I was doing? "Well, yeah, I guess so."

Ace stroked his chin as he mulled that over. "Huh."

Was that a good "huh" or a bad "huh"? And did I just offer to be his *girlfriend*? Where the bloody hell did that even come from? What did I know about that sort of thing…yet again. This was what rambling did. Got you in trouble and signed up for much more than you bargained for.

"You would really do that?"

Uh…I think so? Maybe? If I need to save my job? "Yes,

of course."

He dropped his hand. "I don't get it. Why would you do this for me?" There was sorrow in his voice, but it was the hope on his face that almost broke my heart. *Ah hell.*

"Because I think you're a good guy. Because it's wrong what happened, and if I inadvertently played any part in this whole mess, then I'd like a chance to make up for it. I don't know how any of this stuff works, but…whatever it is you need me to do to help, I'll do it."

The fact that maybe it would also help me keep my job for a little longer belatedly entered my brain, but that wasn't the reason I was doing this. Not at all.

"Are you going for sainthood, Shayne? This shit…it can be a lot. I'd hate for you to get involved."

"Pretty sure I'm already involved. So now we have to make the best of a bad situation, right?"

He shook his head but said, "Right. It's not fair, though—"

"Do you have any other suggestions?"

He smiled ruefully. "I guess not."

"So…we're dating. Publicly."

"Don't worry, I won't try to sleep with you."

"See, ordinarily that would bother me if my boyfriend said that to me, but in this case, I think it's for the best."

Ace ran a hand over his close-cropped hair and sighed, like an enormous weight had been lifted from his shoulders. "Thank you, Shayne. This might…*will* help. A lot."

"Of course it will. And we'll just figure it out as we go." I laid my hand on his forearm, and he smiled, a small but genuine one. Then he looked over his shoulder.

"Better call in the cavalry before they run out of cigarettes."

MARTINA AND ROGER hashed out the details of our plan, which, they admitted, wasn't bad at all, and then they had me sign an NDA that basically threatened my life if I so much as peeped one detail to anyone—friends and family included.

I'd pretend to be Ace's girlfriend until the press died down enough and I was able to find someone to take a more long-term position, as it were. The whole thing left me mixed with emotions—high with adrenaline, relieved at having come up with a solution, sad for the reality of Ace's situation, but most of all, utterly drained.

I'd been there for hours, and when I left, the paparazzi were still camped out outside the gate. A couple of flashes went off this time, but they soon lost interest.

What would happen once the statement went out and Ace and I made a public appearance? Would I be followed? God, I hoped not. At least I'd kept my phone off all day, which helped me live in ignorant bliss for just a little while longer. I wasn't ready to face whatever was on there.

It wasn't until I drove away that Nate's face finally found its way back into my thoughts. He hadn't even been a consideration in the decision I'd made today. Not that he was my boyfriend, but... Well, he wasn't. And it looked like any possibility of that changing in the future would just have to wait.

And damn if that didn't send a stab right through my chest.

Chapter Fifteen
Hair Full of Secrets

"SO? WHAT DO you think? Five-Minute Quickie or Lube It Up?" Ryleigh's foot tapped from behind the counter of Licked as she not so patiently waited for me to give her an answer.

"Can't I choose both?" I asked, and she gave a firm shake of her head.

I'd stopped by Licked after work the next day since I was resigned to driving for the duration of my "partnership" with Ace instead of taking the train in case I needed an escape. Girl talk and dessert always made me feel a million times better, and her naughty-named ice cream and boozy shakes were the best anywhere in the state of California.

And before you think that's just my humble opinion, consider the fact that Licked and Licked After Dark, her companion bar, had franchises popping open all over the country, thanks to a contest and appearance on *Wake Up America*.

While we'd all thought she'd botched her chances of winning after running out of the interview to stop Hunter from getting on a plane, it turned out audiences thought her romantic gesture was endearing and her business impressive. In just a few short months she had offers in eight states with no signs of slowing down. To say we were all proud of her was an understatement.

"Decisions, decisions." I took another bite of each sundae sample. And then another. And then anoth—

"Shayne," Ryleigh said, laughing and moving the bowls out of my reach. I reached for them again, and she swatted my hand. "Pick one. Now. Or God help me, I will never ask you to help me test new flavors again."

Eeny, meeny, miny mo.

"Um. This one." I pointed to the creamy concoction full of chocolate, pecan, and caramel turtle clusters.

She nodded and then wrote the name on a whiteboard hanging near the register. "Five-Minute Quickie it is. Thank you."

"Welcome. Now how about you top that bad boy off? I wouldn't be opposed to a vodka splash either."

"Rough day?"

"Rough day. Rough week. Rough life."

"Hmm." Ryleigh's eyes narrowed as she popped the cap back on her marker. "How about I get you an Overdramatic Valley Girl shake instead?"

"I'm not familiar with that one, but I'd be willing to test it out for you."

She rolled her eyes. "So what's going on? Is Val giving you shit? She called me earlier to book the After Dark for a masked Valentine's Day event, and I priced it a grand above what I normally would."

"And she took it? She's normally such a cheapskate. Or maybe that's just with her employees," I grumbled.

"Hey." Ryleigh leaned over and put her hand on mine. "I know you're super proud and independent, and I'd never suggest you give up a career you love, but if you ever need a side job here, you know it's yours. And I'd pay you a helluva lot better than that dingbat."

"I know. And I appreciate that, I do. It's not really the money, though, that's always tight. Life is just...complicated at the moment."

"Gee, that explanation's not vague at all, thanks."

Scooping another spoonful, I said, "This stuff is a miracle worker, so keep 'em coming."

The jingle of the front door opening and a loud "Aha!" rang out across the room. I whirled around to see Paige stalking toward us, a pile of magazines in her arms.

"I knew I'd find you here, you secretive little wench." She slapped down a *Celebrity Weekly* magazine in front of me, which was turned to page fifteen and had a grainy photo of me leaving Ace's neighborhood in Old Ouiser, albeit in sunglasses and a ball cap. "What the hell is this?"

I frowned. "Damn. They didn't get my good side."

"Please explain why one of my best friends was photographed leaving Ace Locke's freakin' neighborhood. Yesterday it was 'He's gay,' and today it's 'Oops, he's not gay, he's dating the matchmaker.' I mean, *what is this shit?*"

"Wait, you're dating who?" Ryleigh snatched the magazine, and as she skimmed over the article, her eyes grew wide. Then she looked up at me. "I don't understand."

Busted. And it wasn't as though I wasn't dying to give them every dirty detail, but out of respect for Ace, as well as that little thing called an NDA, I had to keep my mouth shut. Which wouldn't be an easy feat at all around the girls.

I shrugged. "We, you know. Hit it off. In Vegas."

"No," Paige said, shaking her head, her blond hair spraying out around her shoulders. "You did not."

"We did so. You weren't sitting with us to know. Now gimme that." I reached for the magazine, but Ryleigh walked off with it and began reading out loud.

"'It has been confirmed by Ace's manager, Mr. Roger Herschman, that the couple has been quietly dating. The pair were reportedly introduced by Val Barberie, the head of Hook, Line & Sinker Matchmaking Company.'"

"And the rest of these corroborate that story." Paige dropped the rest of the magazines in her hands onto the counter with a loud smack.

"Well." I gave them a sheepish look. "Surprise?"

Paige's hands went to her hips. "That's it? That's all you have to say?"

"I was going to tell you—"

"You know," she continued, "I'd expect secrets from Quinn. Hell, I couldn't tell you where she ran off to this week, but you? You seem to be withholding a lot of information lately. Spill it, or I'm driving myself over to this new boyfriend's house and jumping the gate to get the word from him."

With a sigh, I told the girls the story I'd concocted as a cover.

Ace had called me, we'd spent time together earlier in the week, and the gay tabloid piece was the work of a jealous ex, blah blah blah. It was a flimsy excuse at best, even I knew that, but the alternative wasn't something I could live with.

Paige's eyes stayed narrowed the whole time, and when I finished, she pursed her lips.

Come on, just let it go so I don't have to lie to your face any more than I already am.

But neither of them said anything, and Ryleigh went about making a sundae.

"You sticking to that story?" Paige said finally. She had a knowing look in her eyes, but I could see she wasn't going to press for more information. If Quinn had been here, on the other hand, she probably would've guessed the truth in five seconds flat and called me out for it. She missed nothing.

Luckily, Ryleigh chose that moment to slide a new bowl of Five-Minute Quickie my way. "Hey, what about Dimples? What was his name…Nate? I liked him."

Yeah, what about *Nate.* That's all I'd been thinking about all day and exactly what had sent me straight into the arms of the ice cream I was devouring.

I raised an eyebrow. "Weren't you the one complaining he was young enough to babysit?"

"I'm a sucker for dimples, but don't tell Hunter. And he seemed crazy about you, even if he did leave you high and dry," she said with a wink.

Yeah, I hadn't gotten around to telling them about the surprise date we'd had on Monday, *thank God.* Otherwise that would blow the Ace timeline a bit.

"You're avoiding the question," Paige said as she took a seat beside me. "What about Justin Bieber?"

"Um, what the fuck."

"What? They're about the same age, right?"

"No. Jesus."

Ryleigh set a drink in front of Paige and then crossed her arms on the bar. "You're looking a little flushed there, Shayne. Don't tell me I should've given you a Double Dipper special instead."

"No!" Paige gasped and placed her hand over her heart oh so dramatically. "Is our little hooker turning into a big-time madam over here?"

"I'm not double-dipping. Absolutely not."

"Bullllshiiiiiit. If you haven't yet, you will. Or want to."

"You know, now that you mention it, I do recognize that conflicted expression," Ryleigh said, tapping her chin. "Believe me when I say you don't wanna go that route."

And she would know. After reuniting with her high school crush, Cameron Mathis, over the summer at their ten-year reunion, she'd not only kindled a relationship with him, but she had also fallen for his roommate, her now-boyfriend, Hunter Morgan. Both were fuckin' hot, Cameron in a blond 'n' polished business suit sort of way, and Hunter in his blue-collar, getting-dirty-with-his-hands kind of way.

Color us not surprised at all when Ryleigh went with the man good with his hands.

Paige pointed her straw in Ryleigh's direction. "Get off it, woman. Let her fuck whoever she wants—"

"Date," I interjected.

"Whatever. So tell us. Who's bigger? Is Ace's package extra-large delivery, or have steroids destroyed his quivering member?"

I couldn't help but laugh even as her words had me cringing. "I haven't seen either package yet, thank you very much. It's not what you think."

"Fine. So tell us."

"I can't."

"Is Val forcing you on Ace? Oh my gosh, hang on," Ryleigh said, bouncing on her heels. Then she leaned over to

166   BROOKE BLAINE

whisper, "Is he really gay and you're having to cover for him?"

Well, shit.

Before I could deny her way-too-accurate statement, Paige piped up. "Look at her. She's too pretty to beard for some big shot. Hell, she above anyone deserves a sugar daddy."

"You did not just say that." I shook my head and pushed my bowl away. "I'm not looking for a damn sugar daddy."

"Of course not. I said *deserves.* You're practically a saint for putting up with Val, the brainless twins you have for roommates, and pairing off half of the city. Why shouldn't someone take care of you for a change?"

"Aw, would you listen to that? She cares. She really cares," Ryleigh said, and then shrieked as she moved out of the way of Paige's thrown straw.

I sighed. "I appreciate that, I do. But I don't need anyone to take care of me."

"Ugh. Fine. But when are you finally gonna let me convince you to move in with me? Your room would be as big as your apartment right now, plus you'd be able to actually relax without having to listen to *The Bachelor* reruns constantly or having your stuff smell like suntan lotion."

"You wanting me to live with you has nothing to do with using me for my mad cooking skills?"

"No. I'm just selfish and think it would be fun to have girls' night in our pajamas whenever we want."

"You're never home."

"Exactly. It's too damn quiet, and it creeps me out."

I ended the conversation with a "Yeah, yeah," and wished I could take her up on the offer. But there was no way. Paige's place was a huge mansion up in the Hollywood Hills worth several million dollars.

Yeah. Rich bitch was an understatement.

The house had been a college graduation present, not that she didn't make significant money as an in-demand wedding planner. She'd never let me pay her rent, and I refused to be a freeloader. Stubborn Aussie pride and whatnot. And it wasn't like my apartment was so bad. It was a bit run-down, but it had a great view, looking out over Hollywood with downtown L.A. in the distance. During the holidays a Christmas tree was strung up on the Capitol Records building, and the view of it from my couch was the reason I never had to spring for dragging a live tree up four flights of stairs.

"I'll think about it." My standard response every time she asked me that.

"You should think hard. And speaking of hard…" She grabbed two straws and held them up, her eyes twinkling. "Let's discuss how you're not enjoying things down under with two guys right now, you greedy hooker."

Chapter Sixteen
Juggling Balls

I WAS A right coward. I was. There was no denying it, and I wasn't about to try.

Why all the self-loathing, you ask?

It was Friday. And I'd been ignoring Nate's calls for four days.

I know. Don't look at me like that.

Yes, he was this incredibly adorable guy, and most of you would be falling over yourself for him, but if you hadn't noticed, my life was in a bit of an upheaval right now. I wasn't even on speaking terms at the moment with Val—her decision, not mine—and I'd had to spend what would've been our second date last night with Ace instead, going over his schedule and planning future outings so that we could be "casually" spotted by paps.

To say my life was surreal at the moment was an understatement. I couldn't drag Nate into that. Besides, he was this hot college guy, and it wasn't like he couldn't find a replacement in two seconds flat, *right*?

At least, that was what I'd been telling myself.

I didn't have plans with Ace tonight, Ryleigh was spending a night off with Hunter, Quinn was off on one of her mysterious work trips again, and Paige was prepping a weekend wedding, so there I was, putting in a ten-hour day and counting. Thank God everyone had left for the night, and I could get my weekly column up on our website on time.

The column consisted of an Ask the Matchmaker Q&A, which I had to heavily edit because the questions could easily turn into a sex column free-for-all, as well as upcoming events and singles mixers. Our next one was scheduled for Valentine's Day, just over three weeks away, and we already had a waiting list of people wanting to attend. Val had thrown the whole thing on me this week, so it hadn't left much time to start recruiting for my more personal mission. Read: beard needed.

A beep alerted me to the front door to HLS opening, and a quick glance at the time told me it was Roberto making his final security rounds before the next guard took over for the night.

"Roberto, it's just me," I called out, and continued typing.

"I know. He let me up."

My head jerked up at the sound of Nate's voice just as he came to a stop in the doorway to my office and leaned against the jamb. Dressed in dark jeans, a collared shirt, and a navy blazer, and with his chestnut hair stylishly windblown, he looked like a wet dream. *My* wet dream. Somehow I'd convinced myself he wasn't as gorgeous as he'd been in my memories, but I'd been dead wrong. He was so much more than that.

Oh God. This isn't good.

Nate shoved his hands in his pockets and tipped his head to the side. "Not answering my calls?"

My mouth opened to speak, and I willed a response to come, but what could I say? *"Sorry, I'm supposed to be dating Ace Locke and can't commit to more than one relationship at a time, but thanks for stopping by"?*

"You missed our date last night," he continued, stepping up to my desk. "I even stopped by your place, but your roommates said you weren't home. Interesting friends, by the way."

I simply stared up at him, wishing like hell things were different. Because if they were, there was no way I would've missed spending time with him. He'd had my attention from the first moment I'd seen him, and it would suck a fat one to make him leave. But he had to. For my damn sanity.

"Nothing to say? I didn't think it was possible for *you* to go speechless."

Sighing, I pushed away from the keyboard and stood. "Look, Nate...I like you. I do. I'm just not in a great place right now, and the last thing you need is to have to deal with all that."

"Why don't you let me make my mind up about what I'm willing and not willing to deal with?"

"Okay, fine. Spending time with you is the last thing *I* need right now."

"Ouch," he said, his hand going over his heart like he'd been wounded, and then he rounded my desk. "Wait. Is this because I took you to IHOP? In my defense, that was *your* choice, and you ate those waffles like they were the best thing you'd ever put in—"

"No, it wasn't your disastrous date-planning skills."

"Huh. Is it because I tried to steal date night away from Target? I'll apologize, but I won't give it back."

I bit down on my lip to keep from smiling, and he took a step toward me, his hands going to my hips. His tone was serious when he said, "If this is about the age thing—"

"It's not—"

"But if it were—"

"Really, that has nothing—"

"Shh," he said, putting his finger up to my lips. Then he crossed his heart. "If it did, then I solemnly swear never to tell you to get Botox before you're forty."

I broke away from his hold and punched him good and hard on the arm, and he laughed.

"Sorry, I meant fifty. Fifty-five?"

"Asshole," I said, shaking my head. "The answer is at *least* sixty-five, thank you very much. You're lucky I don't call your parents to come pick you up for causing trouble and harassing your elders."

"I asked permission before I came."

I snorted. "Do you ask permission every time you *come*?"

When his jaw dropped, I held up my hand and said, "Never mind." Then I flicked off my computer, grabbed my purse and jacket, and headed for the exit as he followed on my heels. I'd just have to come in early tomorrow to finish the column.

"No, hey, I like this," he said. "Turning the conversation towards the bedroom. I can deal with that."

Before I could reach for the handle, he moved in front of it. "That's not what I was doing. It just came out."

"Happens sometimes." Nate gave me a lopsided grin, and I rubbed my forehead.

"You don't stop, do you?"

"That happens sometimes too."

"Ugh." My head fell back and I growled in frustration.

Why was this guy here to torture me and try to tear through my defenses? Whether I wanted him to or not wasn't an issue, it was that I *couldn't*. But how to explain that to a guy you wanted desperately to kiss you? And more. Much more than that. *Not giving in. Nope.*

"What is it you want from me?" I asked. Though if

the expression on his face was any indication, his mind was
still on the *coming* part of the conversation.

"I want to spend time with you. Go on normal dates
like a night at Arclight and then do cool shit like a Malibu
Wine Safari. Take you to a decent restaurant. Go see a
concert. Check out your underwear collection—you know,
the usual things people do when they're getting to know
each other."

*Resist the dimples. Resist the dimples. And for God's sake,
don't touch them.*

"But...why?"

He looked at me then as if I had two heads. "What do
you mean why? Why wouldn't I?"

"I mean, I'm sure there are plenty of girls in your
classes to go out with."

"And you come across single men every day in this
job. What's your point?"

"My point is..." And then I blanked. It was like those
damn greenish-brown eyes had some sort of hypnotic effect
and had rendered me not only speechless, but brain dead as
well. Awesome. "Uh. I had a point. I mean, I have one, but...
Shit."

Nate tilted my chin up. "I like you. Stop trying to
change my mind."

"I have a feeling you aren't easily deterred."

"I'm not," he said with a grin that soon dropped,
replaced by something that looked a lot like...arousal.
"Don't freak out, but I'm gonna kiss you now."

"That's not a good idea."

"Then stop me."

His hands went to both sides of my face, and slowly he leaned down, both showing his intent and making it clear I could put a halt to what he was about to do.

And I should've stopped him. Part of my brain was screaming at me not to take this any further, that one kiss would lead to another that would lead to another that would lead to…something else entirely. But the other half was in full cheerleader mode, chanting "Don't be a pussy" and doing backflips and cartwheels.

I closed my eyes, as if doing that would keep me from having to make any decision at all. Then my purse was slid down my shoulder, and my jacket was pulled from my grasp, both landing on the ground beside us.

He surprised me when his lips didn't lightly brush against mine as I expected them to. Instead, his kiss was insistent, not asking permission but rather taking it. Forcing my mouth to open to his. Threading his fingers through my hair to keep me from going anywhere, not that I could've at that point. With one taste of his tongue, I was done for.

As he deepened the kiss, he flipped us around so that my back was against the door and he was pressed up against me. Our mouths were hungry, and as the seconds passed, so did all thoughts of work, of Ace, of anything other than the man holding me tight.

He pulled my blouse out of my pants, and then one of his hands traveled up under my shirt to my waist, squeezing gently. When I didn't stop him, he went higher, his fingers ghosting over the front of my purple lace bra. Through the thin material, his hand was warm, and his thumb grazed over my nipple.

I broke from his kiss on a gasp, my hips arching forward into him, and he must've taken that as a signal, because he pulled away and had my shirt up and over my head before I could find my breath again.

He stood there, staring at me for a long moment while we tried to catch our breath, his eyes expressing an appreciation that made my heart stutter. Then one hand went by the side of my head, and the other reached down to—

Flip the lock.

I didn't hesitate. I shoved off the door and found his lips again, pushing his blazer to the floor as we stumbled back against Nicole's desk. A cup holder of pens scattered, her neat piles of paperwork swishing to the floor as if a swift breeze had knocked them off. Or just two bodies about to get their naked on.

As I unbuttoned his pants, he reached to do the same to mine, but then stopped.

"What's this?" he asked, plucking a Post-it out of my bra.

"Oh, uh…it's nothing. Just a reminder." I resumed undressing him, and sadly, the suspenders would have to go, and didn't that almost bring a tear to my eye.

"Did that say 'Remind Bob to put his teeth in before

his date'?"

"Shut up and kiss me," I said, pressing my mouth against his, and then the crumpled square hit the desk.

Suspenders off. Pants on the floor. His. Mine. I somehow managed to get all the buttons undone on his shirt before he spun me around, picked me up, and set me on top of the desk.

Oh, if Nicole only knew how defiled her work area was about to be. But what the hell, she deserved it. *Conniving cuntbag.*

Nate's mouth was on my neck, trailing kisses down my chest. His hands deftly removed my bra, tossing it over his shoulder, and then his tongue teased the top of my breasts. I wrapped my legs around his waist to pull him closer, get his mouth where I wanted it, but his gaze flicked up to mine, and damn if it wasn't mischievous. Painstakingly slowly, his tongue dragged down to my nipple, licking and sucking me into his mouth, and it was a sweet torture that I wanted him to stop but never stop.

I reached between us and took him in my hand, his length rock solid and ready for me. He groaned as I stroked him, and the vibration shot straight to my core. Then he laid me back across the desk, pulling my ass to the edge, and I flinched as the cool wood hit my back. Through my thin cotton hipsters I could feel the heat of him as he slid his still-covered cock between my thighs.

The man was a damn tease, and I told him as much.

"You say that now, but once I get inside you…" He

shook his head.

A shy smile crept over my face, and my hand went to the back of his neck to pull him down toward me and—

"Oh shit." A thought crossed my mind, and it should've been the first one I'd thought of, truth be told.

"What's wrong?"

"Uh…well, I don't know if I have anything in my purse for—"

"I've got it." Nate reached into the pocket of his discarded pants and grabbed a foil packet out of his wallet. As I sat up on my elbow, he stepped out of his boxer briefs and—

"Holy shit."

He looked up, a crooked grin tilting his lips. Then he rolled the condom on his impressive length, and swaggered—yes, that's the only word for it—back between my legs.

"I take it you approve?" he asked, and then leaned down over me, taking the top edge of my hipsters into his mouth. As his hands curled under the material at my hips, I lifted my ass, and he slid my panties down my legs and to the floor.

Though usually a fan of foreplay, I wasn't in the mood for more teasing from him tonight. Maybe it was the sting of denial from the last time I'd tried to get him in my pants, but I wanted it quick, hard, and dirty. And I wanted it now.

When I shoved off the desk, Nate's eyebrows shot

up.

"Care to show me your follow-through, mister?" I kissed him roughly, and after he got over the initial surprise, his mouth was urgent on mine. He backed me up against the desk again, and this time, I broke from his kiss and turned around, sticking my ass out and looking over my shoulder to where his jaw dropped to the ground.

"I take it *you* approve?"

"Fuck," he said, and I gave a wicked grin.

Now if only I could be this aggressive in my career.

He didn't waste time sliding his fingers through my drenched slit, and a loud groan escaped him at how wet and ready I was for him.

I was squirming beneath him before he drew his hand away and lined up his cock, and then he was pushing inside me inch by inch. My puffs of breath steamed across the desk, the incredible fullness almost too much to take, but I pushed back slowly anyway, letting him fill me completely.

Then he began to move, his grip strong on my hips as he thrust inside again and again. What started as easy and tentative quickly turned into the delicious, rough slapping of bodies coming together, chasing our releases like we were in a mad dash toward a finish line.

Sweet God he felt so good, his velvet cock thick and strong, marking me as his. His breath was ragged to my ears, but hell, it could've been mine. There was no way to draw this out, no way to savor it, but I didn't care. I was desperate with need, and my climax hit me out of nowhere, with no warning, no slow buildup.

Arching my back, I cried out as I came, and thank fuck Nate didn't stop or slow the pace. He kept pumping, letting me ride out my release, and then I felt him jerk once, twice, and then a shudder racked his body. I clenched my inner muscles tight, milking him for all he had, and when he finally slowed, his forehead, slick with sweat, lay against my back. Then his hands moved away from my hips to cover my hands flat on the desk, his fingers interlacing mine, and his cock still inside me.

We stayed there as our breathing slowed, saying nothing but saying everything. When Nate lifted his head, it was to trail light kisses down my spine before pulling out. As I sat up, I felt thoroughly used, but in the good way that meant you'd feel it tomorrow, and when you did, you'd smile as you remembered why.

After putting back on our piles of clothing, he helped me set Nicole's desk back to order. Then his arms were around my waist, pulling me closer and nuzzling into my neck. He kissed the soft place beneath my ear and said, "You sealed the deal now. I'm getting us his and hers Jedi bathrobes."

"Oh yeah? Only if you make mine blue."

"I don't know," he said, fingering one of my curls. "I'm partial to red now."

I bit into my lip as I chuckled softly. "Good thing."

His eyes were tender as he leaned in to kiss me

again, softly this time, and it was then that I felt my world spin on its axis. Nothing would be the same after tonight. That thought rang true somewhere deep and closed off, and I was utterly unprepared.

How could this possibly be right? It wasn't the right time, I wasn't in a good place in my work life or my personal life, and how the hell could fate throw Nate my way knowing all that?

"Stop thinking," he murmured against my lips. "Be here with me."

As I let myself get lost in his kiss, I tried to shut my mind off.

I could do this. I could...date two people at once. Sort of. *Right?* This was crazy. I was crazy. Why did Nate have to be so damn persistent? And why did I have to volunteer myself to help Ace, therefore putting me in this predicament in the first place? Perhaps I was a masochist. Or incredibly selfish. I didn't want to give up my job, *or* Nate, so that had to be it. But I would make it work. I would. Because if there was one thing I excelled at, it was juggling balls. And it looked like I'd be doing just that—publicly *and* privately.

Chapter Seventeen
Superman and Spandex

AS IT TURNED out, "dating" two people was easy as pie.

…said no one ever.

"Yes, of course I'd love to go hiking again on Saturday," I said, as I paced my bedroom and tried not to fling myself against the wall in the hopes of scoring an injury that would put me out of commission for a few days at least. I'd already been on two hiking dates with Ace in the past week, and I had blisters in places I didn't even know you could get them. Working out was apparently his version of a date, which was just one of many reasons I couldn't be with a guy like him.

The other being his preference for the *nuts and berries*, of course.

"Great, so you'll come over Friday night, then?" he asked.

"I'll be there." I tried for a smile, one of those that would show through my words, but the reflection in my hanging mirror showed it came off as more of a grimace.

It wasn't that hanging out with Ace was so bad. On the contrary—he was super nice, and the two times I'd been over we'd stayed up late watching movies on his wall-sized TV before I passed out on his couch or in the guest room. I had to be seen staying overnight, of course.

But...damn. Nate had asked me to come over on Friday too, and I was annoyed I'd have to cancel. Again.

There was a knock on my door, and then Paige stuck her head in. "Knock knock, slutbag," she said.

I shouldered my phone and waved her inside. "I've gotta go, but I'll see you then." After ending the call, I tossed the cell on the nightstand. "What are you doing here?"

After locking the door, she proceeded to dump the contents of her bag onto my bed. Wigs...sunglasses...makeup...hats?

"What's all this?" I asked, fingering one of the long blond wigs. "Did you mistake my house for Goodwill again?"

Paige picked up a pair of sunglasses and slid them on my face, scrutinizing them before taking them off and trying another pair. "If you're gonna do this, then you need some disguises."

"If I'm gonna do what?"

She stopped what she was doing, and one of her hands went to her hip. "You know I'm a bottle blonde, right?"

"Yeah?"

"Which means I'm not as stupid as I look." Rummaging through the pile of accessories, she settled for a newsboy cap and then placed it on my head.

"Paige…"

"Shut it. I'm aware that you probably can't say anything because of a contract, so I won't make you break that, but my gut says I'm right, so I'm right. But if you're gonna pull off seeing Nate on the DL, you need to be crafty about what you look like in case you get recognized. Your hair, for one thing, stands out like a freakin' beacon, so it needs to be up and under a hat whenever you go out."

"With which one?"

As I confirmed what she already knew, Paige's eyes twinkled and her lips curved into a smirk. "I've only seen you in workout clothes and a ball cap with Ace, so keep that shit up. And maybe tell Nate you're into the whole role-playing thing so you can rock the wigs."

"God. This is your fetish, isn't it?"

"Just say thank you, Shayne."

"Thank you, Shayne."

"Smartass," she said. "I think you also need to maybe do a darker lip when you're out with Ace, and wear the same sunglasses each time."

"Ah hell." I flopped onto the bed and groaned. "I'm

so not the right person for this sort of thing. What do I know about subterfuge?"

"Hey, even if you get busted, it's more like you're just a hot girl who cheated on Ace rather than someone who covered for him. And honestly? Everyfuckingbody is gay in Hollywood. It's, like, the worst-kept secret ever. The only people that this shit serves a purpose for is conservative middle America, who want to believe their own reality."

I chewed on my lip as I thought that over. "Do the girls know?"

"Does a cow suck its own dick?"

"So eloquently put, Pita." Pita, short for her full name, Paige Iris Traynor-Ashcroft, though when Dick Dawson had coined that nickname years ago, he'd probably meant it as Pain In The Ass and sometimes Paige In The Ass. He wished. *Wink wink.*

"Nah, they don't know. Quinn's not back yet, and Ry hasn't quite clued in to your deceptive ways. Well…that's not entirely true. She just thinks you're a two-timing whore, but she's called me that for years, and it's not such a bad title, really."

"That's just great." Pulling my hair up, I wrapped it in a bun and then put on one of the brunette wigs. With bangs and a straight cut, I looked…weird. *I am way too pasty for brown*, I thought, removing the fake hair. "Hey, I need a final count for the Valentine's mixer at the After Dark. I've got over fifty single guys on my list, so are you in or are you out?"

Paige shook her head. "I freakin' wish I was in. I've got a wedding in Santa Barbara that day, which would be bad enough without the momzilla of the bride micromanaging my every move. Seriously, who gets married on Valentine's Day? It's so clichéd."

"For a wedding planner, you're the most jaded person I've ever met."

"I'm not jaded. I just think monogamy is boring."

"Maybe you haven't met the right person yet."

She gave me a droll look. "Gee, that's not something I hear every day at all, thanks. And pass."

"Yeah, you're right. One-upping Dawson is much more fun than spending time with someone you care about."

"Ugh, you mean *Dick*," she spat. "And don't say that name." She tossed a hat back onto the pile. "All right, I'm leaving these with you. Try not to get busted."

"Try not to hook up with the best man after the wedding," I called after her, to which she responded with a finger before the door shut.

"OKAY, DON'T TAKE this the wrong way, but—" I said, and then a pillow flew at my head, cutting me off. "Hey!"

Ace laughed and looked unrepentant. "Whenever someone says that, an asshole comment follows after."

"It wasn't an asshole comment. I was just gonna say I

never took you for a guy who'd like foreign indie flicks."

Another pillow flew at my head.

"That's not a bad thing," I protested.

"Way to stereotype, Shayne. Care to throw another shrimp on the bahhhbie?"

I threw the pillow back at him. "Yeah, point taken. You know what's stupid, though? We don't even call prawns shrimp."

"Where the hell were you when I needed you? I had to learn that the hard way when I went down under for a press tour. We went to this seafood joint, and I asked if they had any shrimp. I didn't realize there was one whole side of the menu with nothing but the stuff. Prawns. Won't ever forget it."

I burst out laughing. "Ace?"

"Yeah?"

"Don't ever tell anyone else that story."

A muttered curse had me laughing harder as I got to my feet to refill my glass with the to-go Double Dipper boozy shakes that I'd gotten on the way over, courtesy of Ryleigh's cheeky ass. It was Friday, time for our weekly non-consummated sleepover, and we were on the second movie of the night, an Italian film called *Last of the Horsemen*.

"Another?" I asked.

"Nah, or I'll be in the gym all day tomorrow."

"That doesn't make me feel fat at all when you say that."

"You look great. Plus, you don't have to see yourself

on an IMAX screen in 3-D."

"And thank God for that."

After pouring another round, I peeked at my phone again. No messages since the last time I'd looked ten minutes ago.

"You waiting for a call?"

"Huh?" I said, glancing up.

Ace nodded at the cell in my hand. "You keep checking it."

Yeah, I was *so* not telling him that I kept checking it for missed calls or texts from Nate. "No, no, I... Val calls at weird hours sometimes." Shoving the phone in my pocket, I grabbed my drink and then settled back in on the couch. "This movie is really fucking strange, you know that? I'm not sure I understand anything that's happening."

"It's an artistic interpretation of forbidden love."

"Then what's with the horses?"

"Horse number one is in love with horse number two."

"Besides the obvious 'how the hell did you know that' question I'm dying to know, what's the problem?"

"They're competitors in the derby."

"So?"

"And they're gay." He waggled his eyebrows.

I looked back at the TV and tried to see it, but nope. This shit was too far out, even for me. "Don't you wanna watch the new Superman instead?"

"Nah, I lost out on that role."

"Oh. Well, what is Superman anyway other than a bunch of spandex?"

"Agreed."

I sipped my drink in silence and let my mind wander while he continued to be fascinated with the artsy-fartsy crap. The self-control it took not to look at my phone was tremendous.

When I'd told Nate I couldn't hang out tonight, he'd mentioned he needed to get some work done on his final project, an assignment several months in the making.

Schoolwork. It'd been so long since that word was in my life that it was beyond strange to be dating someone who reported to class. But he'd be graduating from the film program in the spring and had already been offered a job at the production company he'd been interning at, so it wasn't *that* big of a deal. And compared to most guys I'd interviewed in their early twenties, he had the maturity of someone much older.

Especially in bed…

"Shayne?"

Shaking myself out of my daydream, I said, "Yeah?"

"You asked earlier what my type was." He nodded at the lanky man on screen with a head full of brown hair and a gorgeous smile.

"A case of opposites attracting, huh?"

"He reminds me of someone I cared about a long time ago."

"So you've always known?"

"That I was gay? Yeah, that wasn't ever a question. Hell, even my parents knew when I was a kid."

"They were supportive?"

"Hell no. The only reason I've hidden who I am in the first place is because they refuse to acknowledge it. And now there are so many others weighing in on every decision I make, and at this point…I would just be letting so many people down, in a way."

"That's pretty fucking fucked up if you really think that way." When Ace raised his brow, I held up my already half-gone shake. "Sorry, vodka said that."

"No, you're right." He rubbed his face, and when he looked at me, his face had aged a decade. "I just don't see how I can keep my career going the way it is if I were to show who I really am."

"Things are changing, though. It's not as shocking or rare for actors to come out anymore." When he started to protest, I held up my hand. "Not that I don't get your unique position because of the kind of work you do, but still. I think you'd be surprised at how many people would be accepting of it, or how many wouldn't give a shit."

"Maybe," he said, rolling his water bottle between his big hands.

"Have you ever thought of maybe doing something not so mainstream? I mean, you're obviously not hurting for money, and you seem to like this"—I motioned to the movie—"abstract, artistic sort of sh—stuff."

He gave a humorless laugh. "Like anyone would hire

me for that, Shayne. Get real. I'm aware it's not my acting ability I get cast for."

"Okay, that's bull and you know it," I said, scooting forward and giving him the wagging finger you got from your parents when you were five. "But what if you started small? I don't know much about that sort of thing, but surely there are low-budget films you could get involved with that would show you take your craft seriously."

"So now you're a matchmaker slash life coach?" His full lips lifted on one side, and then he looked down to where he was rubbing his hands together in what seemed like a nervous gesture. "It's not bad advice. My agent wouldn't go for it, but... I'll think on it. Thanks, Shayne."

"No worries. I can also tell you the future for an additional fee."

Chuckling, he nodded, and said, "Since we're doing this whole 'laying our souls bare' thing, can I ask you something?"

"Is that what we were doing? I thought it was just you."

"Nope."

"Then shoot."

"You don't really like hiking, do you?"

I exhaled in relief. "Oh sweet Mary, mother of Joseph, I thought you'd never clue in." When he laughed, I kept going. "I hate it. Mad hate. I mean, I know you've seen me trip over every single rock going up the hill. I'm not a worker-outer sort of person, but I was trying to love it, really

I was."

"You're a trooper, you know that? In more ways than one, and I appreciate that more than you'll ever know. So if I haven't said thank you for doing this for me, I'd like to now."

The sudden change in conversation from lighthearted to serious had me flushing under his praise. And feeling incredibly guilty at the soft buzz of a notification from my phone that was going off in my pocket.

"You're welcome," I said, looking away from him as I squirmed into the couch. "I'm definitely something."

Chapter Eighteen
Be My
Valentine

AHH, VALENTINE'S DAY. The day of lovers and chocolate, of oversized teddy bears and proposals every two minutes while you're trying to eat your overpriced dinner at a fancy-schmancy restaurant overlooking the ocean.

For me, though, Valentine's Day was just another workday, albeit a huge one. Our annual lonely singles mixer—no, we didn't actually call it that—was being hosted this year at Licked After Dark. Over fifty men and fifty women had signed up, and I had taken on the task of overseeing the event, since Val had decided to get smashed at the bar off ten-dollar Between the Sheets martinis an hour ago.

Yeah, no two-drink minimum here, which could

serve for an interesting night.

I was handing out the last of the nametags with Jenna when Ryleigh sidled up to me and nodded at Val.

"Think we need to call her a cab?" she asked.

"You'd be hard-pressed to get her in one until she's falling off that barstool. I'd say she has about three more to go before that happens. Her alcohol tolerance is through the roof."

"As long as I'm not cleaning up puke. Nothing clears out a room faster, trust me."

"Nah, she'd have to consume something more than vodka and a Tic Tac for that to happen."

Jenna laughed beside me as she packed up the attendee list and spare nametags. "The only thing that woman eats is men and her employees."

"Truth," I said, nodding.

"You know, Jenna, you seem like a sane person, much like my Shayne here. Can I ask why you guys stay on the crazy train?"

Jenna looked over her shoulder to make sure Val was still throwing back her drink, and then said, "I'd never admit it to anyone else, but if there was another high-profile matchmaker in town, I'd leave in a hot second. As it is, though, no one can compete with Val. She probably beat them all back with a stick. Literally."

Ryleigh's lips quirked to the side as she gave me a knowing look. "Did you hear that, Shayne? Jenna is *dying* for someone to steal Val's crown. Know anyone who could do

"Not at the present time," I said, refusing to take the bait.

"Well, she's bound to get knocked off the throne, so until then…" Jenna said, gathering the box of supplies. "I'm gonna go put this in my trunk, since everyone's here."

"Thanks for helping out. Nicole claims to still be in traffic."

"Of course she is," Jenna muttered, and her following curse was lost as she went out the exit.

A huge smile took over Ryleigh's face, and she tugged on my shirt. "Dude, if you started up your own business, I bet Jenna would totally go with you. It's a sign."

"We're not doing this again, are we?"

"The only person who doubts you could do it is you."

"For the five millionth time, woman. Startups require money."

"Quinn would invest."

"No."

"Paige would invest."

"Ryleigh—"

"Hell, so would I."

"Friends and money don't mix. They just don't, and I love you guys too much to fuck up our friendship. Besides, you heard Jenna. Val would *literally* beat me with a stick. Or maybe the bat she keeps in her office."

"I'm not scared of her. I bet she's all talk."

"Don't you have drinks you need to be mixing?"

"Nope, I'm just here to support you and relieve the bartenders for breaks later. Hunter should be here soon, so we'll be partaking in this faaaabulous event if you don't mind."

I picked up the basket of party masks for those who hadn't brought their own and held it out to her. "Can't be here without donning a disguise, so pick one."

"I own the place."

"You still have to wear one. Here, this one matches your dress. And one for Hunter." I handed her a mask, which she grudgingly put on, and then I adjusted my own. I'd picked out an elaborate gold and black one with feathers coming out of the top, and it covered my entire face, except for my lips.

"How come yours is so cute?" Ryleigh pouted.

"Go to one of those costume shops on Hollywood Boulevard and you'll find a bunch of expensive-looking ones for cheap."

"Considering I don't plan on going to any more singles mixers in the future, I'll pass."

"Damn right you'll pass," Hunter said as he wrapped his arms around Ryleigh's waist and planted a kiss on her neck. He looked freshly showered, his longish brown hair still damp, and was rocking a pair of dark jeans and a simple white cotton t-shirt. When I saw the two of them together, it always reminded me of *Grease*, with Ryleigh in her cute fifties-style swing dresses, and Hunter looking like one of the T-Birds, bar the rolled-up jeans.

She'd turned into one half of those lovey-dovey couples she'd always complained about, but damn if they weren't a cute pair.

"How's it goin', Shayne?"

"Best night of my life."

"Your boss grabbed my ass on the way in. Classy broad. I've missed her."

"I can't blame her for that," Ryleigh said, laughing. "If she starts stripping you naked, *then* we'll talk."

"Sorry, Hunter, I can't be held responsible for where Val's fingers go. She won't be here much longer anyway."

Ryleigh pulled away from Hunter then, and whispered, "Hey, I didn't get a chance to ask you if you were bringing a *plus one* tonight." Careful emphasis on the "plus one."

Poor girl; she must not have clued her man in to the whole *Shayne and two guys thing*, even if she didn't quite know the whole reason for that yet. So far, Paige hadn't peeped a word.

"Uh, no, *Ace* is out of the country shooting a commercial for a few days, so he won't be able to make it. But I'll be relaxing later at home." *With Nate.* Read between those lines.

"Ohh yeah, okay. I guess it makes sense Dimples couldn't come to this."

"Bingo." I looked past her shoulder to where Val was cozying up to one of the male clients, and shook my head.

"Looks like I've got to make an intervention, but you lovebirds have fun."

As I moved through the crowd, I briefly checked in with those I passed, and since we'd already done the icebreakers, it looked like most everyone had split off into mixed groups or were paired up on the dance floor. So far, low maintenance…with my boss being the exception.

She was laughing loudly, her head thrown back, and it did nothing to hide her paid-for double-Ds. She was practically falling out of the low-cut scarlet cocktail dress she was squeezed into, and her hand was clinging to one of the poor twenty-somethings I'd interviewed just last week. He smiled along with her, but his eyes darted around like he was trying to come up with an escape plan.

"Andrew, so glad you made it," I said as I came up to the bar and placed a friendly hand on his shoulder. "I was hoping to introduce you to Donna. She just moved here from St. Augustine, so I thought you guys might have a few friends in common." I nodded at the gorgeous woman with dark, creamy skin on the other side of the bar. "Or maybe you could start things off by buying her a drink?"

The relief on his face was evident as he looked in Donna's direction.

"Oh damn. Yeah, thanks, Shayne, I'll do that." Then he gave Val a tight smile. "If you'll excuse me, I should go say hi. It was nice to meet you, Ms. Barberie."

I moved out of the way so he could effectively escape Val's clutches, and when he was out of earshot, I heard a slow clap behind me and turned back to face Val.

"You," Val said, pinning me with a glare, "are a cockblock." Her words slurred on the ends, and her red lipstick had completely come off except for the liner. If you looked up "hot mess" in the Urban Dictionary, Val's face would take up the whole page.

"This is what you pay me for. To match up our clients successfully. No matches, no clients."

Val snorted. "I don't pay you to run off the herd. You're not a herderer. Herdman. Herder of... Ah, shit. Whatever it is. If you see a pretty penis sitting here, hands the fuck off, capeesh?"

"Noted."

"Good." Then she flagged the bartender and held up her empty martini glass. "Another of these and then something to thaw out Shayne's tight ass."

The bartender, whom I recognized as Ryleigh's right-hand woman Zoe, raised an eyebrow, and I gave a slight shake of my head. Someone in this place had to stay sober, and it wasn't gonna be my lush of a boss.

"Are you still here? Don't you have a dingo to catch? A croc to mount?" she grumbled when another drink slid her way.

Clenching my jaw shut so I didn't say anything I'd regret, I backed away before turning and then promptly stumbled into something hard—or some*one*, rather, who caught me by the arms. And that something hard was...Nate.

"Oh fuck, what are you— I mean, uh, hi." *And shiiiiit. What the hell is he doing here? But...I'm glad he's here, but... Oh hell.*

I couldn't be seen with Nate. Some of our clients had already heard through the grapevine about Ace and had asked me if he'd be attending tonight. So if they saw us together, like *together* together, that would be...really fucking bad.

"Hey, are you okay?" His brow furrowed as he looked over my shoulder at Val and then back at me. "Please tell me that's not your boss."

"Boss? Who? Oh, right. She's lovely, isn't she?"

"Is she drunk or does she always say that shit to you?"

I shrugged. "Worse when under the influence, but nothing that surprises me."

"That's not fucking okay, Shayne."

"It's fine. Hey." I moved my face into his line of sight, and his eyes snapped to mine. Then I smiled. "Happy Valentine's Day."

"You're changing the subject."

"Yes, I am," I said, nodding. "I can't believe you're here."

I won't lie. Half of me was giddy as hell, even as the other half was panicking that he might try to kiss me in public. We'd been seeing each other for a few weeks, but during that time it'd been relatively easy to spend time together since, thankfully, he was a homebody like me. The few times we'd gone out, I'd bundled my hair up into a hat and wrapped a bunch of scarves around my neck, but no one had paid attention to us. Paige's accessories had been a godsend.

"Is this okay? Me being here?" he asked. "I know you're working, but I've never seen you in action, and I couldn't wait until later."

"Yeah, yeah, of course. You just surprised me, is all. I'm glad you're here." Then I took a step back to get a good look at him, mostly so I wouldn't wrap my arms around him and kiss the hell out of him. And that was some serious self-restraint, because he was dressed impeccably in a tailored black suit, the collar undone and open, and he'd gone scruffy just for me. Who could resist a man with scruff? Not me. "You look… Wow. Seriously hot. I hate that I'm gonna have to cover you up."

"You mean this?" Grinning, he held up the black and blue mask in his hand. "I just wanted you to see my face so you didn't think I was some stranger running his hands all over you."

"Too bad. I love when strangers grope me."

"Well, I can make that happen too." After donning his mask, he reached out and pulled me toward him as if to kiss me, and I had put my hands on his chest to slow his roll.

"Oh, sorry. I guess you're in professional mode now, huh?" he said.

"Yes, that's exactly it." *No, not just that. I'm a horrible, horrible person.*

I hated holding back from him. Hated that he would hate me when he found out, because God knew if I didn't find someone more permanent to cover for Ace soon, it was bound to get out. And I couldn't let that happen. But finding someone had proved to be trickier than I'd expected, since I couldn't flat-out tell them what they'd be signing up for.

I didn't know how to fix the situation, and Val wasn't helping, since she wasn't the lead on the assignment, Ace had no suggestions, and his team had clearly stated that it was my job and they were too busy still doing damage control, even though the paparazzi had faded since the coming-out announcement had proven to be a "fake." From what I'd heard, most of the people in those tabloids were celebrities who tipped off the paps anyway, so thankfully it'd been a quiet couple of weeks—not that I planned to stop sneaking around and wearing disguises in the meantime.

God…that sounds so bad when I say it like that.

"No problem. I'm more than happy to stare at your ass all night, since I can't see your face." His gaze trailed down my sequined black dress that hit mid-thigh—Val forced us all to wear short dresses tonight; it wasn't my idea—and he whistled in appreciation. "Pantsless again tonight, I see. I'm glad I decided to crash the party after all."

My stomach flip-flopped under his inspection, the same as it always did when he was around.

"I would've worn it later for you," I said with a shy smile. "Unless there was another bloody knee incident, which is still entirely possible."

"Didn't stop you before."

"So. Wanna grab a drink and come make rounds with me?"

"Hell yes I do."

After Zoe slid a pink virgin beverage for me and a blue one for Nate across the bar, we made our way around the room, stopping to check in with everyone, see how things were going. Ask a few questions to get the ball rolling if they were standing there staring at each other. Pushed a few out to the dance floor. Nate was charming, per usual, and I was grateful he had on a mask so I wouldn't have to see all the ogling once they caught sight of his face.

Eventually we settled on the opposite side of the bar from Val, but still within eyesight so I could see when she was done for the night. Or when she decided to fall off the martini glass barstool.

Nate kept his body facing the bar and leaned on his clasped hands. "So we've got to be inconspicuous, huh?"

"Mhmm, we do."

"So I shouldn't tell you I'd like to take off your—"

I slapped my hand across his mouth before he could finish that thought. When I let go, he gave me a cheeky grin. And then said, "Mask."

Laughing, I shook my head. "I don't think that's what you were going to say."

"It was. I'm on my best behavior this evening."

"That's too bad," I said, pulling a small Post-it pad from my cleavage. Nate's eyes went wide.

"Have I mentioned I love that you keep stuff in your bra? Holy shit it's hot."

When I pulled out a pen too, he leaned over to get a glimpse down my shirt.

"Jesus, what else do you have in there?" he asked.

"Sometimes my phone. What can I say? It's like the never-ending Mary Poppins carpetbag in bra form." On the Post-it I wrote: **Maybe I'll let you get a peek later.** Then I pushed the pad and pen his way.

"Ohh, this is tenth grade all over again. Awesome." He peeled off the note and then scribbled a quick line before pushing it my way.

Or maybe I could just tear it off with my teeth.

Such an animal. Is that where you'd start?

Fuck no. You're wearing a dress. It would be orgasms on the dance floor all over again.

I'll settle for the bedroom.

Or the kitchen?

Possibly the shower...

Nate coughed and adjusted his pants. "Fuck." Then:
Did I mention you look stunning?

With my face all covered up? I wrote, grinning.

Can't a guy give a compliment?

I'd prefer the orgasm.

Singular?

Plural. Multiples.

"Oh hell, hang on." Val was teetering, and I quickly shoved the notes in my top and rounded the bar. Nate was hot on my heels, and we got to her just in time to keep her upright and not flashing her bum to everyone.

"I already called the cab," Ryleigh said, coming to stand beside me and grabbing Val's purse from the bar.

"What the fuck do I need a fucking cab for?" Val said, patting her sides as if she had pockets there, and then she pointed at me and slurred, "And where the fuck are my fucking keys? If someone steals my car, you're fired."

"I'll make sure no one steals the Lexus," I said, before mouthing *Thank you* to Ryleigh. Then I took a hold of Val's arm as she wobbled to her feet.

"And these masks are fucking stupid." Val dropped hers to the ground and went to step on it but missed by about a foot. That didn't stop her from stomping around until she nailed it.

"Okay, I think it's dead."

With Nate holding her other side, we helped Val through the throng of guests, many of whom barely looked our way, either too engrossed in conversation, or too used to bars where it was common to haul out the drunkards.

Really super great for business. If only she'd kept her damn mask on.

The cab was, thankfully, already at the curb, and Ryleigh took a few bills out of Val's wallet and gave them to the driver before tossing the purse in the backseat.

"She's at 1440 Miller Drive," I said, tucking Val's legs into the backseat, but she pushed me off.

"I got it, I got it. I can buckle my fucking self, Jesus."

She attempted to do just that five times, the buckles clinking, before finally giving up and throwing them down.

"See you Monday. Drink some water."

Val's eyes narrowed. "Stop with the mama routine, hooker. I don't need a fucking teat to suck. And why the hell are you always dressed like it's a funeral, for fuck's sake—"

I slammed the cab door shut and waved off the driver before she could spew out any more trash in front of Nate.

Damn she'd gotten vile lately. When had that happened? She'd always spouted off, but there was humor behind it. *But now?* She made that "no more wire hangers" broad look like a classy bitch.

"I'm not believing you deal with that every day," Nate said, his eyes tracking me warily.

"Believe it. I should've taken more money out of her wallet as a tip," Ryleigh said, and then did a double take. "Oh hey...Nate. You made it."

He put his arm around my waist, and then caught sight of people exiting the After Dark and stepped back. "Yeah, I wanted to surprise Shayne. Great place you have here."

"Thank you. And...excellent surprise?" She looked at me in question.

I nodded and smiled. "Definitely."

"Okay, well...I'm gonna go find Hunter." Ryleigh ducked back into Licked, and I turned to face Nate.

"Thank you. And I'm sorry about that."

"Nothing to be sorry for."

"So…best, most romantic Valentine's Day ever, right?"

"It's been an interesting one so far, that's for sure." Then he leaned over so that his lips were by my ear and said, "But don't worry. I'll make sure you get what you deserve. And I think I'll start by removing those notes in your bra one by one."

Chapter Nineteen
Cheesetastic

"WHERE ARE WE going?" I asked Nate for the twentieth time in the past two hours.

"Crazy."

I rolled my eyes and leaned back in the passenger seat of his car, letting my hand drift out the window to ride the wind. It was a gorgeous, sunny day in March, and all I'd been told was to pack an overnight bag. "You've already reached that destination, thank you very much. Is there some special occasion we're celebrating that I don't know about?"

"I can't just take my girlfriend away for a weekend?" He glanced over and saw my raised eyebrow and then said, "Okay, fine. But it's cheesy. You'll probably throw up."

"Sometimes I like your brand of cheesy. But if I need to, I'll stick my head out the window."

"Fair enough. We met two months ago."

"Yeah…"

"So, that's it. We met two months ago. On the train—"

"Oh my God, you cheesy, romantic bastard. This is an anniversary sort of thing, is it?"

"Or…a just-because thing."

I shook my head, laughing. "Oh, Dimples, who would've thought such a sentimental sap was underneath those sexy suspenders? Should I start taking you to chick flicks and forcing you to read love stories?"

"Hey, there's nothing wrong with a good love story."

"Is that right."

"*The Great Gatsby. The Remains of the Day.* Love is the central theme, so maybe it's rubbed off a bit."

"I love that you're such a book nerd. It's seriously hot. Is that where we're going? Some place you can read to me in a meadow while I feed you grapes?"

"Not sure we'll find meadows, but grapes are a definite. In some form or other."

"Oooh, well, count me in."

"Seeing as you're already in the car, you don't have a choice."

"And that right there is why I was single for so long. You get in a relationship, and bam! All your free will goes away." As Nate laughed, the twinges of guilt that I'd lived with for weeks now, but tried to keep at bay, resurfaced to remind me they were there.

Ace had been shooting in San Diego for three weeks, and last weekend I'd made a quick "impromptu" visit to the set, which was a crazy experience in and of itself. It had been enough to be seen going in and out of the places he'd be, so we hadn't had to make any public appearances, for which I'd been grateful. I enjoyed spending time with Ace, but every minute with him was one I was missing out on with Nate.

But I wasn't going to think about that this weekend. I was going to enjoy myself with my guy and whatever he had planned.

A few minutes later, we were parked and strolling into the foyer of Bridgefield Winery.

Oh yes. Loverboy had taken me to a winery. Hands off, ladies.

The trickle of a waterfall we passed and the light hum of Italian opera playing in the distance greeted us as we walked up to the check-in desk.

"Wait, are we staying here too?" I whispered.

"That okay?"

"Is that okay? I'm in freakin' heaven."

"Welcome to Bridgefield," the deeply tanned woman behind the counter said. "Checking in?"

As Nate gave her his information, my gaze drifted over to the open glass double doors that offered a gorgeous view of the lush greenery spread out for acres and the hills in the distance. The sky today was a cloudless blue, and without the city lights, we'd be able to lie underneath the stars later, or maybe enjoy the square bonfire pit with the rocking chairs gathered around it. It was so peaceful here, and with the chaos that had crowded my brain for too many weeks now, it was a welcome relief.

As the woman handed Nate a clipboard and pen, she peered at me over her glasses. "You look familiar. Have you stayed with us before?"

My limbs turned to ice as I froze and sent up a silent prayer that she wasn't thinking what I hoped she wasn't thinking. When I didn't answer right away, Nate looked over at me.

"Uh, no," I said, finding my voice and pulling my hat down farther.

I wasn't about to mention I'd gone wine-hopping here with the girls a couple of years back, because first, that wasn't where she would've recognized me from, and second, I was ready to get the hell out of there before the real reason I looked familiar hit her.

"Hmm. I can't seem to place where I've seen you before," she said, pushing her glasses up her nose as she continued to scrutinize me.

Shit, let it go, woman.

"I get that a lot," I said, before casually slipping behind Nate. Then she handed him a keycard and gave him directions to our room and we were off, away from the prying eyes of anyone who could blow my cover.

That had been a close call. *Too* close. I guess I could've pulled out the short black bob for the drive up, but I didn't think it would be necessary to freak Nate out. I'd only been using scarves and hats around him because the wigs seemed a little extreme, but rare moments like this had me panicking that maybe I'd need to put them to good use after all.

When we reached room 112, I teased, "Will you be carrying me over the threshold too?"

Nate dropped his bag just outside the door. "You read my mind."

"Whoa, I was kidding," I said, batting him away. "How about you open the door instead, Romeo."

He laughed as he leaned in for a kiss. "You do know this is a romantic weekend getaway, and I plan on spoiling you, right? I'm gonna need you to get on board with this." His teeth nipped at my bottom lip, teasing until I wrapped my arms around his neck and crushed my lips to his.

"You can do that…in bed. Please and thank you."

With my mouth swallowing his groan, he inserted the room key—though it took several tries—and shoved the door open, and we tumbled inside. I let go long enough for him to grab the bags from the hallway, and as we entered the dark room, the soft flickering of battery-operated tea light candles spread out around the room greeted us. At the end of the king-size bed were more candles, along with flower petals, chilled wine, and glasses.

"Wow," I said softly.

There'd never been any candles and rose petals anywhere in my past relationships. No weekend getaways, no romantic gestures anywhere near this level. Had I just been deprived of romance this whole time, or was Nate an exception to most men?

His arms went around my waist from behind me, warm and strong, and then one of his hands snaked down lower. "You don't mind if I have you all to myself for a private tasting, do you?"

The kiss he planted beneath my ear echoed through my whole body, and I shivered. Covering his wayward hand with mine, I pushed his fingers down even farther, until it reached the apex of my thighs.

My head fell back on his shoulder as he teased me, achingly slowly, over my jeans. Pressed up against me, I could feel his erection growing with every stroke he gave me. Just as my breath hitched and I grabbed the back of his neck, he was pushing me away.

"It's rude to tease," I said, watching as he set the pair of glasses on the table and began to uncork the bottle of wine.

"What? I said I wanted a private tasting."

My bottom lip popped out. "I thought you meant of me."

"Oh, I did." He poured us each a glass of the chilled, golden liquid and handed me one.

"Are we toasting happy anniversary?" I teased.

"How about cheers, smartass, now go get naked."

I took a long gulp and set my glass on the nightstand. With my back to him, I flirted with the edge of my top and then pulled it up over my head, tossing it over my shoulder. He caught it, and when I faced him and unbuttoned my jeans, he held up his hand.

"Don't you fucking dare," he said.

"Oh, I dare," I said, unzipping my pants just as he lunged and tackled me to the bed.

And then…it was *on*.

Nate's hands were on me everywhere, running down my sides, up over my breasts, unbuttoning my bra. He slid it down my arms, and then he straightened, sitting back on his knees. His lips quirked as he looked down to what I was staring at. "You like these?" he asked, pulling on the straps of his suspenders.

"Mhmm, I do."

He unfastened one and then the other. Crawling over me, he pushed my arms up over my head and touched my lips lightly with his. "Then I guess we'll have to put them to good use. What do you say?"

I moaned my approval, and he gathered my wrists together with one hand and wound his suspenders around them with the other. His lips trailed a path of kisses down my neck…my shoulder…settling on the pointy tips of my breasts.

Arching my back up off the bed, I rubbed against him, needing the friction, since I wasn't able to touch. His hips ground into mine, and his hands moved quickly, peeling off my jeans to reveal the ice-blue lace panties I'd bought just for this weekend. Knowing it was the only color he could really see had me consciously picking out clothes just for him.

The warm, wet feel of his tongue between my thighs had me bucking up, a quick swipe that had my breath rushing out. Then the panties were discarded and his mouth was back on me, and *fuck*, I wanted to spear my hands into his hair, to hold him there or push him away because the pleasure was too intense. Writhing underneath him, my arms desperately trying to wriggle out of its hold, I cried out as the wave crested and then crashed spectacularly, sweeping me away with its powerful pull.

I was trembling as I came down from the high, and as Nate's mouth left me, his hands massaged the outside of my thighs to soothe.

When I caught my breath, I glanced over at the wine glasses by the bed. "And here I thought you'd be using the wine for a little private tasting."

"That had been the plan, but fuck, you taste better than anything out of a bottle."

Oh fuck me, that might be the best compliment I'd ever heard.

As he kissed his way up my body, I lost myself in his touch, his caress, both gentle and strong, and in the dirty sweet nothings he whispered as he filled me so entirely that I couldn't imagine ever feeling complete without him.

THREE HOURS AND four—count 'em, four—orgasms later, we were still tangled in the sheets, the lights off and the doors leading outside open so the wind could breeze in and we could see the stars.

"It was like this where I grew up," I said. "So quiet at night and you could see out for miles."

"Must've been nice. The view wasn't anything like this in Michigan. All I remember is snow for months."

"Snow is pretty."

Nate's chest vibrated with laughter. "Yeah, because you've never been in it."

"True. Maybe you'll take me there sometime."

"Maybe so." I could hear the grin in his voice. "Speaking of…do I get to meet your parents anytime soon?"

"Uh, you really want to talk about my parents while we're naked?"

"You're avoiding the question."

"I'm not—" I started, and then shook my head. "Sorry to dash your dreams, but they're not visiting until next year. So *if* I'm still putting up with you then, I guess I'll let you tag along," I said with a wink.

He clutched at his heart. "*If*, she says. Don't you guys Skype every week?"

"Hold on. You want to Skype with me and my parents? Really?" A slow smile spread across my face. "You liiiiike me, you want to kiiiiiss me—"

"Oh bugger off," he said, and that had me laughing. "See? You're already rubbing off on me."

"Maybe don't say *that* particular expression when you meet them."

"So it's *when* now, huh?" His grin turned arrogant.

"Yeah, I guess I'll claim you."

"That's good to know," he said, as his hands played in my hair. "So you know the project I've been working on?"

"The one you've been talking about but not talking about for weeks? No, I have no idea," I said, grinning as I nudged him with my knee. "Please tell me more of nothing about it."

Nate was on top of me in a flash, his eyes twinkling as he pinned me to the bed. Laughing, I struggled to escape, but gave up when he interlaced our fingers over my head.

"We're booked for showcases next month. I want you there."

"Mhmm, I think I can make that happen," I said, lifting up to catch his lips in a kiss, but he dodged out of my reach.

"Promise?"

A fleeting thought of checking in with Ace went through my head, but even if something came up with him, there was no way I would miss Nate's big event. It was only one night, after all. He could deal.

"On second thought, I might be busy that day…" I teased, pushing my hips up against his.

"Don't make me tie you up again and force you. I'll do it."

I pulled my left leg out from underneath him and wrapped it around his hips, pushing him down onto me as I arched into him again. "How bad do you want me there?"

His eyes glazed over with lust at my sexual invitation.

"Pretty fucking bad," he said, licking his lips as one hand came down to hold the leg I had around him firmly in place. His mouth went to my neck, brushing so light against my skin that I shivered. "Tell me...will you come for me?"

"Come for you...or with you?"

"With me," he said, his lips grazing mine. "Always."

A whispered "yes" lingered in the air as I rolled on top of him, giving just as good as I'd been given.

Chapter Twenty
Pervy Pete

WHY IS IT always when things are going well that they inevitably turn to shit? Just out of the blue, bam, it hits you, and you're knocked off course.

It was a rare rainy day in April, and I was just wrapping up my column for the week when my cell phone rang.

"Hey, Ace, what's up?"

"Sorry to make this quick, but I'm in the middle of a shoot. Something's come up for Friday, and I'll need you."

"Friday, like *this* Friday? As in tomorrow night, you mean?"

"Yeah. Sorry, I know it's last minute, and I was gonna just go alone, but Roger and Martina seem to think you need to walk the red carpet with me. There's another fucking story coming out in next week's tabloids, and it would be a stronger show to ward off the shitstorm."

Oh my God. Not Friday. Not Nate's project Friday.

"But—"

"Don't worry, I'll make sure you've got something to wear. I'll have Roger work things out with your boss so you can get something tomorrow—"

"Wait, uh…you don't have to do that." Shit shit shit. "What I mean is, um. I can't…go with you. I already made plans—"

"I'm sorry, I know this makes me such a huge asshole, but I need you, Shayne. I hate having to even admit that, but…if we don't show up together, I'm fucked and this is all for nothing. Please."

"Isn't there something else we could attend instead? Something Saturday or Sunday?" Literally *any* time other than tomorrow night. *Please, God, don't do this to me.*

"Oh…well, if it's not possible, I'm sure I can figure something out—"

A muffled sound as if the phone dropped or switched hands, and then—

"Shayne." *Oh hell.* Ace's right-hand man had, of course, heard the conversation. Great. Just great.

My eyes squeezed shut as I ground out, "Hi, Mr. Herschman."

"I just wanted to remind you of the contract you signed with us. And that the penalty for breaking said contract is a pretty hefty fee, to the tune of two million."

"I'm more than aware of what I signed." And more than aware that even if I worked every day of my life I'd still never make that much money.

So what was the alternative? Jail? Getting sent back to Australia? If it wasn't so fucking terrifying, it would almost be laughable.

"Then it'll be no problem for you to do your job and attend the event with Ace tomorrow. And you won't give him a hard time for asking something simple of you. I'm sure your plans can be easily rescheduled." His voice brooked no argument. It also said that if I tried to fight him on this, that he would personally see to it that I attended, even if he had to drag me kicking and screaming bloody murder all the way there.

But Nate's face was all I could see, and the burden of what I had to do weighed heavily on my shoulders. I tried to swallow past the lump in my throat, but I felt like I was choking. *No. No, I can't go. No, I won't go. I don't care how much money you sue me for.* That's what I wanted to say, what was on the tip of my tongue. Instead I said, "I understand."

"That's what I thought. Martina will find you tomorrow and get you set up with something to wear, as Ace said. You'll be at his house at four on Friday for hair and makeup, and then you'll ride together."

"Right. Of course." My voice sounded so small I didn't even recognize it as mine.

"We'll see you then." He ended the call before Ace

had a chance to get back on, and I instantly felt sick to my stomach.

What the hell was I going to tell Nate? *"Oh, I can't attend your big final project that you've been working so hard on because I have to go walk a red carpet with my faux-boyfriend. You know, the one I said I wasn't dating in Vegas but ended up in a contract with? Oh, did I forget to mention that? Well, you know now, and also your friends will tell you once clear pictures without a fucking disguise are plastered all the hell over every magazine and newspaper."* No big deal. I just had to go break his heart, which in turn would break mine.

Fuck. Fuck fuck fuck fuck. How was this my life?

IT'D TAKEN THREE hours for me to work up the courage to go see Nate. He'd been expecting me to head over right after work with dinner I'd ordered from the Aussie bakery nearby, even though he was swamped with final project details, of which he was still keeping a super secret.

He opened the door with a huge smile, and I wasn't even in the door when he grabbed me by the waist, kissed me, and pulled me inside.

"Just the break I needed," he said, kissing down my neck and then taking the bags I held and dumping them on the counter.

"Sorry I'm late."

"Nah, I was just taking a break, so it's perfect timing." He kissed me again, his lips lingering on mine, but then he leaned back, his brow furrowed. "You okay?"

I mustered a smile, even though every beat of my heart pumped the dread in my veins deeper and harder until I was consumed. But I couldn't hide it from Nate. Not for long, so I told him the truth. "Not really."

"What's wrong? You starving? I know how you get when you're hungry," he said with a grin, and let go of me to pull the Styrofoam cartons out of the to-go bag. "I got port to go with it, the kind your dad mentioned you like—"

"I can't go tomorrow," I blurted out.

His hands went still, and his head craned to look at me. "What?"

"I can't go tomorrow. To your big night."

"Yeah, I heard you, but I was hoping there was a 'just kidding' coming."

I took a big breath, and then gave him the story I'd come up with on the way here. Lies upon more lies. What else was new for me lately? And who the hell was I? "Val informed me today that she has an out-of-town emergency, and I have to handle a big client mixer on her behalf. Two of her investors will be there, and it's a huge deal for the company. I tried to get out of it, I swear, but she wasn't having it."

The story would check out fine because Val was indeed out of town until Monday, but not for an emergency, like I'd said. No, she was off enjoying herself on some tropical vacay, as she was wont to do more often than not. Must be nice.

"And no one else can do it," he said. Not a question. A statement that said he was sure someone else *could* do it, and I just hadn't said no.

I crossed my arms over my chest so my hands would stop shaking. "No, she doesn't trust anyone else to handle it."

"I see." He stared down at the counter for a long moment before pushing off it and walking past me.

"Nate, I'm sorry—"

"I'm sure you are."

"Of course I am. But what can I do?"

"You can say no, Shayne. You can say I'm sorry, but we'll just have to reschedule. You have choices. You do what you want to do."

"But I *don't* have a choice, don't you understand that?"

"You know, you keep saying that like you're stuck where you are. No one is keeping you there."

"What, so you want me to quit my job?"

He stayed silent, staring at his hands as he sat on the edge of the couch.

"Nate, I can't quit my job. I love what I do." His eyebrow winged up, and I said, "Okay, I don't love where I'm at, but I do love what I do. I'd never ask you to give something like that up."

"Is that what I'm asking you to do?" His head cocked

to the side, and his eyes studied me as though I were someone he'd never seen before. I didn't want him looking at me that way. I wanted the happy-go-lucky Nate who had opened the door. The one who believed I wasn't the asshole who would blow him off.

Perching on the end of the chair opposite him, I said, "It makes me sick that I can't go, and if I could be there I would. I mean that. I'm so proud of you, and I *want* to be there to see what you've accomplished. More than anything. Please believe me."

He picked at his hands. "This little school thing, or whatever you think it is…it means a lot to me."

My eyesight grew blurry around the edges as the tears threatened, and I swallowed hard. "I know it does. And it's not a little thing at all."

Nate didn't say anything to that, just had his head in his hands. After silent minutes passed, he rubbed his face and stood up, heading back to his desk.

I just watched him, not sure whether he wanted me to stay. Wanted me to go. Wanted to yell. He rearranged the books on his desk and flipped the monitor back on.

"I don't know what else to say."

"Then maybe you should go." His face was hard, closed off. He looked so much older in that moment than I'd ever seen him, and I hated the cause was me.

I recoiled. "You want me to leave?"

His shoulders lifted in a shrug, and my heart sank. I knew the reaction wouldn't be a good one, but I hadn't expected the complete shutout. I'd thought he'd be upset and pissed off and then forgive me and say maybe next time. I should've known better.

"If that's what you want."

He looked back down at his desk. "I've just got a lot to work on, so it'd be best if you did."

"Nate—"

"Shayne," he said, his gaze coming up to meet mine. He started to say something else then shook his head. "I'll call you later."

I didn't want to leave, not yet. What if he decided this was too much of a deal breaker and I never came back? *Surely not.* Work happens. He'd understand...eventually. "I'm really sorry, Nate. I tried."

"Yeah, I heard you the first time," he said softly. "You can let yourself out. Take the food with you."

I was too much in shock to say anything back, so I stood and walked numbly to the front door, passing by the food left out on the counter. I didn't want it, and he'd need it later. When I opened the door and looked back at him, his back was facing me, and it was all I could do not to go back inside and *make* him forgive me. Instead, I would give him space, and I let the door click quietly shut behind me.

AFTER THE TEARS unleashed and then finally came to a

stop on the drive home, I left a message on Val's machine
and told her I was gonna chuck a sickie the next day.
Because apparently I had to go shopping for a fucking dress
for a fucking premiere so I could officially come out as Ace's
fucking girlfriend, in essence cutting off all ties to my real
fucking boyfriend.

And yeah, my punishment and bad karma had been
coming for a while now, and I'd been lucky my double-
dealing ways hadn't bit me on the ass yet, but I needed more
time. I needed this all not to happen until I could figure out
how the hell to fix it, but let's face it—I'd been in fix-it mode
for weeks and weeks now and hadn't gotten any damn
where.

Normally when I was upset, I'd stop off and grab a
pint of ice cream at Licked, but I wasn't in the mood for any
more lying today. Yes, I was avoiding my friends. Add that
to the "Shayne is a horrible person" list. So I made a detour
to Trader Joe's for cookie butter and cheap red wine instead.

When I got home, the apartment was thankfully
empty, a rarity nowadays, but the twins were in Palm
Springs for a few days, so I would take advantage of the
dead silence that mimicked the numbness I felt inside.
Maybe I'd take a long, luxurious bubble bath to go with my
gorge-fest, along with a little mindless reading to quiet the
chaos that would soon come back with a roaring vengeance
to vie for attention inside my brain.

That wasn't asking too much, was it? A nice, quiet
night at home to pretend my life wasn't a complete fuck-up.

So not what I got.

My enjoyable evening started with plumbing issues. It took a good ten minutes of running the water for the rusty, orange-tinted liquid to go clear—damn old pipes— and then another ten for the shitty water pressure to fill the tub. Trying to fit myself into the small, bubble-filled bath was a challenge, my limbs contorting into awkward positions so that I was covered, but it was either legs under and top half out, or top half in, legs out.

See? Baths always seemed like such a good idea in theory, but until tub makers decided to wake up and realize people were taller now than back when they'd been invented in the nineteenth century, it would continue to be an uncomfortable experience for anyone over five-two.

Oh, and for the record, Dawn dish soap makes for an inexpensive alternative and gives great foam. #CheapideasbyShayne

I crossed my legs Indian-style and lay back, and the water finally covered most of me. Closing my eyes, I counted backward from a hundred, clearing my mind of everything threatening to invade my quiet time. In this space, there wasn't work stress or lies. No men to complicate things. No money problems or car issues. Just peace and tranquility.

"Shayne!"

The pounding on the front door jolted me awake just as I'd finally begun to drift off somewhere between sleep and consciousness.

Nope. Ignore. Pretend there is no old landlord beating down your door to tear you away from this mountain of bubbles that you worked so hard to build. There are also no such things as cell phones, crazy people, love-life problems, or anything stressful. Nope. There is only bubbles. And a half-eaten jar of cookie butter by the tub within arm's reach.

My hand grazed through the top layer of foam, and when I scooped a handful, I blew on it and made a wish before letting my eyelids shutter down again.

Bang bang bang. "Shayne! Open open."

When the assault against my front door continued, I growled and sat up, the water lapping over the edge of the tub. Then I stood, grabbed my robe, and muttered obscenities as I stomped out of the bathroom. Wet footprints on the fake hardwood linoleum trailed me as I made my way through the living room, and then when another knock sounded, I swung open the door.

"There better be a fire," I warned, holding my robe closed in one hand and gripping the door with the other.

My landlord, a squat man with a beer belly, stood there with a flashlight in his hand, which was probably what he'd used to beat my door half to death with. He didn't even try to hide his open perusal. Instead, he twirled his handlebar mustache and whistled to show his appreciation.

I didn't refer to him as Pervy Pete for nothin'.

"I didn't realize I was interrupting," he said, his south-of-the-border accent thicker than usual, and he looked anything but apologetic.

I clenched my robe tighter in my fist. "Is there an emergency?"

"What?" He took his gaze off the top of my robe, which was at eye level for him, and looked up at me. "Emergency? No. Electric out." He waved the flashlight behind him, to where the building sat in darkness. It was probably safe to assume that our entire block was lights out. Great. I hadn't noticed in my candlelit haven that I was more than ready to get back to.

"Okay, well, thanks for letting me know. Feel free to go wake the others now." As I went to shut the door, he stepped into the doorway.

"You have batteries?"

I blinked. "You're here for batteries? Seriously?" *Does your car not work for a store run?*

He held up the damn flashlight again and showed me the empty compartment where a pair of cells should go.

"Oh my God," I muttered, and headed to the kitchen, where we kept a drawer full of miscellaneous household items, a.k.a. the junk drawer. Of course Pete would pick me to come to out of the fifty-plus residents that lived here.

"What size?"

Pervy's gaze rested on my chest. "C. C is gooooood."

I forced myself not to roll my eyes and grabbed the last pack I had. His eyesight must be out of whack, because I barely filled a B-cup, but I wasn't about to argue that point with him. "Here. Off you go," I said, ushering him back out the way he came.

"Thank you, Shayne. I bring them back—"

"Not necessary," I said, practically pushing him out the door.

"Okay, I bring you my homemade tamales—"

"I'm good, thanks, Pete." My words rushed out, and I shut the door and locked the deadbolt.

He pounded on the door again. "Shayne! Rent due."

With a sigh, I opened the door. "Rent due, yes, I know. Friday is always payday, so we'll drop it off to you after work."

If it wasn't the roommates giving me hell, or the orange water, or the helicopters constantly roaming super loud overhead, it was my creepy landlord.

What the hell am I still doing here?

The bubble hill was half deflated when I got back to the bathroom, and when I stuck my hand in the water, it was lukewarm.

Just great. *Nice, relaxing evening, my ass. This just sums up my life, right here.*

Leaning over, I pulled the plug from the drain and then scooped up my cookie butter, cradling it in the crook of my arm. I stuck the spoon of sweet gingerbread in my mouth and swiped the candle with my free hand. I set it all on my nightstand and then curled up in the center of the bed in the darkness, the candle and the faint city lights down below the only light in the room. For the first time in a long time, I felt alone, and I had not one fucking clue what to do. If ever there was a time to call in my tribe, it was now.

With a deep breath, I reached for my cell and dialed a number.

Chapter Twenty-One
Rally the Troops

NOT EVEN AN hour later, and the troops had rallied, the girls all meeting at Paige's house, since parking was such a bitch at mine, not to mention the electricity was still out.

"All right, Shayne. You've called us all together tonight for a reason, so…time to come clean. The jury awaits." Paige swept her hand toward Quinn and Ryleigh, who were settled into the plush cream couches and looking at me expectantly.

"Can I do a shot first?"

"Uh oh." Quinn looked between us. "Should I get the popcorn?"

Paige shook her head. "No shots. No popcorn. Spill. Now."

"Okay." I rubbed my hands on my pajama pants, and then said, "I stuffed up." When they all stared at me, I continued. "I mean, I'm in a…sort of bad position, and I need your help."

The girls all responded at once, talking over each other.

"Is it money?"

"Did something happen with Val?"

"Did Ace get caught with a supermodel and you need us to hide his body?"

Everyone stopped and turned toward Ryleigh at that final comment. She looked between us and said, "What? I'm good with an ice cream scoop, so I'm sure I could handle the shoveling."

Paige groaned, and then motioned for me to keep talking. "Hurry up and spit it out before Ryleigh has us committing a felony tonight."

I took a breath that expanded my lungs until they ached, and then let it out on a rush. "The night I met Ace in Vegas, it *was* as a client meeting, like I told you. But what I didn't say was that I discovered something during that meeting, and I wouldn't just be finding one match for him, I'd be hired to find two—one publicly, and one privately. I relayed the whole thing to Val when I got back, and then the next thing I know, Ace's secret is splashed all over every tabloid magazine in the country, and he's freaking out, his handler people are freaking out, and they're like, fix it, fix it, so in a panic, I volunteered to be his public girlfriend in part to keep my job. They made me sign this super-strict NDA, which I'm totally breaking right now, so hopefully I don't get sued for the pennies I have in the bank, because that's all I could afford to give them anyway. So I lied to Nate, I lied to myself, and I lied to you guys, but Paige figured it out and I made her promise she wouldn't tell you, because being a two-timing wench is so much better than being a lying beard, which is what I am, and I suck. I know that. I'm a horrible person, and I'm sorry I couldn't tell you, but…well, there it is."

Quinn and Ryleigh blinked at me.

Squirming in my chair, I said, "Say something. Anything."

"This is some crazy shit," Quinn responded.

"I know."

"So you're still a part of this charade because of Val."

"Pretty much."

Ryleigh scooted to the edge of the couch and fidgeted with her ring. "And what about Nate?" she asked softly. Then she shook her head, her eyes turning sad. "He doesn't know any of this, does he?"

"No, he doesn't. I couldn't legally tell him either, and now I'm in this bad situation, and I don't know how to get out."

"Dude," Quinn said. "You've got to tell Nate the truth."

"Ace too," Ryleigh added. "If he realizes he's ruining your life and *your* chance at a happy relationship at his expense, I bet he puts a stop to the whole thing."

Before I could protest, Quinn held up her hand.
"Fuck the legal bullshit and come clean. That's the only
choice you have unless you want things to blow up in your
face, and I promise, that'll happen sooner than later. Sounds
like you've gotten lucky."

"Well, it's probably already blown up in my face,
seeing as I told Nate tonight that I couldn't go to his
showcase tomorrow because of this red carpet thing with
Ace. And his final project is a huge deal for him.
Like...huge. So yeah. Nate will barely look at me, much less
talk to me."

"Oh, Shayne." Ryleigh shook her head, her eyes full
of pity.

"If I tell him now, I'll lose him anyway. It's a lose-
lose situation."

"Too fucking bad," Quinn replied. "You're breaking
the NDA to tell us now, so it's ridiculous for you to keep it
from him. And yeah, most likely he'll fucking run, because
that's a lot for a guy his age to handle. Hell, it's a lot for
anyone to handle. But just maybe he'll see the spot you're
in."

"I doubt it. He doesn't think very highly of Val or my
job."

"Aaand that's another thing we need to discuss.
None of us do," Paige said, and then stopped herself when
my head jerked up. "I mean, not that we don't think highly
of you and your matchmaking skills, but dude. You've got

to get away from that woman *and* that company. We've been telling you that for years."

"And the longer you let Val dictate your life and threaten your job, the more miserable you're gonna be. We won't let you fall, Shayne." Ryleigh reached for my hand and gave it a squeeze.

"I appreciate that, but—"

"Do it. Leap off the damn cliff," Quinn said, as if it were that easy and she'd made the jump a thousand times.

"When you decide to take our advice and get the fuck away from Val, can we do something awful to her? Send her a chocolate basket spiked with laxatives?" Paige asked, but Quinn shook her head.

"Nah, something more untraceable. Cyanide. Arsenic."

Paige stopped and stared at Quinn. "Seriously, what the hell is it you do all day, woman? Does it entail having easy access to cyanide?"

"I'd tell you but I'd have to kill you," she replied, and shrugged.

Paige waved her off and said, "Okay, maybe nothing that will kill her, but something that would make her and that little wench, what's her name? Nicole? Yeah, something that would make them super uncomfortable and exploding from both ends for days."

"Hell, sugar-free gummy bears would do that, and it's easier to feign innocence than poison them. I learned that the hard way when I was stocking the toppings," Ryleigh said, holding her stomach. "Go read reviews for that stuff when you need a laugh."

"Yeah, I'll do that," I said, and my voice sounded dead even to my ears.

"Hey. Where are your Post-its? We'll just write down what you need to do, and when you cross off each thing, you'll feel much better." Paige squeezed my shoulder and walked us over to the couch. When we sat down, they all gathered around and enveloped me in a group bear hug that gave me the warm and fuzzies.

"Simple as that, huh?"

"Simple as that," she confirmed.

Quinn rested her chin on my shoulder. "You got this. Talk to Nate. Take the weekend to figure out what you want. And then lean on us."

I DIDN'T CALL Nate right away. I knew he wouldn't answer. But I sent him a message before bed to say I missed him, that I was sorry again, and asking if we could meet tomorrow.

When I woke the next morning…no response.

Another message sent and still nothing when I went to meet Martina and spend Ace's money on a ridiculously priced designer gown for the evening. There was a gorgeous satin dress that fit like a glove, but it was blue. Blue. As in the only color Nate could see on me, so that one was out.

Maybe it was silly, but if I couldn't spend his big night with him, I wasn't about to wear something that would remind me of him the whole night. I didn't need any reminders. And God forbid he ever see the pictures of me with Ace, but I didn't want him to see me in that color with someone else.

Like I said. Silly.

I went with a sequined silver number that touched the floor and had me wondering how the hell I would walk in heels and not trip over it. The last thing I needed was to call more attention to myself on the red carpet by falling ass over face, but that was no doubt what would happen tonight. Awesome.

More messages and phone calls left. Still nothing from Nate when I left the shop. Nothing when I got home. Nothing after I'd showered and shaved. *Ugh.* I had to leave for Ace's house in a couple of hours, but maybe I should just head over to Nate's now and pray he was there and had ten minutes to spare—

The shrill sound of my phone ringing cut through the air, and I tripped over myself in the rush to get to it.

"Nate," I said, breathless as I answered the phone.

"Hey." A pause. "Why are you breathing so hard?"

"I was trying to get to my phone, but...well, my feet got in the way."

"Oh."

Oh? That was it? No joke at my clumsy-ass expense?

Okaaaay, that didn't bode well, did it?

"I saw you called a few times. I've been downstairs at school all night, and I don't get great reception. Was there something you needed?"

Something I *needed*? Oh bloody hell, just say it, then. "Actually, yes. Could I stop by your place for a few minutes?"

"You could, but no one's there."

Uh. "Okay, well, wherever you are. The venue, whatever that is."

He sighed. "I don't really have time right now, Shayne. I'm getting everything ready for tonight—"

"I know, that's what I need to talk to you about."

"What, did you change your mind about coming?"

"Well…no—"

"Then it'll have to wait until tomorrow."

"But it's important. Please? I won't take long."

"So tell me now."

Now? I wasn't about to tell him on the phone. "I can't talk about it over the phone."

"You would if it's that important."

"It is important, but it's not the kind of thing I want to tell you over the phone."

"That's all I can offer you right now. Take it or leave it."

Fucking ouch. I weighed whether I should just tell him everything now, but surely waiting another day wouldn't make a difference.

"Look, I've gotta go."

"Nate," I said, gripping the phone in my hand. "I'm sorry."

"It's fine. Seriously. Don't sweat it."

"You know I want to be there, right?"

"Honestly, Shayne? No, I don't. But if this job with your joke of a boss is that important to you, then you should go."

His words were a slap in the face that had me recoiling. "That's not fair."

"You know what's not fair? That you let that psycho run all the fuck over you, and you don't do a thing about it. You're this incredibly hardworking, talented woman, who has no problem saying what's on her mind except with her. Why is that? You're not a doormat, Shayne, so stop acting like one."

Wow…had all that been building up overnight or longer? The phone shook in my hand, my heart skipping erratically in my chest. "I…was not…expecting…that. So…you think I'm a doormat."

Nate sighed, and I could picture him running his hand through his hair. "I don't think that. I'm just frustrated that you don't stand up to her—"

"What would you have me do? Quit my job? Take up begging for dollars on the train?"

"That's not what I'm saying—"

"Sure sounded like it. Until I can figure out a Plan B, I'm stuck where I am, so get off my back."

The sting of tears had me pinching my eyes shut so they wouldn't fall. We were silent except for our breathing, and I hoped he couldn't hear the hitch in my throat.

When he finally broke the quiet, he said, "Look, I'm sorry. I'm just exhausted. I haven't slept in three days, I'm stressed about tonight, and I've got less than four hours to get everything set up with the team and make things perfect, or I can kiss my dream job goodbye. Okay? And yeah, I'm upset that you won't be there, because this is important to me, but fuck. I don't want to fight with you, Shayne."

Swallowing hard, I struggled to make my words come out without wavering, and I almost succeeded. "I don't want to fight with you either. If I could be there, I would."

"Yeah, I know you would." The sound of loud voices chattering rang out on his end of the line, and he sighed again. "I've gotta go, but I'll try to call you after it's over. If not then, I'll come see you tomorrow. If you want me to."

"Of course I do. I'm sorry."

"I'm sorry too."

Then he clicked off, and the tears I'd been holding back came out full force. I had to get myself out of the deep hole I'd gotten myself into, but how was I supposed to do that without hurting Nate, Ace, or both, on top of losing my job?

Where the hell was a fairy godmother when you needed one?

Chapter Twenty-Two
Erase and Rewind

OH GOD. I looked bloody ridiculous.

Okay, so maybe ridiculous would be the wrong word to anyone else looking at me. To them, I might look sort of glamorous, like I could walk a red carpet and not be an embarrassment to Ace. The floor-length silver gown was satin and practically painted on me, my face was airbrushed, my lips matched my hair, and the heels were entirely too high. Total glam bomb.

But all I could think was, *How the shit am I going to walk in these shoes or breathe in this dress? And how long will it take to wash the five pounds of makeup off my face or the two cans of hairspray holding my curls in this fancy bun?*

I was going to fall on my face, I just knew it.

The town car had picked us up from Ace's house and was now navigating the streets of downtown. In my state of nerves, my mind a million miles away and focused on Nate, I hadn't even bothered to ask where we were going or what movie we were going to see. If it was even a movie.

As we pulled up to the venue, my brow furrowed. We were across the street from the main entrance of Nate's uni, which meant I was way too close for comfort. What if Nate was somewhere close by? He'd never mentioned his project being shown on campus, but I'd just assumed. So if he stumbled onto our event?

Fuuuuuck.

"The premiere is here?" I asked, but before Ace could answer, the car slowed to a stop and the door was opened.

Ace smiled at me. "You're up first."

Right. Of course. And I needed to be graceful getting out of the car and all that jazz. As I took the hand of the man holding open the door, I carefully stepped out onto the sidewalk, making sure to keep my dress lifted enough so that my heel didn't catch the end of it. It didn't. *Thank God.*

When Ace made his way out of the car, it was then that I noticed there wasn't a red carpet. And there wasn't a large crowd or cameras everywhere. There was a steady stream of people walking into the building, but other than that, it was the same reaction we would've garnered had Nate and I been going inside instead—none.

"Is this the back way?" I asked as I took Ace's proffered arm and he led me down the tiled walkway, followed closely by his driver slash bodyguard.

He chuckled. "No, it's not a huge event."

"It's not?"

"Not at all. Remember when we talked about indie films and getting back to basics?"

"Yeah…"

"Let's just say you inspired me."

"How's that?"

"You'll see."

"Gee, that's not cryptic at all," I said as he held open the door and we walked into a rather large foyer with an ornate chandelier hanging from its center to light up the space. To the right there were a handful of photographers snapping photos of attendees on a small red carpet that ran a few feet and was backed by what Ace called a "step and repeat" backdrop with the list of sponsors.

A woman with a clipboard came over then, introducing herself to Ace, and then leading us over to the photographers. When Ace and I stepped up in front of the cameras, they went wild. His arm went around my waist, pulling me close, and I tried to mimic all those celebrity couple pictures I'd seen in magazines. The head angled slightly toward him, the big grin, one leg in front of the other for a longer line. No idea if I was nailing it or trying too hard. I hoped for the former.

"Just like a pro," Ace said with a smile, his fingers giving me a gentle squeeze of encouragement.

After they got their shots, Ace gave them a nod and

thanks and then I took his arm again. After the flashes, I was seeing double, and would've tripped all over my gown had I not had something to hold on to.

I frowned and squinted at the backdrop. "Does that sign say USC?"

He nodded and then pointed back toward the entrance we came from, at the buildings across the street. "Film school was where I started, so I thought I'd give back a little. Help someone else catch their break."

"Film school," I repeated, hoping I'd misheard—and misread.

"Yeah, you know, branch out by starting small. Isn't that what you said?"

"Uh...did I?" Fuck, it was hot in here, and I patted my forehead with the back of my hand before fanning myself. A low hum sounded in my ears, the rush of blood as my heart rate picked up. Surely this was just a coincidence. It had to be. Yeah, I had a lot of karma coming back my way, but the others involved were good people...

Fuck, I needed to sit down.

"Are you okay?" Ace asked, his forehead crinkling. "You did eat today, right?"

"What? Oh. Uh yeah."

"Just making sure. I know what low blood sugar looks like." Then he leaned in and whispered, "The last five girls I dated lived off cigarettes and champagne. Fainting spells every damn day."

"I don't...smoke," I managed, fanning myself faster.

Was the air on? Did they have a freezer I could hide in? My eyes searched the room, but Ace was pulling me in the opposite direction.

"Ah, there's the man of the hour," he said, as he led me over to—

Nate.

He turned around just as we came to a stop, and when he saw me, the biggest dimpled smile I'd ever seen crossed his face. "You made it."

Oh my God. It was slow motion as he reached for me, pulling me into a tight squeeze. As his lips brushed against my cheek, I couldn't move, couldn't speak. My arms were frozen at my sides as the reality that my life was about to crumble to the ground punched me in the gut.

"I'm so happy you're here. You have no idea how much it means to me," Nate said, and then pulled away, that big-ass grin still on his face. Then he noticed who was standing next to me, and he put his hand forward to shake Ace's. "Hey, man, thanks so much for coming. And I see you already found Shayne. That's great. I figured since you two are friendly, it'd be a cool surprise that you worked on the film."

"Absolutely, it was my pleasure." Then he gestured toward me. "So you already know Shayne?"

"Of course I do. She's my—" He stopped when he saw Ace's hand move to my lower back. His brow furrowed and he blinked, as though to make sure he was seeing things right. Then, when Ace pulled me closer, Nate's eyes jerked up to mine.

It was like a car spinning out of control with no way to stop it as the horror of realization in his eyes clashed with the absolute despair I knew were in mine.

No. No. *No.* My mind went from numb and hazy to instantly clear. All the things I should've said before this moment, the contract I should've broken for the man in front of me, the lies I never should've told…it all hit me then that I'd played this game wrong. So very, very wrong. And now it was time to pay, in the most fucked-up, combustible way possible.

"She's your…?" Ace asked when Nate didn't answer.

Nate's eyes were pleading, begging me to tell him that what he was seeing wasn't the truth. That I wasn't a liar, that I was his and his only. They told me exactly what he wasn't going to say out loud: *Why would you do this? I trusted you. I cared about you. Is this some kind of fucking nightmare?* And finally, *I don't understand.*

When I didn't refute his assumptions, Nate's gaze dropped to the floor and he swallowed hard. Then a moment later, he lifted his head and met Ace's stare straight on, giving him a tight smile. "Friend," he said finally. "Shayne is just a friend."

"Ah, it's amazing how small the world can be, right?" Ace said, squeezing me to his side.

Nate's jaw clenched at the move. "Right. Listen, I've got to get things ready, but Monica over there with the clipboard will show you to your seats."

"Great, thanks. Good luck in there."

Nate gave a curt nod and, without a glance in my direction, headed into the auditorium. When he disappeared into the room, I briefly wondered if I'd imagined what had just happened. But then Ace spoke, and that hope was dashed.

"Are you sure you're okay?" he asked. "You look a little pale."

"What?" I tore my eyes away from the auditorium doors and looked up at him. "I just…don't feel so great. Is there a restroom?"

He searched out the foyer and then walked me over to one on the far side of the room. Thank God he had his arm still around my waist, because my legs were two seconds from giving out underneath me, and the last thing I needed him or any of the other guests to see was me collapsing into a broken mess.

As I crouched down in the last stall of the restroom, I pulled at the sides of my eyes so the tears wouldn't fall.

How could I go in there and sit with Ace and face Nate again? This was his night, the one I should've been by his side for, and there I was shoving another man in his face. He didn't know it wasn't what it looked like, and when would I get a chance to tell him? After what he'd just seen, would he even hear me? And did I blame him? Not one damn bit.

The cold tile against my arm helped the lightheadedness fade, and I rested my head against it and closed my eyes. I'd been too late. I'd wanted to tell him, wanted to come clean, but it had been too little, too late, and now things were fucked to hell.

My stomach roiled, and if there'd been anything in it, it all would've come up. But I hadn't eaten anything all day, my nerves had been too shot, and now it felt like some eerie sense of foreboding. My body somehow knowing what would happen before my mind had a chance to catch up.

"Shayne?" Ace's voice echoed in the restroom, and I quickly got to my feet and smoothed my dress. "You're not passed out in here, are you?"

"N-no, I'm okay," I said, willing my voice not to shake, though it did anyway. I took a deep breath, wiped my brow again, and then exited the stall. Ace was standing in the doorway, and I gave him a thin smile. "Sorry. Better now."

"Just making sure," he said, and then looked over his shoulder. "It's starting soon, so we should get to our seats."

"Okay. Be right there."

He ducked out as I washed my hands and checked my face for any sign that my life was falling apart. My eyes were tinged pink, and I was definitely flushed, but you couldn't tell by looking at me that I was cracking underneath.

I took Ace's arm again as we headed into the auditorium, led by the woman Nate had pointed out. The room was packed, and all eyes were on us as we walked toward the front of the room, where a huge white screen had been erected on the stage.

Of course the woman pointed us to seats that were in the front fucking row, only feet away from where Nate stood at a podium getting set up with a wireless mic.

That's it. I want to shrivel up and die.

When Nate turned around, his eyes went directly to mine, sending a stab of pain directly into my heart. The hurt was still there, but now something else accompanied the pain.

Nate was *pissed*.

He sent one final dagger my way before buttoning his suit jacket, and standing beside fellow classmates and an older gentleman who, I presumed, was one of his instructors.

"Good evening, and thank you all for coming," the older man's voice boomed into the microphone. "As the dean of the School of Cinematic Arts, I'd like to welcome you to our spring showcase, featuring our most promising graduate students."

A round of applause, and then the man spoke in detail about the school's program before introducing the student filmmakers standing next to him. I couldn't have told you anything he said. My focus, as much as I tried to look away, rested solely on the man in the navy suit I'd helped pick out two weeks ago. The man who was actively looking anywhere and everywhere except in my direction, his body a ball of energy that was restless and bursting to break free.

"The first film featured this evening is a contemporary short by Nate Ryan, featuring Sophia Jones and Howard Klein, with a special appearance by Ace Locke, who's joining us tonight," the man said, gesturing in our direction as thunderous applause met my ears. Out of the corner of my eye, I could see Nate politely clapping, but his eyes stayed on the dean. Just as well. I couldn't handle meeting his eyes either.

"Mr. Ryan will be taking questions for ten minutes following the film and then we'll break briefly. Please enjoy."

There was another round of applause, and then the lights went dark and the screen on the stage lit up. A blurry red circle appeared, taking up almost the entire expanse, and then slowly the camera pulled back. As the object came into focus, it became obvious that it wasn't actually an object at all. It was a young girl, with flaming red hair that covered her crouched form like a shroud as she gazed down at a group of boys roughhousing on a beach from her perch high above. Her expression was wistful, and when one of the boys looked up, she jerked back, out of view. Again and again, the same action shown throughout the years, the girl growing into a young woman, the boy into a young man, but no words exchanged, no interaction other than the brief acknowledgment of the other.

But there was a tenderness there, and it was that same young boy who grew into a man that turned the tide after several years, finally approaching her from behind.

The story wasn't overcomplicated. It was a simple love, theirs, as undeniable and natural as an ocean breeze, but it was what he'd achieved visually that was the focus. You couldn't take your eyes off the screen for a moment. He pulled you in with close-ups, panned out to visually stunning landscapes, the colors and textures so rich and vibrant it was like you were there. The soundtrack rose and fell, perfectly matching the emotion of the actors. I almost didn't recognize Ace as her overprotective father, his performance so gentle, such a light touch, but one that tugged the heartstrings. The film was everything that encompassed Nate—a beautiful, artistic soul with love at its core.

When the screen went black and the lights came back up, the audience was up on their feet, a roar of applause echoing around the room, and as I stood up, tears stung my eyes. I was overwhelmed by what I'd just seen, my heart full, and just proud. So unbelievably, terribly proud. My eyes sought out Nate, and when they landed on his from where he now stood behind the podium, my heart thundered in my chest. I'd felt his gaze on me during the film, but I hadn't dared turn his way, hadn't wanted to see a look on his face like the one I saw now.

"Thank you," he said, when his eyes moved over the crowd. He swallowed hard and then tried for a smile, but there was no light behind his eyes. "I appreciate you all coming out tonight, and I'm honored to stand before you to present my final work here at USC. It's been an extraordinary experience, and I'm excited to move on to the next step in this journey. I'll take any questions you may have now."

Several hands went up, and Monica handed a microphone to an audience member.

"Congratulations on a beautiful piece of work. I was wondering what the inspiration for your project was?"

Nate was silent for a long moment, his eyes downcast. Then he stroked his jaw and said, "Love."

The woman waited for him to continue, and when he didn't, she asked, "Could you expand on that a bit?"

"I suppose the inspiration came from a personal experience. When two people can come together it's always a sort of miracle, whether they're from different backgrounds, have different beliefs, and with all the challenges they face both individually and together. Love doesn't discriminate, it just...happens. I wanted to showcase that, without distractions, without unnecessary conflict." His eyes went to mine before quickly moving away. "Just something pure and untainted. Strong."

Pure. Untainted. Strong. I stopped breathing.

An older gentleman stood up, taking the microphone. "The film was both stirring emotionally and stunning visually. What message were you hoping the audience would come away with?"

"Well, if I've done my job right, you leave feeling..." He paused and wiped the sweat from his brow. I was close enough to see the slight shaking of his hand, which he then ran through his hair. "…hopeful."

When the man nodded and passed the microphone to the next person, Nate shook his head.

"I'm sorry, that's all the questions I'll be answering this evening," he said, before unclipping his microphone and setting it on the podium. His legs took long strides up the aisle, and as he left the auditorium, I jumped up after him.

It didn't matter that I was there with Ace. It didn't matter that I would probably break my ankles running in heels. And it didn't matter who saw me do it. His words had been a stake in the heart, and there was no way to stanch the bleeding, not without him.

He was halfway across the foyer when I called out for him, but he didn't turn around. His hands were at his throat, undoing his tie and then ripping it off as he stalked for the front door.

"Nate… Nate, stop, please."

He jerked around so fast, I almost lost my balance. He pointed at me, his jaw clamped tight, and the muscles in his neck corded. "Don't." Then Nate's eyes shot over my shoulder as Ace came up behind me.

"What's going on?" he asked, looking between us.

"Not a thing," Nate answered, the skin around his eyes bunching as his pained stare seared my skin. "Not a damn fucking thing."

Then he pushed out of the door, leaving it to slam shut behind him, and when I wobbled on my feet, Ace gripped my arms to steady me.

"What the hell was that?" Ace's tone had gone from concerned to authoritative, and when I began to sob, he quickly ushered us out to the car. He let me cry without any more questions, and not even rubbing my arms stopped the shivering, nor did it soothe as my mind went wild with random thoughts. Would I ever see Nate again? Would I get a chance to apologize? Had his parents been there? But of course they had. I hadn't met them yet, but they knew who I was, and now they'd been privy to the embarrassment and hurt I'd caused their son. *Great. Just...*

Ace's voice was low when he finally spoke. "You're involved with him." Not a question.

I nodded.

"And he didn't know about me." Another non-question.

My eyes lifted to his, and he sighed, rubbing his hands on his slacks.

"Why do I feel like somehow this is my fault?" he said quietly.

"No. It's mine." I turned to face him and then asked, "How did... I mean, how did you—"

"Become involved?" He rubbed his hand over his buzzcut. "I'd stopped by his class one day a few weeks ago while visiting with my old professors. You and I had talked about starting small, and getting back to the root of things. They told me about this student of theirs, one with an incredible gift for storytelling, and that he still needed someone to fill a pivotal role in his project. I took a look at some of his other work and approached him about helping out. I just thought..." He sighed again. "I just thought it would've been cool if someone had done that for me when I was in school. We all start somewhere, and hell, the kid's talented, so you never know where he'll end up or how high he'll go. And, you know, I thought he looked familiar, but I didn't piece it together until now. But he was in Las Vegas that night I met you, wasn't he? The guy that was staring at you?"

"Yes."

"So he knew who I was. To you, I mean."

"He knew I'd met with you that night, but he didn't know why. He assumed we were friends."

"You care to explain the rest?"

Not really. I wanted to melt into the seat, but I owed him an explanation.

"I met Nate shortly before meeting you. Kept running into him, and he was so persistent..." I said. "And then, somehow, that story about you in the paper happened, and...I was sort of thrown out without a net, without any idea what I was supposed to do or if it was my fault, and when I saw you that day at your house, you were so miserable and lost...I just reacted. I didn't think about the consequences."

"So by helping me, it's fucked whatever you have going on with this guy."

"No, that was my choice."

"Yours? Or Roger's? Martina's idea, maybe? What about your boss, Val? Did you really have a choice, or were you forced into it, Shayne?"

"I still would've helped you."

He sat there quietly, a storm brewing behind his dark eyes. There was a grim twist to his mouth, and when he spoke again, his voice was rough as sandpaper. "Do you love him?"

I didn't hesitate. "Yes."

"Fuck, Shayne," he said under his breath. "Just fuck."

Chapter Twenty-Three
New Dawn Breaking

I'D BYPASSED THE first three stages of grief and gone
straight to the fourth stage—depression. Or maybe I was still
a mix of all of them—the denial that the relationship with
Nate was over, anger at myself over the whole damn thing,
bargaining…okay, well, I hadn't bothered with the
bargaining stage. There was no way I'd ask him to take me
back after the embarrassment and hurt I'd caused, even if I
wanted to. And I didn't want to. I'd hit the fourth stage of
grief and accepted my depression.

It was two days after what I was referring to as the
Oh Shit Event, and thank God it was a Sunday and I didn't
have to leave the house for work until tomorrow. I'd finally
showered last night after the girls had come by and pushed

me into the bathroom. Standing under the hot spray and letting it wash away my tears until the water turned cold hadn't eased the tight fist clenched around my heart and stomach, but at least I was cried out for the moment.

Had I really been so stupid? It had been like tempting fate the whole time, just waiting for the ball to drop. I'd thought I'd been doing a good thing helping Ace, but to the detriment of not only myself, but my relationship with Nate.

My Nate. The most amazing human on the planet, who didn't deserve what he'd seen two nights ago. Just his name had me wanting to shrivel up and die, and that was before I let myself remember the way he'd looked at me with the saddest eyes I'd ever seen.

Did he hate me? Rue the day I was born? I could deal with that more than I could deal with the hurt. It was too much to hope that he'd gone through the stages of grief and come out fine on the other side. I hated the expression FML, but it was true at the moment—fuck my life.

Because there I was, yet again. The destined-to-be-single matchmaker. I kept doing it to myself, always with good intentions but shitty follow-through.

My cell phone's blaring ringtone pushed me out of my thoughts, and I fumbled for it on the nightstand, knocking over my alarm clock in the process.

Not Nate. Not one of the girls. Not Val, *thank God.* It was Ace, and shit if I wasn't in the mood to talk to him. But I answered anyway, my voice coming out like rough gravel.

"Ace, now's not a good time—"

"Turn on channel four," Martina said before the line went dead.

What? And why is Martina calling on Ace's phone?

I hit redial, but when no one answered, curiosity hit. Dragging myself off the bed, I shuffled into the living room, picked the discarded bikini top off the remote, and flicked on the TV. *Dirty-ass roommates,* I thought, kicking their flip-flops under the coffee table.

When I stopped on channel four, the camera zoomed in on Ace as he walked up to a podium on a small stage, buttoning a sharp blue suit that showcased how large his frame really was. Unlike the last time I'd seen him, his expression was calm and resolute, and he nodded at the crowd of what looked like press before he spoke, his voice strong and clear.

"Thank you all for coming given the late notice. There have been quite a few stories going around in the press lately, and although I don't usually address issues concerning my personal life, and don't plan to do so again in the future, I would like to clarify something with you all today.

"It was never my intent to have this conversation, not today or any day. My private life is just that—private. But in the process of protecting my privacy, others were harmed to the detriment of their own lives. So this is me clearing the air." He paused and looked down at the podium, as if gathering his thoughts. Then his head lifted, his expression determined, eyes blazing.

"The truth is…a story came out about me a few months ago, and while most of what you read in the press is usually false, this one happened to stumble upon the truth. I did indeed meet with a matchmaking company, and it was for two reasons. The first being I was looking for someone for myself, and it's been difficult in my position to do so, regardless of what you've seen of me in magazines. The second was to find someone who would serve as a significant other to the public. Meaning someone who would act as my girlfriend for you all and anywhere there might be paparazzi lurking. Now, you may be asking why I'd need a separate public and private partner. And the reason for that is because I've been living a lie."

Murmurs from the crowd rose, and Ace lifted his hand to silence them.

"I'm well aware of what my coming out to you all today might mean." The murmurs grew to a roar, and Ace had to put up his hand again. "Yes, you heard that right. Telling you I'm a gay man might mean I lose the career I've worked so hard for. But as much as I hope that's not the case, I can no longer live with myself if I can't be open about who I am. There are many out there who struggle in the same way I do. With what their friends might think, with what their family tells them is wrong in God's eyes or in theirs.

"But I'm here to tell you there's nothing wrong with us. I'm not any less of a human being, of an actor, of a brother, son, lover, or friend, and neither are you. If who I choose to love weighs on your decision to see my films, if it somehow diminishes me in your eyes, then that's your decision, and there's not one thing I can do about it. I hope that's not the case, though. That I even have to make an announcement in this day and age is unfortunate, but the reality is, I've lied for too long, and I've involved others now. There's one person in particular who has gone above and beyond for me, and it cost her the person she loves. That's my fault. And right now, I'd like to personally offer them both an apology." Ace looked directly into the camera, his eyes penetrating straight through as if he were across from me and there was no one else in the room. "Shayne, I'm so sorry, and I'll do anything I can to make things right for you both. You came to my aid when I was at my lowest point, and because you're a selfless, generous human being and I was desperate, I let you. But that stops now. I owe you so much, so if and when you decide to start your own company, I'd like to not only invest, but I'd be honored to be your first client."

As the crowd went wild with questions, my jaw dropped, and the remote fell out of my hand and clattered to the ground. *What did he say? My own...? Has he lost his mind?*

My cell phone began to ring from where I'd set it on the coffee table below me, but I couldn't tear my eyes off Ace long enough to answer it. Had he really just come out on live television in front of the world? And not only that, but he wanted to—I could barely fathom the words—*fund* my own company?

I had to still be in a delirious state, because none of this made sense. After all the time spent covering for him, why had he come clean and opened himself up now?

That little voice in the back of my head told me exactly why. *Because of you. Because of Nate.*

Well, it was too late to save my relationship with Nate. With the way things had exploded, there was no coming back from that. But for Ace…this was a good step, a great step, and a flicker of pride alleviated the oppressing darkness in my chest.

My phone was still ringing on a continuous loop, someone calling and hanging up, calling and hanging up. One look at the screen when I glanced down had me grinding my teeth.

Val.

Two choices. I could either turn off my phone and probably lose my job, or…I could answer. *Oh for the love of…*

"Hello, Val—"

"What the fuck is this bullshit with Ace on my screen right now?"

Just jump right into it, why don't you. "I-I don't know—"

"Did you honestly think you could fucking double-cross me and get away with it? Your *own* company? Have you lost your pea-sized brain?"

"Whoa, hang on a sec. I don't even know what he's talking about right now. I swear, this is the first I've heard about any of this."

"Sure it is. Tell you what," she said. "You come to the office and talk me out of packing up your shit right now, and maybe I'll hear you out."

"Don't do that. I'm on my way. This is just a misunderstanding, and—"

"It better fucking be, hooker. It better fucking be."

Then she hung up, and I stood there, dazed, with my phone in my hand. Wait—why was she at the office on a Sunday? *Hell.* Looked like I'd have to put real clothes on after all.

When I looked back up at the TV, Martina was standing next to Ace and pointing to a reporter in the crowd, who asked, "Mr. Locke, is there someone special in your life right now?"

Ace gave him a side grin. "Not at the present time, no. But when there is, I still won't tell you."

A chuckle from the crowd, and then, "Mr. Locke, are you saying you'd like to be a client at this matchmaking firm?"

"Only if that firm is run by Miss Callahan. Listen, we all want to find love. Why not let someone with a talent for pairing up couples work their magic?" As he winked, his usual charm came back out to play, and his shoulders relaxed.

As he continued to answer questions, I threw on some clothes and was out the door. I didn't put it past Val to already be dumping the contents of my office into a garbage bag, so the sooner I got there, the sooner I could get a handle on the situation.

But why?

Those two words sprang into my head out of nowhere. *But why* would I want to stop her? Obviously the reason was because I needed my job and loved it. And I needed my job so I could pay rent at a place I hated. And just as I merged onto the 101 heading downtown, the lighting bolt hit.

I didn't *have* to live there anymore. Paige had made it abundantly clear more times than I could count that her place was my place, and as much as I hated the thought of taking advantage, she *had* offered. And if I was honest, the thought of getting away from the twins and my perv-monster landlord was so appealing I couldn't even fathom coming back to the shithole.

So…if I wasn't struggling for rent, there was no reason to stay at a place with a boss I didn't respect, who didn't respect me back, and who had morphed into this demented creature of evil who thought it was okay to treat people like flea-infested, rabid dogs. There was no *reason* I should have to put up with that any longer. None at all. Anything, and I do mean *anything*, was better than having to deal one more day with her.

And it was then that I knew.

I was done.

I was so completely over Val, over the years of being at her beck and call, and over having any association with her or her company, that my plan of heading down to HLS to stop her from packing my shit changed to heading down there to help her pack it.

Even if Ace wasn't serious about investing, I'd figure something out, and I'd find a way to do things on my own terms, without compromising what was left of my integrity to do it. I may have royally fucked things up with Nate and the whole situation with Ace, but I wasn't about to let that happen again.

The first smile in days spread across my face, like a new dawn breaking, and I pushed down on the accelerator.

Chapter Twenty-Four
Fuck You Very Much

AS I WALKED into HLS, the office was silent, the lights
dimmed. Strolling past my desk, I felt not one iota of
nervousness at what I was about to face. No, I was ready to
kick the superbitch down a rung or five.

"Stop dawdling and get in here. I can hear you
breathing," echoed Val's voice from down the hall.

Pushing open her door, the first thing I noticed was
that she was lounged back in her chair with her leopard
heels kicked up and crossed on her desk. A scowl was on
her burgundy-painted lips, and she didn't move as I entered.
Instead, her eyes watched me with the focus and intensity of
a hawk getting ready to strike its prey.

"About time you got here. What, did you get lost?

Forget the way back to the place that made you famous?" She sniffed, raising her chin. "Infamous, more like."

"I could never forget you, Val," I said, smiling sweetly before I dropped the bomb on her. *Oh, this was going to be fun.* But then my eyes went back to the second thing I'd noticed when I'd entered, not that I could help but look, because perched on the edge of her desk was the most enormous hamper I'd ever seen. My thoughts immediately went back to the conversation I'd had with the girls a few days ago, but surely it wasn't…they hadn't…

"Wow, that's an impressive hamper. Who sent it? And is that…chocolate-dipped fruit?" I asked, stepping closer to get a better look, but Val sat up and seized the note attached to the top before I could get a peek.

"None of your business. And it's called a gift basket, not a fucking laundry hamper." Then she opened the note and a savage smile crossed her lips. "'To the woman who deserves the most exquisite delicacies life has to offer…you are truly one of a kind.'"

Oh my God. Oh my God, Paige…

As Val ripped through the cellophane, I had to bite down hard on my lip to keep a straight face. Then she plucked off one of the chocolate-covered strawberries and made a big show of eating the damn thing, as if to rub it in my face.

I couldn't hold back the laugh anymore, and I covered my mouth and coughed like I was having a fit instead of laughing over the fact that she was eating a laxative dessert basket. God bless my friends and their timing.

"What?" Val asked. "You want one of these, do you? I'd share, but I noticed you sporting puddy pockets lately. You could probably use these instead." She pushed a half-empty container of orange Tic Tacs across the desk toward me.

"I'm sorry, the what pockets?"

"Puddy pockets. The saggy bits under your ass. You might want to do something about those. Like squats. Or munch on some lettuce." She finished off the strawberry and reached for one of the bananas on a stick.

It was unbelievable to me, in that moment, that the woman across from me was ever someone I knew. When I'd first met Val, she'd been a fireball, but there was vulnerability behind that hardened exterior, and she'd let that wall down a few times for me to glimpse over at her faded, unkempt lawn, the one she metaphorically spray-painted green to hide her sad, empty life.

But you can't spray-paint shit and call it grass. Over the years, she'd turned into some kind of robot, like the Botox had frozen not only her face, but also her heart and the blood in her veins. The change had been so gradual that I hadn't even noticed the extent of how bad it'd gotten. Like the story of the frogs in a lukewarm pot on the stove who didn't jump out and save themselves because the heat was turned up so gradually that by the time they noticed, it was too late.

Or something like that.

"No," I said, crossing my arms.

"No what?"

"No, I won't be munching on lettuce or doing squats, because I don't have anything on my body anywhere that sags. But when I do, I sure as hell won't be injecting myself full of toxins just to keep my old ass clinging to twenty-five like I'm trying too hard."

Hot *damn*. That'd felt good. I kind of wanted to pat myself on the back.

Val slowly rose to her feet, her frame towering in those five-inch heels, but I didn't shrink back. "What the fuck did you just say to me?"

"You heard me," I said, staring her right in the eye. "I'm not your errand girl, your assistant, your bitch, and as of today, I'm no longer even your employee. So you can find someone else to do your dirty work."

She blinked at me for a long moment before a sneer crossed her lips. "Please. You wouldn't know what to do without me. And even if you were serious, you couldn't go anywhere without a referral, and after that little speech, you can kiss it goodbye."

"You've never said one good thing about me and my work, so why would I expect you to start now?"

Val sighed and came around her desk to rest on the edge. "Is this about the Ace thing?"

"The Ace *thing*?"

"You're mad because I tipped off the press about the

gay thing," she said, waving her hand.

"You *what?* But you said—"

"Oh for fuck's sake, Shayne, grow up. Business is business, and that story has had this place going fucking nuts with referrals for weeks now."

"Which would've happened anyway if we had taken Ace on as a client and you hadn't gone running your mouth. How could you do that? *Why* would you do that?"

Val ignored the question as she examined her nails one by one. What a vain, conniving little—

Wait. That was it. I'd been with her at too many meetings and seen her in action throwing herself at too many men to have missed it, but it was obvious now.

"He turned you down, didn't he?"

Her head snapped up. "I beg your pardon?"

"Oh my God," I said, pointing a finger at her. "At that first dinner meeting…he didn't take you up on your advances, and that pissed you right off. You didn't tattle on him to the press merely to get business. You did it because your fucking pride took a hit. Holy shit."

"That's so far from the truth—"

A hysterical laugh bubbled up in my throat. "No, it's not. I'm right. I'm so right, and I can't believe I didn't put it all together before. This whole time I thought it was Nicole, but it turns out she's just a bitch, not the narcissistic, deranged nutcase that you are."

"You're gonna pay for that, you little twat," Val said as she pushed off the desk and took a menacing step toward me. I pulled the mace I usually carried in my purse out of my pocket and held it up, and she halted.

Hey, she had a bat in the office. I had to come prepared for unhinged.

"You take one more step and I'm spraying this bad boy right up your nose."

She narrowed her eyes. "You wouldn't dare."

"I would dare, and I'd love for you to try me." My hand didn't shake, and my grip stayed firm on the can. Is it bad I really did want her to move so I could use it?

With a sigh, Val tilted her head to the side. "So what is it, Shayne, huh? Would you rather I swaddle and rock you when you have a bad day? You know, when I found you, I was under the impression you could be self-sufficient, that you were the kind of gal who'd go after what you wanted and take no prisoners. Imagine my disappointment when I realized that all I got was a do-gooder like yourself, one who needs to be coddled. And unfortunately for you, I lost my patience for that sort of thing a long time ago."

"Wow," I said, reeling, but keeping my hand up. The fire in my veins went from simmering to boiling, but somehow, I kept my voice steady. "All I ever wanted was to do my job to the best of my abilities. Not coddling. Not praise. Not recognition. I never asked you for anything, not even a raise, which I've more than deserved for over seven years now. You want me to imagine your disappointment with me? Imagine mine when I realized I had a thundercunt for a boss. I am nothing like you, thank God, and the sooner you and this joke of a company are out of my life, the better off I'll be."

The veins in Val's face looked ready to pop, and her nails were digging into her palms so hard they were white. "You… You were nothing when I found you, and you'll be nothing without me either, you little tramp. Don't you ever forget that. You could never do what I do."

I couldn't help the grin that spread across my face as I shook my head. "You're right about that, Val. I could never do what you do." And then I shrugged. "I'll just do it better."

And then I backed out of her office while she stood there like a bomb ready to explode. After slamming the door behind me, I victory-danced my way down the hall but then realized I had one last thing I was dying to say.

When I stuck my head back inside, she was clutching her stomach, but dropped her hand when she saw me.

"Sorry, I forgot one thing," I said, and then wrinkled my nose before looking her up and down. "Eat shit, Val."

THE ONLY THINGS I'd taken with me from HLS had been the collage of wedding invitations on my wall, the backup drive of our client list and information, and my Rolodex. Oh, and my fluorescent Post-its with the fancy holders, because hello, priorities. Then I'd dropped off a quick note for

Roberto at the security desk, and I was home free. And oh my God, the relief. With the windows down and the fresh air breezing in, I felt like I was flying.

No more Val.

No more HLS.

No more money, which was disturbing, but I'd think about later. Dammit, I felt so good I needed a round two. While I was taking out the trash, so to speak, it was time to deal with the other oppressive weight holding me down.

Two hours later, I'd thrown all my stuff from the apartment into garbage bags and shoved them into my car. Turned out I didn't have much worth the effort of taking with me. Now that I had no job, I had no income, and I'd be damned if I was staying with the Barbies for one more minute. Not when I had an alternative.

I was just filling a laundry basket with the last of my haul when the twins came barreling inside, reeking of suntan oil, sweat, and margaritas.

"All right, I'm out," I said, brushing by them as I headed for the door.

Kassy's head spun toward me. "Out? As in moving out?"

"Yep. Surely you two have friends who can move in and help with the rent, right? And if not, just flash Pete your boobs for a discount."

"Really? That works?" Kassy tapped her lips as she thought that over, and then her face lit up and she said, "Kels, we should totally ask Mariska to move in."

"Ooh yeah, or Ashley. Oh my gosh, dibs on your room!" Kelly leapt up and ran past me into my bedroom, which was bare except for the furniture. Not like I'd need my Craigslist hand-me-downs where I was going.

"Bye to you too," I muttered.

"Thanks, Shayne!" Kassy was already punching numbers on her phone, and I heard, "Hey, Mariska? You'll never believe it," as I opened the front door and ran smack into Pervy Pete.

He looked at my laundry basket full of clothes and all the knickknacks I'd thrown on top and said, "Going somewhere?"

"Yep." I shifted the basket onto my hip and then pulled the door shut behind me. Then I passed him without a care in the world and without looking back at the place I'd called home for too many years.

"No, Shayne. You no go. Contract—"

"Oh riiiiight," I said, spinning around to face him. "I did sign a contract with you, huh?"

"Yes, so you no leave—"

"Actually," I said, dropping the basket at my feet, "I *am* leaving. And our little contract is null and void. It can carry on to Kelly and Kassy, but I'm peacing out. You'll have to find a new neighbor to harass."

"You leave, I sue."

And I swear to God, when he said that, I laughed. Hysterically. So much so I had to bend over with my hands on my knees to catch my breath after a full two minutes.

"You're a funny man. Really." Then I crouched down and rummaged through my basket until I found my checkbook and a pen. After quickly scribbling enough to cover my portion of a month's rent, I held up the check. "Here's my thirty-day notice. If you try to stop me, I'll contact the police about the way you've drilled peepholes into the bathrooms, or the way you come into our apartment and sniff our clothes when we're not home, both things I'm sure you realize are against the law."

"I not do—"

"Oh, yes, you do. I've got pictures and several videos on my phone, you dirty old man. Dare me to use it, Pete."

His mustache quivered, whether from anger or from being two seconds away from bawling, I didn't know and didn't care. And then, because I was on a roll and the guy was a disgusting degenerate, I stepped in real close and said, "And don't think they wouldn't love to hear about who you've got hiding away in your apartment. They'll have them deported before you can say, 'But Shayne, I need you to give me your double-Ds.' You got me, Muchacho?"

Pete's jaw fell slack and his eyes almost fell out of their sockets, so I took that for a yes. Smirking, I picked up my basket and headed for the stairs, where Old Ouiser was packed to the brim and waiting. When I passed his mother standing at the window, a horrified expression on her sweet face, I whispered, "Don't worry, Maria, I wouldn't do that to you." Then over my shoulder, my voice stern, I called out, "I mean it, Pete."

And Pervy did the first smart thing he'd probably ever done in his whole life—he didn't follow me.

AS I DROVE up the hill that led to my destination, poor Old Ouiser chugging along, I had to mentally pat myself on the damn back for growing a vagina of steel.

Damn that'd felt good. I was two for two in the shock-the-hell-out-of-assholes game today, and the huge smile that had my cheeks burning was the first one I'd had on my face in what felt like too long. I'd never felt so free, with so much weight off my shoulders—no more ruse for Ace, no more horrible boss, no more sharing an apartment with skanks. I was lighter than air, but I knew once the high wore off that the scared-shitless feeling would come rushing back in soon enough. Especially when I checked my bank account.

I wasn't going to think about all that right now, though. Instead, I was going to take things one day at a time, and check off the tasks as I went. The first and most important being a roof over my head.

When I pulled into the circular stone driveway, I expected nerves at showing up unannounced, or at least panic at leaving everything behind. But it felt like the right thing to do, and so I pulled out the basket from the backseat and then went up to ring the bell. When Paige swung open the door, I looked back down to the basket of clothes I was holding and then blew a wisp of hair out of my face.

"It's not too late to take you up on your offer, is it?" I asked. "Because I just told Pervy Pete to fuck off or I'd deport his family, so I'm probably not allowed back at my apartment...or the premises, so it's either sleep here or the train, and I thought I'd at least try here first. Oh, and I quit my job. Tell me I'm not crazy."

Paige shook her head and took the basket off my hands, effectively shutting me up. Then a megawatt smile took over her face as she nodded for me to come inside. "About damn time, you stubborn woman."

Chapter Twenty-Five
Pull up Your Big-Girl Panties

"OH FUCK ME gently with a chainsaw, I can't believe you called Val a thundercunt," Paige said, laughing as she helped Ryleigh bring over a round of Bustin' Balls shakes from Licked next door. The girls and I were at the After Dark, and they were helping me map out a business plan.

Yep, you heard that right. A *business plan*, which still sounded foreign to my ears, but they swore we could do it.

"I did say that. She didn't even flinch. Or maybe she did, but I couldn't tell, since her face doesn't move."

"It's too bad you told her off so quickly. I was hoping you'd see her shart her pants first." Paige caught a cherry with her mouth and then gave me a sassy wink.

"I can't believe you spiked her gift basket with

laxatives. That might be the best thing anyone's ever done for me."

Paige pointed at Quinn. "Actually, she made me do it. She said, and I quote, 'No way in hell is that psychobitch gonna fuck over our girl.'"

"Aw," Ryleigh said, batting her lashes. "You guys are so sweet and thoughtful. Seriously, we all lucked out finding each other. Do you remember when Shayne sacrificed her underwear to get me away from that creepy guy at Halo that one time?"

"Please don't remind me. I try not to think about the fact that he might have a shrine to my cherry panties." I shuddered and took a long gulp of my shake. "All right, Quinn, call this meeting to order."

Quinn held up her glass and said, "To sending our sweet Shayne out into the world to kick a little ass. We're gonna be four for four, bitches. Taking over the world, one business at a time."

As we all held up our drinks in cheers, Ryleigh said, "Damn straight. But what is it you do again?"

With a roll of her eyes, Quinn threw back her drink, and I had to laugh. One of these days, she was bound to fess up or slip up. We'd come up with such fantastical possibilities as to what her day job entailed—assassin, undercover agent, high-priced escort—that whatever she really did to spend her days would probably be nowhere near as cool. So, assassin Quinn it was.

"All right," she said, wiping her mouth and then

banging her fist on the table like a gavel. "I've got the rundown of what we'll each be helping you with so you don't get overwhelmed and end up crying in Paige's master bathroom all day." Then she passed out folders to each of us, and when I opened mine, I whistled.

"Wow, someone's organized. If it'd been up to me, I'd just have a wall of sticky notes."

"I wouldn't be surprised if you've got some in your purse," she replied. When I pulled a stack of them out of my bag, she pursed her lips. "Exactly. Okay, so the first thing on the list is what you need to obtain a business license, and for that, Ryleigh will be helping you. You can tell who's doing what by the colored tabs for each section. Since she's also helping you with your financial planning, her tab is green."

Paige groaned as she flipped through the folder. "You're killing the badass mafia image I have of you, Quinn. Please don't tell me you own pocket protectors or play Dragons and Dungeons or whatever it's called."

"Nothing wrong with a little role-playing, as you well know." She flipped her jet-black locks over her shoulder. "Now, I'm the red tab, and if you'll turn to that section, it'll show you a list of properties I've already been scoping out as possible locations. Don't stroke out at the price tag, please, because these were all priced well under what was on the expense sheet Ace gave you. It's just a matter of deciding where in the city you'd like to base the company, how much space you need, etcetera."

"Holy shit, can I be Ace's beard for a little while? I'd

like to expand. Instead of just wedding planning, I could also coordinate bachelorette and divorce parties. I'm a good investment," Paige said.

Quinn shook her head and continued, "What you need to do is start touching base with your old client list and get your website and social media set up, since you already have experience doing that at HLS. You want to get your name out there and have a few clients under your belt before we go full blast with the marketing, which we'll get to once we narrow the rest of this down."

"We still need to think up a good company name," Ryleigh pointed out.

"The only reason we're still brainstorming is because Cocks in the Henhouse has been ruled out. Lame whores," Paige said.

"We're not naming it *that* either." I sent a pointed look Paige's way and then dropped my gaze back to the folder. "You guys…this is too much. I don't even know what to say."

"Say you'll send your clients here for their engagement parties," Ryleigh said.

Paige nodded. "And then send them my way for wedding shenanigans."

I looked around the table at my friends in amazement. Each of them was successful, fiercely independent, strong-willed, generous, and so freakin' talented in their own way, and it was then that I realized…I was one of them. Like, *really* one of them.

No, I hadn't grown up wealthy, and no, I hadn't had much luck in business in my twenty-eight years, but I wasn't on the outskirts looking in on this kickass group of women… *I* was talented in my own right, and I could do anything I set my mind to, especially with them by my side.

It had taken this long for me to get that through my thick skull, but I finally got it. Besides, what did I have to lose?

Needing to get started before I got all teary and emotional, I cleared my throat and said, "All right, slutbags. Let's do the damn thing."

THREE HOURS AND two more rounds of drinks later, and I had paperwork that I'd need to file filled out, we'd gone over expenses, and I'd also narrowed down the list of potential locations to four, which I'd be visiting this week with Quinn and Ace, if he was free.

I was feeling pumped and confident, especially when I checked my voicemail and listened to Jenna's message about joining me when I was up and running. *Hot freakin' damn.* I felt like Tom Cruise in *Jerry Maguire*, with one celebrity client and one coworker willing to jump ship from the sharks because they had faith in my ideas. All I was missing was the goldfish.

As I helped carry empty glasses back over to Licked,

my eyes zeroed in on a tall, dark-haired man standing by the ice cream counter in jeans, a formal white shirt, and…suspenders.

My heart seized in my chest as I came to a stop. Surely that wasn't…it couldn't be… Then the man turned around and pushed a thick pair of glasses up his face, and I let out the breath I'd been holding, though it wasn't one of relief.

He caught me staring at him and looked down at his clothes self-consciously. "Too much?" he asked.

Shaking my head, I smiled sadly. It wasn't his fault I was wishing he was someone else. "Not too much at all. Perfect, really."

Had there been anything or anyone more perfect than Nate? Was I a fool like the girls said for not begging forgiveness? Maybe I just didn't understand how he could begin to forgive in the first place, but…perhaps they were right. Or maybe it was just wishful thinking.

I jumped when Ryleigh put her hand on my shoulder.

"You okay?" she asked, her brows knitting as she looked between me and suspenders guy.

"Uh, yeah. Fine." I gave her a tight smile. "All good."

She raised an eyebrow but didn't call me out on my lie. Instead, she took the empty glasses from my hands and headed to the back to drop them in the sink.

"You know," Quinn said, coming up beside me and linking her arm through mine as she walked me back over to the After Dark, "your horoscope today reminded me of Nate."

His name jerked me back to reality. "What?"

She pulled her cell phone out of her purse and opened her astrology app. "'A past love may resurface when and where you least expect it this week. Be prepared to open yourself up to all possibilities.'"

"It does not say that," I said, snatching the phone out of her hand and then repeating, word for word, what it *did*, in fact, say. "Huh. Well, for all I know, they could mean Crazy Cal from six years ago."

Quinn gave me a knowing look. "Or it could be the sign you've been waiting for to go after the other thing you want. There's nothing and no one stopping you now but you." She shrugged and then shoved the phone into her tight black leather pants. "Just think about it."

Chapter Twenty-Six
Meals for ~~One~~ Two

THERE I WAS again. A wild Thursday night in the meals-for-one aisle. But this time, I'd come armed.

With a candy bar clenched in my fist, I sat with my back against one of the cool glass doors, my legs splayed into the aisle in front of me, and staring up at that stupid, wretched sign. The one that was destined to describe my life from this point forward.

For all eternity, I was destined to match lovers, but never *be* a lover. Which was to say, my attempt at a startup was actually going well. So well, in fact, that although I hadn't yet found an office space, the clients that had followed me over from HLS were willing to meet at local coffee shops over espresso and banana bread instead. And with Ace's investment, and the flux of interested potentials that had heard about me from his press conference, I'd be able to afford to bring Jenna on board as soon as we found our headquarters.

I guess it was true what they say, whoever "they" happened to be—that when one part of your life is finally doing well, the other part can't seem to get its shit together.

My thoughts, as they always did, drifted to Nate. He'd be graduating in a couple of weeks. Would he stay here? Head to New York? Somewhere else? Did he think of me? And not in the *thank fuck I dodged a bullet with that one* sort of way, but the *I miss her* way.

That was asking a lot, though. There was a reason I hadn't reached out to him even after Ace had come clean in front of however many hundreds of thousands of people had seen his press conference.

Nate deserved better.

I bit off another piece of chocolatey peanut goodness and crunched on it while a woman pushing a cart down the aisle did her best to pretend I wasn't there. Her best wasn't good enough, though, because I caught her judgmental "call security, stat" side eye as she passed. When she caught me looking back, she pushed the cart faster, away from the crazy hobo camping out in front of the Lean Cuisines.

Whatever. She didn't belong in this aisle anyway, if the titanic-sized rock on her left finger was any indication. The family-size Hungry Man's, that was where she belonged. And if she tattled and had an employee ask me to leave, my answer would be that I was indecisive and still debating between the angel hair pasta with shrimp or the lasagna frozen dinners. No harm, no foul.

The sad thing was, I technically didn't even need to be here anymore, since Paige kept the kitchen fully stocked and there were grocery stores much closer to her place. *Our* place, I silently corrected. But I couldn't bring myself to break my weekly visits, and for some reason tonight I had no desire to leave. They'd have to kick me out.

After shoving the rest of the chocolate in my mouth, I balled up the wrapper and tossed it into the shopping basket ass-planted next to me. Then I ripped open another one. My phone displayed the screensaver when I hit the home key, which meant no messages. No phone calls. No emails. Nobody by the name of someone that rhymed with "great" trying to get in touch with me.

With a grunt, I dumped my phone back in the basket, and when I looked back up, I almost choked.

Standing just under the meals-for-one sign, like I'd willed him into existence, was Nate. Scruffy Nate with hair that needed a trim, but hell, it was hair that was made for running your fingers through it. In black pants, a white collared shirt, and grey suspenders, he looked every bit how I remembered him from the last time I'd seen him, but he was different too. It was in his eyes. Where I'd expected to see them lit with fire, there was no anger, no hurt. His expression was open and curious and...something akin to amusement?

Probably because he'd just caught me in the middle of gorging. I quickly swallowed and wiped my mouth. And then...yeah, and then I just stared at him, because not one word came to mind. What did you say to greet people again? It started with an H, I knew that much, and I sounded it out so whatever letters came after it would show up.

He didn't say a word as I stumbled over mine. Instead, he sat down on the other side of the aisle, leaned against the glass door, and crossed his arms.

"H-hi," I said finally. There, *fuck*. Was that so hard? Apparently not, because then I couldn't shut up. "I was just thinking about the second time I ever saw you and how I'd been cursing that stupid sign up there and calling Target an asshole for trying to make a dating aisle in the middle of the frozen foods section. And then half of me thought it was genius and that I should set up shop here because at least then I wouldn't starve. And then you showed up and said something about my pants making you hungry, and honestly, I was just grateful I was wearing fucking pants, even though I'd forgotten to throw on a bra that day. Not that you knew that, because I was holding on to those pizzas like a life raft, but yeah. Tit bit nippily that night, but don't worry, I remembered to wear one tonight. I think." I held open the collar of my shirt and peered down at my white lace bra. "Yep, all tucked in."

Nate tilted his head to the side as he stared at me. Well, stared at my face, not the boobs in question. *God*, why was I thinking about that instead of the fact that he was there, in the flesh, sitting across from me and memorizing my face?

This had been all I'd fantasized during my waking hours, when I hadn't been consumed with the setup of my company, which was working under the name Sayonara Spinsterhood and Sweatpants because, well, *Paige*.

I cleared my throat and tried again. "I mean, hi."

He nodded toward the chocolate bars in my lap. "Can I have one of those?"

My eyebrows shot up, and when I saw that he was serious, I nodded mutely and then slid an unopened one across the aisle.

Peeling off the wrapper, he kept his eyes on mine and then took a bite. And then another, his crunching the only sound I could hear. When he'd finished, he licked his fingers one by one, and I could only watch in fascination because something about it was almost intimate, but then again, it called to mind nights in his bed, and on his table, and on the rug.

Focus.

"Can I ask you a question, Shayne?"

"Yes."

His hazel eyes pierced mine. "Is your phone broken?"

"Is my... What?" So not what I thought he was going to ask.

"Your phone. Broken? What about your car? Your legs? Email? Note-taking abilities? Messenger owl? All of that broken?"

"What are you talking about?"

"I'm talking about why you didn't track me down, Shayne. I'm assuming you didn't want to, since I'm easy to find."

My mouth opened and closed several times, but I couldn't squeak anything out. Had he *wanted* me to go after him? And why the hell? I'd not only embarrassed him, but fuck, had it been me, it wasn't something I could probably get over even with an apology.

But then again…Nate wasn't like anyone I'd ever met.

"Nothing to say now?" he asked, but he wasn't mad. No, nothing on his face was accusatory. Merely curious.

"Excuse me, but you two need to move." A woman in a red shirt and a nametag that said *Manager* stood above us with a disapproving expression. "We don't allow loitering on the premises."

"We'll be gone as soon as I get what I came for," Nate said, his eyes still on mine.

"You need to leave now before I call security to escort you off the—"

"Can you just give us a minute," he said, finally snapping his head up. Then he held up his hand and said, "I'm sorry, but that woman over there did something super shitty that she needs to apologize for, and I'm not leaving until I get it." Then he looked back at me and said, "Anything you want to get off your chest, Shayne?"

"Sir—" the manager started again.

"Five minutes," he said, and she huffed but shut her mouth and looked in my direction to hear whatever apology he was waiting for.

"You want me to say I'm sorry for hurting you? Nate…I could never apologize enough for what I did. It's all I think about. If I could take it all back—"

"You wouldn't, because I wouldn't let you," he finished.

I shrank back. "Excuse me?"

"I've already talked to Ace, and I'm well aware of why you did what you did. That's not the apology I'm looking for."

Blinking, I said, "You don't want me to tell you I'm sorry for hurting you? If that's not what you want from me, I don't know what to tell you. Whatever it is, I'm sorry, a million times over. Had I known you wanted me to, I would've begged you to talk to me, to take me back and try to understand, but you deserve someone who wouldn't lie to you in the first damn place."

"Aha," he said, pointing at me and looking up at the manager. "You see that? That was like some kind of backwards apology shit."

She shrugged and said, "I'm gonna have to agree."

"What?"

I tossed my chocolate bar into the basket and crossed my legs. "Why don't you just tell me what it is you want, and I'll repeat it back to you then."

"Okay, here you go: 'Nate, I'm so sorry I made you think I didn't give a fuck about you. I must've lost all brain function during my weeks-long stay in the hospital, because anyone who's seen a romcom knows that at the end of the movie, the person who did the wronging is the one that goes after the wrongee. So I apologize for fucking up the formula and making you chase me here. Please take me back.'"

I gaped at him. "What the hell is wrong with you? Are you on drugs?"

"Say it, Shayne."

"You want to be with me? Like, really want to be with me?" There was no way he was being for real about this. *Or is he?*

"I'm not fuckin' around," he said.

"But...seriously? Is this a joke?"

Nate threw his hands up. "Is it so hard to believe that somewhere along the way I fell for this crazy girl with the big smile that has a tendency to trip over her two left feet and somehow still make that look hot? That I might actually care enough about her to understand that even when she has good intentions, it can somehow skew into what-the-fuck-were-you-thinking territory, and even knowing that, I see where her heart is?"

"Nate, listen. That crazy girl you met that was letting loose on a pantsless Metro ride? That's not really me. That's me plus two liters of vodka and a heap of peer pressure. The girl who falls all the time? Yeah, okay, but I don't see how that's even remotely attractive. The girl in ice cream pajama pants eating candy bars in the middle of a store that, yes"—I looked up at the manager—"I plan to pay for. Yeah, that's more who I am. And that can't possibly sound appealing to you in the long run, not really."

"I already know all that about you—"

"But did you know I order really embarrassing drinks at coffee shops?" I asked, getting to my feet as he followed my lead but stayed across the aisle. "Ones with ten names in them that end in the word *frappuccino*. And sometimes I wear my jeans every day for a week because they get more comfy and I'm lazy and hate to do laundry. Oh, and I still listen to NSYNC CDs, especially the Christmas album, even when it's not Christmas because they put me in a good mood and I can do all the dance moves, not that I'd ever show anyone outside of the shower. I like the smell of musty spaces mixed with mothballs because it reminds me of my nan's attic, which is super weird because most girls want candles that smell like roses or cookies. I don't like to watch Disney movies because they make me cry, something you'd probably be ecstatic about getting out of. I'm a shitty cook, no matter what my friends say, which is why I'm always in this damn aisle, but I can bake a mean pina colada cake, so you know you'll probably end up diabetic. You're a fit guy, so you'll want me to go hiking or running with you, and you should just know right now that my idea of exercising is walking in heels at work. Which I don't plan to do anymore anyway."

He crossed the aisle. "Shayne—"

"There's more—"

His finger went to my lips, and I fell silent. Then he brushed a stray curl from my face, and his hand cupped the side of my neck. "I promise never to take you roller blading or hiking or anything else that might require a fully padded body suit. The music thing...eh, we'll have to compromise on it, but I'll never complain about being fat and happy as long as you don't."

I sniffled. "But what about the mothballs?"

With a long sigh, he shrugged. "You're a freak. Guess I'm sorta into it."

"Uh, you're both freaks," a voice behind us said.

Our heads jerked in the direction of the manager, who was backing away as if she was ready to get the hell out of our way in case she caught something infectious. "We close in half an hour, so just"—she waved her hand at us—"keep it PG."

"People," Nate said, shaking his head. Then his gaze traveled down between us, and he licked his lips. "I've missed those pajama pants."

"I missed these suspenders," I replied, snapping one like a rubber band.

His dimples deepened, and then he cupped my face, his forehead resting against mine. Such a simple act, but it was all that was needed to have the anxious nerves evaporating like the ocean on your skin under the hot sun.

"Nate?" I said, breathing him in and opening my eyes. "I'm sorry."

"I know."

And then he kissed me, and it was butterflies, and fireworks and explosions, but most of all, it was the assurance that he knew who he was kissing, really knew, and wanted to anyway. My hands threaded through the soft strands of his hair that now sat just above his collar, and his stubble grazed against my cheek as our tongues tangled. And then it occurred to me that this was the first time I'd ever been able to do this with him in public. To do more than hold his hand, without a wig, without a hat, just open and exposed and without any other cares in the world.

And it felt fucking fantastic.

When he pulled away, he kissed the tip of my nose and then lifted his eyes to the sign above him. "You know…I think that sign's a little misleading." He looked behind me to make sure the coast was clear and then pulled a Post-it pad out of his pocket, along with a Sharpie. After scribbling something across it, he peeled off the sticky note and slapped it on the sign, right over the word "one," so that it now read:

MEALS FOR *TWO*

"Much better," I said, my arm going around his waist as his wrapped around my shoulders. We stood there looking at his handiwork until the intercom came on, alerting shoppers that the store would be closing soon.

Nate picked up his empty basket and put it

underneath mine to share. His brow wrinkled as he looked up and down the aisle at the selections behind the frosted doors. Then he winked at me and said, "There's nothing here that's appealing to me anymore. I'm suddenly in the mood for ice cream."

"Yeah, that sounds good. We can stop by Licked if you— Ohhh," I said as my brain finally picked up what he was throwing down, which should've been blatantly obvious by the way his eyes never left my pants. "Lead the way home, then, Mr. Ryan."

Six Months Later

"WHY THE HELL am I blindfolded? It's not like I don't know where my new office is. Or the fact that the girls will be there, because I *did* invite them for drinks, ya know." Shayne sounded faux annoyed as I led her up the sidewalk and into the building that housed her new business, Happily Ever After, Inc. I halted her so I could open the door and took a moment to admire the way her long blue dress molded to her body like a second skin. As she brushed past me, I stepped in behind her, and then grabbed her hand as we walked over to the bank of elevators.

    "I figured you missed wearing disguises," I said, punching the up button, and the doors immediately opened.

"Aren't you hilarious. If I fall on my face—"

"Do you honestly think I'd let you fall?"

Her teeth came out to bite her bottom lip as a smile threatened to break free. "Maybe…if you needed a good laugh."

"Nah. The only way I'd let that happen is if I hit the ground first."

"Aww. So you fall, I fall. That's so cute."

"Well, more like *you* fall, I try to hold us up, but yeah, something like that."

She giggled as we reached the seventh floor, and I held her around the waist as we exited the elevator and headed to her new office.

"You ready?" I asked when we came to a stop in front of the door.

"I think I'm gonna spew I'm so excited," she said, holding her stomach, and then she took a deep breath and let it out slowly. "Can I take the blindfold off yet?"

"No."

"Okay. What about now?"

"Nope."

"Now?"

"Shayne," I growled.

"Okay, okay."

I rapped on the door three times and then pushed it open. As we entered, I took off her blindfold and flipped the light switch.

"Surprise!"

Shayne jumped about a foot as the thunder of voices vibrated across the room. The space was packed with people, all new clients and former ones that had made the jump from HLS, as well as Shayne's girlfriends, and even her—

"Mum? Dad?" she said, her eyes wide before she ran straight into their open arms. "Oh my gosh, what are you doing here?"

"We couldn't miss our baby girl starting her new business, now could we?" her dad said, kissing her temple. He was about the same height as Shayne, with the same eyes, but that was where the similarities ended. She had her petite mom's coloring, right down to the ivory skin and wild red curls, though she kept hers cropped just above her shoulders.

Shayne was shaking her head in disbelief. "You flew all the way across the Pacific just for this?"

"Of course, baby. Not to mention there was someone we've been dying to meet." Her mom looked over at me before stepping forward and holding out her arms. As I embraced her, she said, "So good to finally meet you in person, Nate. You're so handsome. That video chat thing doesn't do you justice." Then she pulled back and looked up at me. "And look, you're even taller than our Gracie girl. Garry, can you believe she found someone bigger than she is?"

"Mum!" Shayne protested.

"Oh, darling, I don't mean big as in your thighs," she

said, and then turned to me and whispered, "She's so sensitive about her legs, you know."

"Uh, Carolyn, why don't we let Shayne make her rounds and catch up with her later, hmm? I'll get you some punch. We'll see you in a bit." Garry put his arm around his wife and led her over to the banquet table that the girls had set up with finger foods, desserts, and drinks.

Shayne rounded on me and shook her head, though she had a huge grin on her face. "Let me guess. That was all your idea."

"Guilty."

"You're pretty amazing, you know that?"

"Why yes, I do."

She playfully slapped at my chest and then frowned. "Is my makeup all smeared now?" she asked, her beautiful eyes looking up at me as she swiped underneath her eyes.

I shook my head and brought her hand to my lips to plant a soft kiss across her knuckles. "Nope. You're perfect."

She beamed and then leaned in for a kiss—

"Oh, break it up, you two, and come greet your guests," Paige said, as she came up beside us and stole Shayne away. "Nice touch with the blindfold," she called out to me over her shoulder.

"Nate, hey." A hard clap on my shoulder had me turning around to see Ace standing there.

I greeted him with a clasped hand and a pat on the back. "Good to see you here, man. Thanks for coming."

"Wouldn't miss it. The place looks great." He looked

around the open space, decorated in airy beach colors that Shayne had said reminded her of childhood summers spent at the beach where she grew up in Wollongong. And I only remembered *that* piece of information because I'd made her say it five times fast, and shocker of all shocks, she did.

"The girls went through the client list that's scheduled for the next couple of months and invited all these people. This whole thing is just going to explode, you know that, right?"

"If this is where she's starting, that's damn impressive. And thank fuck she's away from that psychopath of a boss. That woman's attempt at conversation was to unzip my pants under the table."

"And I thought her grabbing my ass was bad," I said, laughing. "But seriously, thank you for helping make her dreams come true. The girls said they've never seen her so happy."

"No, I don't believe that for a second." He looked me dead in the eye. "But as far as the business side of it goes, I mean it when I say it's the least I could do for...hell, all of it. I'm just glad I screwed your head on straight before you lost her for good."

My eyebrows shot up. "Whoa, man, word choices."

"Oh, shit. Yeah, you know what I mean—"

"What the *fuck* are you doing here?" Paige shrieking from behind me had us shutting up and turning in her direction. A man in a casual suit, the top half of his shirt unbuttoned, was barely in the door before Paige stomped over, attempting to usher him back out. With a self-satisfied smirk, long dirty blond hair pulled back, and sporting what looked like eyeliner, he looked like something out of one of those glam rock bands or some shit. Come to think of it, he'd been at the club in Vegas with us back in January. Didn't look like those two were on any better terms.

"You're becoming a broken record, Pita," he said, his smile lazy. "One of these days you could greet me by simply saying hello."

Her hands balled into fists as they went to her hips. "You mean goodbye. This isn't a brothel, Dickwad."

"Judging by your appearance here, I'd say that statement is false. Besides, I heard this is the hot new place to pick up chicks."

"There won't be any reason to pick up anyone when I cut off your balls and serve them as an appetizer at my next wedding event."

The man bristled. "You get so flushed and passionate when you talk about my balls. Please continue."

Wheeling around, I pushed Ace toward the drink table before they started throwing things at each other's heads.

Even as I chatted with Shayne's parents and struck up conversations with the other guests, I kept one eye on my girl, and I couldn't help but be awed by the effortless way she put everyone around her at ease. Pride swelled in my chest, and well over an hour passed before the crowd parted enough that I could make my way over to her.

"I don't think that smile has left your face since we walked in," I said, coming up behind her.

"Oh my God, Nate, I'm floored. Sensory overload, seriously."

"Well, there's just...one more thing," I said, taking her hand and leading her over to the wall of windows that overlooked the city. It was a stunning view, and Shayne would have the same one from her office that was to the left.

Shayne raised an eyebrow. "Another surprise? It's not Val, is it?"

Laughing, I shook my head. "Fuck no, and security downstairs knows she's not allowed within ten feet of the building."

"Guess I can put my mace away, then."

"Nah, keep it on you in case someone gets too handsy with my girl."

"Your girl, huh?" She smiled as she stared up at me, her expression so full of joy I wished I could keep it on her face forever.

"Are you opposed to that?"

"Not in the slightest."

"Are you sure?" I asked. "Because I've got to ask you something..."

Shayne's eyes shot straight to where my hand was reaching into my pocket for what I wanted to give her. When I pulled it out, I held it behind my back.

"Do you remember our conversation on our first date?"

"You mean the IHOP date?"

"That would be the one. Do you remember when we talked about bucket lists and what I told you?"

Shayne's hand grew shaky in mine when she gulped and whispered, "You said you wanted to fall in love."

I smiled and nodded. "I did say that. And—"

"Oh my God, you're not going to propose, are you?" Paige sounded horrified as she came to an abrupt stop next to us, her martini splashing over the lip. The room went dead silent as everyone turned in our direction.

Oh shit.

"Paige," Shayne said through clenched teeth. "Shut *up*."

"Dude, at least get down on your damn knee," she protested.

Okay, this is not going like I planned it.

Clearing my throat, I turned my attention back to Shayne. Yeah, now I was sweating like a motherfucker.

"There was something else I mentioned on that list," I said. "And I thought it might be a nice addition to what you've got going on here."

Shayne's forehead pinched ever so slightly. "And what would that be?"

I looked over my shoulder and nodded at Ryleigh and Hunter, and her gaze followed. When they pulled back the curtain from the corner of the room, it took her a moment to realize what it was she was staring at, and then she gasped.

"Is that a—" She took a few steps forward, her hand still in mine, and touched the thin red iron bars that crisscrossed up and down the outline of the large heart sculpture. I'd had Hunter custom-build the piece with a partner of his over the last few weeks, and it stood about seven feet tall and the same distance wide.

Shayne's eyes were watery as she looked up at me. "Is this for what I think it is?"

Bringing forward the object I'd held behind my back, I nodded. Then I opened my palm, and she gingerly picked it up. The padlock was the same shade as her hair, brilliant and fiery, and as she fingered the inscriptions, she smiled and a tear dropped. Our initials were carved into one side, and on the other, the date of—

"The day I met your Star Wars underpants." She laughed, and the sound was like a thousand twinkling chimes on a breeze. Then she winked. "I mean you."

"I thought maybe your clients could come back and...you know." I gestured toward the sculpture. "Fill up the heart."

"Fill up the heart," she repeated, staring in awe at what stood in front of her. "I don't know what to say." Then she brushed a stray tear from her cheek as her friends gathered around her.

"And we made one for all of us too," Ryleigh said, showing Shayne the bright pink lock with all four of their initials and the word "Forever" on the bottom.

Shayne looked around at all the family, friends, and

others supporting her dream and said, "You guys, this is so much. I wouldn't even have any of this if it weren't for all of you."

"Yes, you would," Paige said. "You're too fabulous to sit in someone else's wake."

"You've got a rival to take down and lonely people all over L.A. knocking down your door," Ace piped up. "Besides, I want my own lock on that tree, so you better get to work."

"No pressure or anything," Shayne said, laughing, and looking back down at the lock in her hands.

"So, Miss Matchmaker," I said, "whaddya say? Care to get love-locked with me?"

"Hmm." Shayne's eyes were teasing as she tapped her lips. Then she looked over her shoulder and said, "Hey, Quinn. What's my horoscope say?"

Quinn opened up the app on her phone and grinned. "It says, 'A new venture in love or business will be extremely profitable and long-lasting.' Sounds promising."

I wrapped my arms around Shayne's waist and pulled her close. "I think it means love *and* business."

"Oh, you think so, huh?"

"I know so."

"Want to do the honors together, then?" she asked, her eyes shining.

"Hell yes, I do."

After opening the lock with the key from my pocket, we each grabbed hold of it and aimed for the same spot, front and center, directly in the middle of the heart.

And then, my friends, as was appropriate at a business so aptly named, we lived Happily the Fuck Ever After.

HITCHED
Book Three of the L.A. Liaisons Series
Coming Soon

Thank you for reading Hooker. I hope you enjoyed my sassy
girls!

* Want all access to my latest book news + exclusive
excerpts, teasers, & giveaways?
Subscribe to my newsletter at www.BrookeBlaine.com!

* Reviews are vital to authors. All reviews, even just
a couple of quick sentences, can help a reader decide
whether to pick up our books. If you enjoyed this book,
please consider leaving a review on the site you purchased
from. I'll make sure Ryleigh whips up a Spank You, Sexy
Bitch shake in your honor!

Special Thanks

First and foremost, to my favorite Aussie—from the brainstorming sessions to the breakdowning sessions (yes, it's a word) to the gorgeous formatting to the fantastic book trailer to laughing even when reading my book for the millionth time. I can't tell you how much I appreciate you. If I tried, it'd be the size of a novel. Thank you, Ella, for being my person.

It truly takes a village to release a book, and I'd like to thank my talented team:

My phenomenal cover & promo designer, Hang Le, who I just adore. Arran McNicol, my smartass superhero editor. Jay Aheer of Simply Defined Art for the gorgeous teaser photos. Judy's Proofreading for her fabulous catches—even working on vacation! Mickey Reed Editing for polishing up my blurby blurb. Mary with Between the Sheets Promotions for taking charge of Hooker's cover reveal, blog tour, and release blitz like a boss. Renee K for keeping my Aussie-isms on track. The fab ladies of FTN for the daily giggle snorts and venting sessions, both of which are always much needed. To my Tribe, my family and friends who keep me sane and give love and support no matter what—my mom and seester, Stacy W, Jen G, Donna, Bianca, Ann. I love you all so much, I'm so glad you're my people! To the women and men (man? Oh, who am I kidding? It's you, Bill. Lol) of The Naughty Umbrella—I get to squeeze hug so many of you this year, and I can't wait!! Cassandra Caress, Karen Branton, & Michelle Lov Engler—I see you three sharing my books constantly, and it blows my mind. Thank you! To the bloggers who have picked up my books, reviewed them, and shared them with the world—a million thanks and spanks. And to you reading this right now…I hope you enjoyed Hooker and will stick around for the many more stories to come!

About the Author

About Brooke

You could say Brooke Blaine was a book-a-holic from the time she knew how to read; she used to tell her mother that curling up with one at 4 a.m. before elementary school was her 'quiet time.' Not much has changed except for the espresso I.V. pump she now carries around and the size of her onesie pajamas.

Brooke enjoys writing sassy contemporary romance, whether in the form of comedy, suspense, or erotica. The latter has scarred her conservative Southern family for life, bless their hearts.

If you'd like to get in touch with her, she's easy to find - just keep an ear out for the Rick Astley ringtone that's dominated her cell phone for ten years.
If you'd like to get in touch with Brooke, she's easy to find - just keep an ear out for the Rick Astley ringtone that's dominated her cell phone for ten years.